W E COULDN'T make out the wording of the signs until we reached the actual edge of the desert, which was a distinct boundary, a strip no more than ten yards wide, where the ground got sandier and the grass got sparser. Beyond that, the sand was as thick and white as in a brand-new sandbox.

What each of the signs said was BEWARE OF SAND HANDS.

"*Sand hands?*" Robin said. "*Sand hands?* What in the world are *sand hands?*"

We all looked at each other. We all shrugged.

"I never heard of anything so ridiculous in my life," Robin said. He took a step into the sandy area before the desert. And another. Still nothing happened. He took another step and his foot sank deeper in the sand than he had anticipated, causing him to stumble. He pulled himself upright, then pitched forward again. "Hey!" he yelled, surprised. Then, "Hey!" he cried again. And there was fear in his voice.

From where we stood, we saw . . . Well, it sure looked like a hand to me. A human hand. It had hold of Robin's right ankle, and it tugged. Robin's entire foot disappeared under the sand . . .

Other Books by Vivian Vande Velde

USER
unfriendly

Vivian Vande Velde

sandpiper

Houghton Mifflin Harcourt
Boston New York

All rights reserved. Published in the United States by Sandpiper, an imprint of
Houghton Mifflin Harcourt Publishing Company. Originally published in paperback
in the United States by Harcourt Children's Books, an imprint of Houghton Mifflin
Harcourt Publishing Company, 1991.

For information about permission to reproduce selections from this book, write to
Permissions, Houghton Mifflin Harcourt Publishing Company, 215 Park Avenue
South, New York, New York 10003.

SANDPIPER and the SANDPIPER logo are trademarks of Houghton Mifflin
Harcourt Publishing Company.

www.hmhbooks.com

The text of this book is set in Berling LT Std.

The Library of Congress has cataloged the hardcover edition as follows:
Vande Velde, Vivian.
User unfriendly/Vivian Vande Velde.
p. cm.
Summary: Fourteen-year- old Arvin and his friends risk using a computer-controlled
role-playing game to simulate a magical world in which they actually become
fantasy characters, even though the computer program is a pirated one containing
unpredictable errors.
[1. Fantasy games—Fiction. 2. Computer games—Fiction. 3. Fantasy.]
I. Title. PZ7.V2773Us 1991
[Fic]—dc20 90-21060

ISBN: 978-0-15-216353-2 paperback

Manufactured in the United States of America
DOC 10 9 8 7 6 5 4 3 2 1

4500363125

This book is dedicated, with appreciation,

to Ed and Gary
  for taking the time to explain
  the game to somebody's mother,

to Norm and Barb
  for support and help above
  and beyond the call of duty,

and to Jane
  for unrelenting enthusiasm.

contents

USER
unfriendly

CHAPTER 1

Day One

THE FIRST THING I noticed was the smell.

Take that back.

The first thing I noticed was the stink. I nearly gagged, and rolled over from my side onto my back.

The second thing I noticed was that I was itchy all over. But before I could get too busy worrying that Shelton had set me down on an anthill—and figuring what I'd do to him if he had—I realized that I was lying on straw. The reason this place smelled like a barn was because it *was* a barn.

I moved the crook of my elbow over my nose. It didn't help. From just off to my right there was a soft *whuffing* noise. I turned my head and found I was about five feet away from this incredibly *big* horse. I mean, I've seen pictures of horses, and I know people used to ride them and all, but I'd never expected them to be so huge. The thing shifted its weight, setting this absolutely enormous hoof even closer to my head. Terrific. Twenty seconds into the game and I was about to get my face stepped on by the local transportation.

I wondered if anybody ever paid his money, got killed in the opening moves of the game, and spent the whole campaign in the cool gray gauziness that the computer calls death. It would only last an hour, but it would feel like five days. That hardly seemed fair. Surely there was some rule prohibiting it, or people would demand a refund. I backed off from that thought and from the thought that went with it: There was, in this particular campaign, no one to enforce the rules. Rules had already been broken just to get us here.

But then the computer conditioning kicked in.

I mean, I still remembered who I was and all that. But everything just sort of suddenly kind of *shifted*. Sure, I knew I was really Arvin Rizalli of Mrs. Kascima's eighth-grade class at Saint John the Evangelist School; but I *felt* like Harek Longbow of the Silver Mountains Clan, an elf warrior of the fourth level. All at once I had all these dim sort of . . . I guess you could call them memories . . . about how to ride a horse and take care of it, just as if I'd been doing it all my life. Just the way a fourth-level elf warrior would have.

I got to my feet and scratched the underside of

the horse's neck. "Easy," I murmured, though before then I'd been the one in need of calming. As if from a great distance, I recognized my sense of surprise at the prickliness of the horse's hide and my sense of alarm when it tossed its head, its breath warm on my arm. But the Harek in me wasn't worried at all.

I looked around the stable. (And suddenly I knew it *was* a stable, and not a barn.) It was small, dark, smelly—even by medieval stable standards. Daub-and-wattle construction, I observed, though on my own I wouldn't even have been sure what that meant: twigs held together by mud and dung. Not a real high-class establishment. The door was open, letting in some light. Morning, I judged.

Well, the adventure wasn't likely to come to me here. *Shelton Jankowitz, I hope you know what you're doing*, I thought.

But it was too late for that.

I peeked out the door and found myself looking down a small village street. The stable was up against another building. An inn, I guessed, spotting a sign with a barrel painted on it.

Where were the others? One part of me, the Arvin part, answered that they were asleep in Shelton's basement rec room. All of us were. Shelton had parked himself in front of the computer, fat lot of good that would do him in the stage of sleep called REM—Rapid Eye Movement state. My mother, of all people, was on the recliner. Dawn Marie shared the love seat (of course) with Noah. Sometimes it seemed to me that the two of them must be attached with an invisible strand of Super Glue, but they're tenth-graders and sometimes tenth-graders get like that. Giannine was in the lounge chair. Cleveland, Dominic, and I were stuck with the pillows sprawled on the floor.

But where we really were was unimportant. What counted was where we felt we were. Or rather, where the computer hookup made us feel we were.

Find Rasmussem, that was the one directive from Rasmussem, Inc., and there had been no reason for Shelton to change it when he'd pirated the program. Sometimes Rasmussem was a person, sometimes a place, occasionally an object—according to those who had played before. Shouldn't be too hard to find; it wasn't meant to be a puzzle, but only an introduction to the campaign for the player characters.

I headed for the inn, figuring that'd be the place to meet people, to ask questions.

But the inn was, in its own way, even worse than the stable. The floor was rough-hewn planks of wood.

There were candle holders attached to the walls, though without any candles. I knew what they were by the globs of dripped wax and by the black, sooty crescents on the walls and ceiling. I was willing to bet the owners of this place wouldn't provide light except when it was absolutely necessary. Their customers were probably the sort who stole candles.

I walked in feeling self-conscious. My clothes were straight from an old Hildebrandts print, but there was no telling what had resulted from the combination of my instructions, Shelton's perception of them, and the computer's ability. If we had been doing this right—if we had gone through an official Rasmussem outlet—I would have had the benefit of all their expensive biofeedback equipment, which would have responded directly to my conscious desires. Of course, if we had gone through Rasmussem, it would have cost a fortune, and we would have had their rules to contend with. Still, it was very disconcerting not to know what I looked like. I hoped I'd get a chance to see my face before the others did.

The room was hazy with smoke from the fireplace. There were maybe three dozen people sitting at beer-barrel tables, mostly humans, mostly guys— except for the serving wenches and a few women who looked even meaner than the men. My impression was that everybody knew everybody, except, of course, for me.

I hate being places where I don't know anybody.

I approached the bar, where a man with a gold hoop in one ear wiped up spills with a gray rag. I leaned against the bar, which was sticky despite the bartender's efforts. "Excuse me—"

"What'll it be?"

"I was wondering—"

"What'll it be?"

"I just have a question—"

"I only answer questions from patrons. What'll it be?"

I felt the pouch at my belt. I would have been provided with a few starting gold pieces. At the last second I came to my senses enough to bite off a request for soda. "Do you have coffee?" I asked. My mom says coffee stunts a kid's growth; but I figured if it hadn't stunted me by fourteen, why worry about it now?

"Coffee?" the barkeep said. He flopped the rag over, and it smacked the bar wetly. "Never heard of it."

I sighed. "Could I just have some water then?"

He gave me this look like I was a real pain in the you-know-where.

"I'll pay."

He folded his arms and stared at me coolly. Finally, just as I was beginning to squirm, he took a tin mug from under the counter and wrung his rag over it. "One gold piece."

Cute. People were beginning to watch. Rough-looking people, with swords and eye patches and missing teeth. "Maybe I'll have a beer," I said. I didn't have to drink it.

The barkeep dumped the gray sudsy water onto the floor, barely missing my foot. He refilled the same mug with amber foam from a barrel behind him.

"Thanks so very much," I said.

Apparently sarcasm didn't faze him. He held one hand on the mug, the other out for the gold piece.

I handed it over. "I was wondering where Rasmussem is."

He let go of the mug only after biting the coin. "Information costs."

"I just paid you."

"You just paid me for beer."

I took another coin from my pouch and held it over his extended hand. "Where's Rasmussem?"

He wriggled his fingers. "Pay and I'll tell."

I sighed and dropped the coin.

He made it disappear into his apron pocket, then resumed wiping the bar.

"Well?"

"Well, what?"

"Where's Rasmussem?"

"Here, you dumb twit. This is Rasmussem. The Rasmussem Inn. Dumb twit of an elf, don't even know where you are." He shook his head.

Nice world. And I was going to spend five days here? I was insane for letting Shelton talk me into this, and I probably deserved whatever I got. I took my drink and found an empty table in the corner by the door.

Being careful not to spill, though they didn't look too careful about that sort of thing here, I tipped the mug to catch my warped reflection in the metal surface. My hair was long and very light blond. Sort of the color of the stringy stuff you have to pick off of corn on the cob. It was a shock. What I had asked for, but a shock.

My blue-gray eyes were the shade of faded denim, and the eyebrows tipped upward, giving me the appearance of cool disdain. The pointy ears were a bit too large, and I pulled the hair in front of them; but that made me look like a girl. Next time, I thought, I'd have Shelton make the ears shorter. And wasn't that a laugh? Two minutes ago I'd been hating it, and here I was saying "next time" with the campaign not even started yet. Maybe this was going to be fun after all, despite the bad start.

I'd just thought that, when someone kicked open the door beside me. It was a dwarf, looking meaner than the men or the women, and he was dragging a dead body behind him.

CHAPTER 2

Player Characters

SEVERAL PEOPLE JUMPED to their feet for a closer look. Others quickly settled up, gulping down their drinks or abandoning them, eager to get out before trouble started. Those who were quickest to the door collided with a group on their way in—townspeople who'd followed the dwarf and his grisly burden from the street. Instant traffic jam, right there by my table.

I took a swig from my mug, because that's what people on TV do to steady their nerves. But the liquid was more bitter than I expected, and warmer and fizzier, which made me cough and sneeze at the same time. *Wonderful start*, I thought, wiping my face on my sleeve. I became aware of something resting against my ankle and looked before I thought not to. It was the corpse's hand. His glazed eyes seemed to be looking directly at mine.

I've never liked the kind of stories with exploding

heads or severed limbs or brains trickling out of people's ears, and I gulped. This was make-believe, I reminded myself: a computer-generated image that looked and sounded and smelled and tasted and felt so real because it was hooked up directly to my brain. But make-believe just the same.

It didn't help.

"Quiet!" bellowed a voice about two inches from my ear. The crowd inside the inn settled a bit. From the edges of the group people were still demanding to know what was going on, or complaining that they couldn't see.

The dwarf climbed onto my table. The noise level dropped several decibels more. "I am Feordin Mace-wielder, son of Feordan Sturdyaxe, grandson of Feor-dane Boldheart, brother to Feordone the Fearless, great-grandson of Feordine Stoutarm who served under Graggaman Maximus."

With dwarfs, this can go on forever. They always introduce themselves by introducing their ancestors. *All* their ancestors. And the names always sound alike. As Harek, I had memories of seeing dwarfs kill people for trying to rush them through the litany; they killed them and then recited over the dead bodies, starting again from the very beginning.

But this dwarf, Feordin, must have come from an undistinguished family line. Or he recognized the need for uncommon urgency, for he stopped after a mere four generations and pointed to the corpse by my foot. "And that man,"—as if on cue, everyone took one giant step back, so that I had a clear view of the man's arrow-ridden body. I gulped, but my stomach didn't lurch this time. Computer conditioning again: as an elf warrior, I wouldn't be unsettled by death. "That man," the dwarf said, "was a soldier, dressed, as you can see, in the livery of the Grand Guard of your king, Ulric, known as The Fair."

The computer had planted a memory, something I would have known as an inhabitant of this land. Ulric, I knew as soon as I thought about it, was king of the human community. He was respected—as not all human kings were—by elves and dwarfs and halflings alike. They sometimes called him "The Fair," which referred both to his reputation as a just ruler and to the straw-colored hair he'd had in his youth. Now more often he was called "The Old King." He'd had three wives—one at a time, of course—but they'd all died. He'd outlived four sons also, and had only one daughter, Dorinda. Blond-haired, blue-eyed Dorinda, ten years old and loved by everyone. Ulric had formed the elite Grand Guard—twenty-five of the fastest, strongest, best men in the kingdom—to watch over her and accompany her wherever she went.

And one of them was dead.

"Orc arrows," I murmured, noting the raven feathers and the pattern of fletching.

Feordin heard and turned on me. "Oh aye," he said, his tone indicating I was the biggest jerk he or his ancestors had ever met. "Orc arrows."

A woman who was dressed in a plain green gown stooped to get a closer look. "Not likely a Grand Guardsman would find himself surprised by orcs," she said. It was the same thing Feordin had hinted at with his tone. The same thing *I* knew. Orcs couldn't tie their shoelaces without a captain to tell them to and three sergeants to show them how. I'd never said the guy'd been killed by orcs; I'd just said orc arrows.

The woman stood. Dawn Marie, I was sure of it, butting in where nobody needed her. "Where was the body found?" she asked Feordin.

The dwarf nodded his head to the left, west. "Toward Sannatia," he said, a name that meant nothing to me.

But it meant something to most of the others. "Ah," the crowd murmured in a tone that gave me goose bumps.

"What's Sannatia?" someone else asked, sparing me the burden of having to play the jerk again. This person looked like a native American Indian. I figured he was from our group. For one thing, while we can be whoever we want, from whatever time period or piece of fiction we choose, the nonplayer characters that the computer provides are all matched to the setting. Probably Dominic, I decided, who usually chose to play trackers and rangers and solitary warrior types. Another way I knew he was one of us was from the incredulous looks he was getting, like all the towns-people already knew what Sannatia was.

The dwarf looked at him contemptuously. "The deserted city," he said. "Nobody lives there."

The Indian shrugged.

"Nobody," Feordin repeated, "*lives* there." He paused to let that sink in. "Twenty years ago it was a settlement, a big one. Mostly there were humans, but also dwarfs lived there, and elves and halflings. Thousands of people. There was an army garrison there, and seven or eight temples. A bazaar second to none. The city was said to be so crowded you could hear the noise of it from five miles away, and at night the lights could be seen from as far away as the River Gan."

And? I thought. *And?* I waited for the other shoe to drop, for the part of the story that could make the townspeople here say, "Ah," in that combination of awe and fear.

"And then," the dwarf said, "between one day and the next, they were gone. The buildings were undamaged, the livestock unharmed in their pens, but the people were gone. Nobody remained. Whatever had happened, you'd have thought that the soldiers at least would have put up a fight; but the garrison storerooms were provisioned, the weapons clean and neatly stacked, the horses safe in the stables. Just . . . no people. King Ulric sent soldiers to investigate. But though the miller and his wife who live across the desert at Miller's Grove saw lights over the desert sands, just as they did every night, the soldiers never marched back. Since then, no one who has spent the night in Sannatia has ever come out again. And every night, the lights of the city still brighten the western sky."

There was a moment of silence. The woman in green said, "Still, if that's where the king's daughter has been taken . . ."

People shook their heads and walked away, afraid

to get involved. In a moment the crowd was nearly gone. Only nine people remained around me and my table. These would be the seven other members of my group, plus two nonplayer characters, computer generated to accompany us on the campaign. I looked them over and tried to decide who was who.

The woman in green had her arm around the waist of a man also dressed in green, who in turn had his arm around her. Dawn Marie and Noah. I just knew it by the gooey expressions on their faces.

"Hi," the man said. "I'm Robin Hood and this is Maid Marian."

Of course they were.

"I'm unofficial king of Sherwood Forest and bane to the wicked sheriff of Nottingham. Expert thief extraordinaire. Climbing walls, opening the unopenable, and picking pockets my specialty." He held out his hand, revealing a small knife held flat on his open palm.

The Indian must have recognized it. He slapped his hand against his buckskinned thigh, against the empty knife sheath. He snatched the weapon away from Robin, who just grinned.

"And this is my . . ."—Robin smiled at Marian—"able-bodied assistant, a swordsmaster of unsurpassed ability."

Marian blew him a kiss.

"Harek Longbow of the Silver Mountains Clan," I said to put an end to all this mutual admiration before I threw up.

"Cornelius," said an old man dressed in a robe and conical hat embroidered with silver stars and moons. He swept off the hat. "The Magnificent." That was probably Shelton, who always chooses to play a magic-user.

A man in a plain brown robe and a haircut like Saint Francis bowed. "Abbot Simon," he said. "At your service." Oh-oh, a cleric. They have magic powers too, so that killed my theory about Shelton's having to be the wizard.

"Feordin Macewielder," said the dwarf. "Son of Feordan Sturdyaxe, grandson of Feordane Boldheart, brother to Feordone the Fearless, great-grandson of Feordine Stoutarm who served under Graggaman Maximus." He knew too much about the opening situation to be one of the group and had to be a computer-generated aid. But on the other hand he *was* black, and I know how proud Cleveland is of his African heritage.

The Indian, who I had already pegged as Dominic, was still sulking that Robin Hood had managed to steal his knife. "Nocona, chief of the Comanches," he grumbled.

There was another elf warrior in the group, but this one was a woman. "My name is Thea Greenleaf," she said, looking right at me, "of the Greenmeadow Clan."

Another of those computer-generated memories kicked in. There was long-standing rivalry between the Greenmeadow Clan and my own Silver Mountains group. Giannine Bellisario? I wondered. Or was Giannine the swaggering halfling woman who pushed her way to the front? She might have been only four feet tall, but she had biceps bigger than anybody else's here and she wore a metal bra, which may have accounted for the sour look on her face. "Brynhild, of the Sisterhood of the Sword, and better than any man here." She spat on the floor, which I thought was pretty rude whether she was Giannine or a computer facsimile.

Things were going too quickly, and I was getting lost about who must be who. But there was no doubt about the last character, the fourth woman in this group. This was one of the Rasmussem's serving wenches, dressed like a gypsy in an embarrassingly low-cut blouse. "I'm Felice," she said, with a self-conscious giggle. "Isn't this fun?"

Mom. How humiliating.

CHAPTER 3

Provisions

I TRIED TO LOOK LIKE "Ho-hum, don't bother noticing me because I'm nobody you know," but Mom
picked me out straight off. Mothers have a knack for
that sort of thing, like being able to tell when you're
spitting your lima beans out into the napkin instead
of swallowing them, or knowing just when to say, "It's
too quiet in there—what are you doing?" Recognizing
their kid from a lineup of warriors, thieves, and assorted nonhumans must be one of those gifts that
come with motherhood. She fixed me with this kind
of goofy smile of hers that let me know I was getting
off lucky—that she could have ruffled my hair and
said, "Hi-ya, Arvin."

The other elf, Thea, came to my rescue. "What do
you do, Felice?" she asked.

"Do?" Mom repeated.

"Warrior-maid?" asked Brynhild, but she didn't look very hopeful. "Magic-user? Thief?"

"Oh." Mom looked directly at me. "Am I supposed to tell?"

I squirmed and pretended not to realize she was asking me. Everybody had to know who she was. The only way I could escape dying of embarrassment was to hope that they didn't know me.

"Yes, my lady," Cornelius was telling her, "you most definitely are supposed to tell."

"Oh," Mom said again. "I'm a thief." She put a finger to her lips in a "don't tell" gesture and giggled again.

"Six fighters," Maid Marian counted out loud, as though someone had died and left her dungeon master, "two magic-users, and two thieves. Good mix."

"I'm so pleased you're pleased," Feordin grumbled. "Are we going to stand around introducing ourselves all day, or does anybody actually plan to do something?"

"First order of business is weapons and equipment," Robin Hood said, cutting off Marian, who was obviously winding herself up for a rebuttal. "What say we all meet back here in a half hour at the latest?"

Made sense to me. The only ones who already had weapons were Nocona, with his knife—while he had it—and Feordin Macewielder, with—appropriately enough—a mace. But even they would need supplies for the quest. The group started to break up. I avoided meeting my mom's eyes. As a thief, she'd be looking for stuff totally different from what I'd be needing as a warrior. She was better off with Robin Hood anyway.

There was only one armorer in the town, and from him I bought a leather breastplate. Chain mail would have been nice, but it was twice as expensive. That's the kind of pennypinching that can cost dearly later in the game, but I'd already spent more than I should have, trying to buy information at the Rasmussem.

From a booth on the same street I also bought a bow and a quiver with two dozen arrows, but for swords and knives, I had to go to a blacksmith. It took me all of five seconds to decide the guy must be the Rasmussem barkeep's not-so-friendly brother. All the while I was there, he cleaned his fingernails with a knife as long as my arm.

"May I see that one?" I asked, pointing to a long sword that hung over his work area.

With a sigh as though I'd been there all morning, he fetched the weapon and slammed it down on the counter, then resumed picking under his nails.

I lifted the sword.

Take that back.

I started to lift the sword. Pain shot through my arm as though I'd whacked my elbow against a brick wall. The sword dropped from my numb fingers and I doubled over.

The blacksmith looked at me for a few seconds while he cleaned off his blade on his pants leg. He started in on the other hand. Philosophically he said, "I always heard tell elves couldn't handle iron. Never seen one dumb enough to try before."

"Glad to be of service," I wheezed once I got my breath back. "Do you have any bronze?"

"Couple pieces." He grinned, and I knew it was coming before he got it out: "Course, bronze costs more."

I ended up with a sword and a dagger. I really wanted a shield, but I remembered one campaign—one of the old-fashioned ones that we'd played with dice and graph paper and miniatures—where I'd had to leave behind treasure. Shelton, as dungeon master, had gotten real picky and pointed out that I could only be credited with what he figured I could reasonably fit into my pockets, a fraction of what I was due. So now instead of a shield I got a large sack, and a length of rope, which I figured was something that could always come in handy, and a water skin, since Feordin had mentioned a desert.

Walking back to the Rasmussem, I started to worry about Mom. She was a reader of high-fantasy adventure stories, not a gamer. She'd been interested in what was going on, those times the group had met at our house, and had liked to listen to the campaign scenarios. She'd never been able to figure out the dice, though, and had certainly never asked to play. I wondered if she'd have asked to join us this time if Dad hadn't been gone all week on a business trip. What if, I thought, lovebirds Robin and Marian hadn't split up, despite their different classifications, and had left her on her own? What if we had to go out looking for her?

No such luck. She was already there; *everyone* was already there. Waiting. For me.

"What happened?" Brynhild demanded. "We were about to send out a rescue party."

I tried to ignore her and kept my back to Mom so she wouldn't see my face go red.

"Harek, do you have any money left?" Marian asked. "We pooled our resources and bought some food supplies, but we'd like to take what's left and get a pack animal to carry all this stuff."

This wasn't a half bad idea. I only wished somebody else had come up with it. Dawn Marie was just too bossy for me to take to her suggestions easily. I handed over my last gold piece and we all trooped out of the Rasmussem. I worked hard to make sure there was somebody between me and Mom at all times.

There was only one public stable in this town, and only one animal within our means. This was a shaggy, swaybacked thing who, we were told, answered to the name Phoenix. Even at three gold pieces, we were getting gypped.

There were ten other horses—nice respectable-looking horses—and I gazed at them longingly.

"Excuse me," Mom said. "Excuse me. Stablemaster person?"

The owner of the stable was this big, hairy guy who looked like he ate people's moms for breakfast. He folded his arms across his chest and glared at her.

"You see," Mom explained chipperly, "we're on an expedition to rescue the king's daughter. So, really, it'd be nice if you could give us some sort of discount for humanitarian reasons." She gave him her brightest smile. "Don't you think?"

Her enthusiasm had already begun to wilt under his scowl when finally—finally—he said, very slowly, very distinctly: "Tough. Luck. Lady. If it's the king's business you're on, then you'll be expecting a reward. If there's a reward involved, you can afford to pay me fifteen gold pieces."

While Marian and Cornelius tried to convince him that we didn't have fifteen gold pieces, I noticed that Mom was trying to get my attention. Not another brainstorm, I prayed. I pretended I didn't notice.

"Psst," Mom called in a loud whisper, "Harek."

Feordin poked me in the ribs with the handle of his mace. No way I could pretend I hadn't noticed that. Reluctantly, I faced her.

She was giving me these meaningful glances, looking from me to the doorway. Meaningful, I could tell. Meaning *what*, I couldn't.

"What is it, Felice?" Thea asked, pulling her over closer so that we formed a tight huddle, me, Mom, Thea, and Feordin.

"Any reason," Mom whispered, "we can't steal that horse? Any reason we can't steal all eleven horses?"

CHAPTER 4

Horses

CROUCHED BEHIND THE STABLE, after the stable-owner had thrown us out, we discussed Mom's plan.

"Well," Mom said, "what immediately comes to my mind is a diversion." She looked to Robin, the other thief. "Is that too common?"

"Not at all," Robin said. "Cornelius? Abbot Simon? Is it too early for a magic spell?"

"No," they said simultaneously—no clue there as to who was real and who was computer generated. The computer would have given us nonplayer characters to complement the rankings we had declared at the outset, and Shelton would have given himself at least a dozen spells to use. This was perhaps the main reason why he'd worked so hard to crack Rasmussem's program: his dissatisfaction over the rule that says first-time participants are to be admitted at beginner level, working upward from session to session, regardless of previous experience with other versions of the game. Shelton had been playing for five years to achieve his standing and he wasn't willing to work his way through the ranks a second time.

The rest of us aren't as devoted to the game as Shelton is, but all the same, considering what Rasmussem charges per session, it *is* exasperating to have to start without experience points. Warriors, thieves, magic-users: we all have to gradually build up our skills, and the game is kind of boring when you're just starting out. That's why we made Mom a full-fledged thief instead of an apprentice, even though she'd never played the game in any form before.

"I think," Cornelius said, "some sort of illusion would do nicely."

I started to rack my brains, determined to prove my worth in *something*

"The king himself, come to requisition the horses?" Feordin suggested.

Cornelius considered, then shook his head. "Too risky. These people are likely to refuse him."

"Duplicate horses?" Robin said. "We could switch them for the real thing."

"Too time-consuming."

Suddenly it came to me. Proud of myself I said, "Pay them in fake gold."

"Too dull."

Well, thank you very much.

"Some natural disaster?" Mom suggested. "Like a storm, or flood, or earthquake?"

Cornelius stroked his long white beard.

Suddenly there was a sparkle in Mom's eye. "Or a dragon?"

Cornelius grinned. Everybody grinned. Nocona patted Mom on the back.

"Dragons aren't a natural disaster," I grumbled.

"They are around here," Brynhild snapped.

Wasn't anybody on my side?

Cornelius scanned the sky, then pointed out a small fluffy cloud near the horizon. He rolled his sleeves back. *"Suki choolu,"* he said, or some such. *"Ollafranix propus."* He wiggled his fingers and got bug-eyed.

The cloud drifted closer, which made it look bigger, and now I could see that it wasn't as white as I had originally thought. Cornelius was more interesting, with his face all red and sweaty, looking like he was about to burst a blood vessel or something.

"*Churlindoe, hermandix, flez.*" And so on, and so on.

I stifled a yawn and checked to see how the rest of the group was reacting. They were staring at the sky, enthralled. I took another look and saw that the cloud had taken on the color of a burned-out lightbulb. Thunder rumbled. Wind tugged at our clothes and hair. And the shape kept changing. Too fast for wind currents, it seemed to throb, reminding me of the film we'd seen in science class of a beating heart. Lumps formed, and lumps on top of lumps. Then curves, and angles, too precise for something as insubstantial as a cloud. The color darkened noticeably even as I watched.

Townspeople stopped whatever they'd been doing and were looking upward in dismay. The thing definitely looked like a dragon silhouette now, and was almost directly overhead. Lightning flashed in the vicinity of the creature's head. Simultaneously, thunder cracked, loud enough to make me jump. I blinked, to get the jagged image of the lightning out of my eyes. But part of it remained: a chip of unnatural brightness where the dragon's eye would be. People on the street started to back away. Those still in their homes began to slam their doors shut, to latch their windows.

And then the cloud began to rotate. From a side

view to head-on it moved, with its lightning-chip eyes too bright, too horrible to look at. It opened its huge mouth, displaying gleaming teeth and—it took a moment for me to register it—a blood-red tongue. It gave a cry, its voice the roar of thunder, and it swooped down on the town.

People scattered, screaming.

Even knowing what it was, I was tempted to do the same.

Cornelius's dragon breathed out fire. Buildings burst into flame—the Rasmussem Inn, the stalls of the arms merchants, a cloth seller's shop. The stable.

People ran back and forth, unable to decide which was more dangerous, indoors or out. The wind caused by the beating of the dragon's wings stirred up the dust of the street till our stinging eyes ran with tears. The smell of the dragon's sulfur breath tingled in my nose and throat. And the fires blazed unchecked.

Behind us there was a particularly bloodcurdling scream. The door to the burning stable banged open. The stableowner lurched out, flames running like liquid over his body. I could feel the heat of him, could smell the charred flesh.

Mom grabbed Cornelius's arm, breaking his concentration. "Are you sure this is just illusion?" she demanded in a voice of horror, as the human torch ran down the street, and the townspeople fled from him.

"Of course," Cornelius said. "Look. Nothing is actually being consumed by the fire."

For once I didn't mind my mother's intervention; I had needed the reassurance too.

Cornelius raised his arms again, but the spell had been interrupted and couldn't be resumed. What he had created would run its natural course, but he couldn't add anything.

I was unable to drag my gaze away as the walls of one of the shops seemed to collapse, scattering glowing embers halfway across the street. I could taste ash on my tongue. Cornelius certainly knew his stuff.

"Harek. *Harek.*" It was Thea, dragging on my arm. The others were all heading inside the burning stable, which appeared close to collapse itself. It couldn't hurt us. Even if we seemed to catch fire, the effect would go away when the spell faded.

Which suddenly made me wonder. "Cornelius," I called, running to catch up. "How long does this spell last?"

He shrugged.

Wonderful.

These townspeople were going to be awfully mad when they realized what we'd done.

The horses, unfortunately, were just as fooled as everybody else. They whinnied and reared in terror as tongues of flame flickered across the straw and up the supporting timbers. Even Phoenix, the drooping, swaybacked mare we'd almost bought, kicked at her stall, which was more energy than I'd have thought she had.

Each of us picked one of the ten other horses. Enough tack for all of them was hanging on the walls, but since I was the last one in, I had to take the saddle that appeared to be on fire.

"Steady, steady," I murmured to my chestnut-colored horse as he tried to circle in the narrow stall. I knew what to do, but it wasn't easy. Fastening the bridle first, I looped the reins around one of the timbers to hold him fast. He couldn't turn his head, but I could see his white-rimmed eyes trying to catch glimpses of me from the sides. "Steady." If those hooves came down on me, or if he bit me, the computer stimulating my brain would cause me to feel pain.

I checked to see how the others were doing. Better than me, but not by much. The only exception was

Nocona. Being Indian, he didn't have to bother with a saddle, and he seemed to have a natural way with the horses. Not only had he gotten his horse bridled already, but now he was preparing Phoenix so we could use her for carrying packs. Even as I watched, he wrapped the lead rope around her stall's gate and looked us over to see who he should help.

Me, me, I thought, but I wasn't going to ask, and he went to my mom.

"You all right?" I heard him ask.

"Just getting a headache from all this smoke," Mom answered.

I jerked my hand back in time to avoid my horse's teeth. "Stupid horse," I muttered. "Can't you feel it's not burning you?" In fact, the flames seemed to be fading, not quite so intense as before. "Spell's going," I warned the others.

But instead of being thankful for the information, Robin said, "Come on, Harek. How come you're always last?"

I gave the cinch belt one final tug, then looked up. Glaring. Daring Marian to pipe in with agreement. She didn't.

Mom did. "Ready, Ar—Harek?"

I backed the horse out of the stall and swung up

onto him. Conditioning was with me: the action felt natural and easy. I dug my heels into the chestnut horse's sides, and he was so high-strung we practically flew out of the stable, despite the semblance of fire by the door.

The others were right behind me.

Outside, Cornelius's dragon still swooped and incinerated. None of the townsfolk seemed to have noticed yet that there was a patch on the creature's tail where you could see through to the sky beyond.

Our horses' hooves thudded against the packed dirt of the street as we headed west. Away from the fire. Out of the town. Toward Sannatia.

CHAPTER 5

Forest

As soon as we passed the last buildings of the town, we were surrounded by tall trees. They pressed thick against each other, overhanging the narrow path on which we rode. Roots and creepers snaked across the way, forcing us to slow the horses' pace. In places, two or three of us could ride abreast. Mostly we went single file.

We rode in silence, each of us glancing back frequently to see if we were being pursued and scanning forward for any new danger. We could hear all sorts of small skitterings, and once a dark shape hurtled itself into the underbrush as we rounded a curve, but so far the biggest danger seemed to be the path itself, and the likelihood that one of the horses would trip and injure itself or its rider.

After a while the final traces of Cornelius's imitation fire disappeared from my horse's saddle. The dragon and the fires it had set in the town must have disintegrated by now also. There were going to be an awful lot of people mad at us. But, so far at least, nobody was following.

After it seemed as though we'd ridden for our full five days' allotment, at a point where the path ran alongside a wide stream, Robin said to Feordin, "Tell us about the land. What do you know of it?"

Feordin shrugged. "Nothing. I've never been west of the town."

Terrific. And here I'd thought he was our guide.

"Didn't you come this way with the dead guardsman's body?" Thea asked. "Where did you find it?"

"I didn't find it at all." Feordin was beginning to sound pricklish. "One of our people did, a forester, and he brought it to another forester stationed closer to the town, who brought it to me at Forester Head-quarters. Apparently the first man found the body where the forest meets the desert."

Nocona pointed to the ground ahead of us. "You can see where the body was dragged along here, no more than six, seven hours ago."

Well, maybe *he* could.

From up ahead came a scream, loud and terrified, as if someone alarmingly close was getting murdered.

In the stunned moment while the rest of us sat there giving each other dumb ooh-what-do-you-think-that-was? looks, Thea Greenleaf reacted. She dug her heels into her horse's flanks and forced him into the underbrush, following the stream where it curved into the forest away from the path.

I tore off after her even before the others. Sure, I was eager to get personally involved in this adventure that everybody else seemed to be running for me, but mostly it was the computer-ingrained rivalry: I couldn't let a Greenmeadow elf show me up.

I leaned forward to avoid the whipping branches, flattening myself against my mount. My horse's hooves thudded loudly, echoed by the others who'd taken up the chase. Ahead the trees thinned. There was another scream, closer this time. Whatever was happening, it was happening in that clearing.

Thea broke through the trees several seconds before I did. In the time it took me to catch up, I saw her swing her bow around and pull an arrow from her quiver.

I reined in beside her. We were on a gently inclined bank. The stream widened here, from something you could almost jump across, to a wide pool with this big rock in the middle of it. A lot of splashing was going on near the rock, but for a second that was all I could tell.

"Something's got her!" Thea cried. She had her arrow readied, but whatever she'd seen was no longer visible.

Then somebody's head broke through the surface of the water. Judging by the long hair it was a woman, but the distance was so great and everything happened so quickly, I couldn't be sure. She disappeared back under the water, fast enough to make me agree with Thea that she had been pulled under. I could see one of the woman's hands, still scrabbling for a hold on the rock, but then this thing that looked like a vine snaked out of the water and started prying at her fingers.

Thea shot her arrow, which was a risk considering all the thrashing that was going on. Her aim was good, though: the end of the vine split off, and for a second the woman almost heaved herself up out of the water. But her body was covered with more of those vines, writhing and twisting and obviously intent on pulling her back in. She got out one more scream, which was cut off with a gurgling sound as she went under.

I could hear the clatter of the hooves of our companions' horses on the stony bank even as I urged my horse down and into the water. There was no way we could save that woman in time by shooting off the vines one by one.

My horse balked, and I could understand why: the water was frigid and scummy and stank of rotting vegetation. I forced him forward, my sword ready. The water churned, but the woman didn't resurface.

Though the water was no higher than the horse's knees, he'd go no farther. I jumped into the frigid pond, close enough to see the woman's face under the water, a tendril around her neck.

The water was up to my chest as I hacked at the vines—and they were vines, despite the fact that they seemed to have a will of their own. When I cut them, they were pulpy and they oozed what looked like that white glop in milkweed. The water was so roiled from our struggles—me, the horse, the woman, the vines—I couldn't even tell if there were a bunch of separate plants or whether all the vines were attached to some central stalk. But they were all around the woman and she was flailing about. I had to be careful not to strike her. Under the water, her face and her fair hair had a greenish tinge.

I could hear my friends calling out encouragement, and there was splashing as some of them waded into the stream. Grabbing hold of the shoulder of the woman's dress, I started to drag her up out of the water.

Her hair and face, which had looked green under the water, were *still* green. And the vines . . . I couldn't tear my gaze from the vines. They were growing from her body. She smiled, showing what seemed to be hundreds of tiny, sharp teeth, stained pink as though she'd been eating . . . as though she'd been eating . . .

Before I could bring myself to finish that thought, she kicked my legs out from under me. The water closed over my head, cutting off sound, isolating me.

I could hear the blood pumping through my arteries and the roar of the water pressing against my ears. Keeping my mouth and nose shut I tried to figure out which way was up. But the woman—the creature—was hanging onto me, dragging me down, holding me down.

I swung my sword with all my force, which, underwater, was nothing. A vine blocked me, then coiled itself around my wrist. The water pressed against my face, against my chest. At the pool at our school I'd never been able to make it all the way across underwater, and the water sang into my ears that I wasn't going to make it now, either. *Stop struggling*, the water whispered. *I'll be gentle*, it whispered.

The water was icy cold, and suddenly drowning didn't seem as bad as it was cracked up to be. Except somebody had hold of my hair—and *that* hurt—and whoever it was dragged me to my feet and held me upright. All I wanted was to sit down in peace, but by the way I was being jostled I could tell—even with my eyes closed and my ears still blocked with water—that whoever was holding me was also fighting the naiad or kelpie, or whatever the green monstrosity was that had lured me into the stream. It certainly didn't seem fair on my part to make my rescuer work at two things at once, so I concentrated on keeping my balance, opened my eyes, and said, "Mom?"

My mother was fighting the water creature with her bare hands—Mom, who calls me or Dad, then leaves the room if a spider needs squashing; who lets the Home-School Association walk all over her; who won't stand up for her rights with her co-workers. She was biting, scratching, kicking, punching.

And the creature was backing up, trying to get away.

I was aware of people behind us and Marian commanding: "Harek, Felice—duck!"

I ducked, Mom ducked, and Marian's sword swept through the air, taking the water creature's head off as neatly as a Weed-Eater decapitating a daisy.

It wasn't as yucky as it could have been, the creature being a plant and all. The head plopped into the water, then the body tipped over. The vine around my wrist slipped off. All the vines twitched for almost a half-minute more, as if they couldn't tell they were done for and were wondering what they should do next. Then the water got all white and cloudy and started to bubble.

Nocona pulled me in the direction of the shore, while Robin and Marian helped Mom, whose face had suddenly gone all white and scared now that the danger was gone.

Back on dry ground, we whooped and hugged and congratulated each other on a fine first adventure.

I turned to thank my mother. "You done good," I told her.

She stood there, dripping wet, looking at me, and the only sign that something was wrong was that her bottom lip quivered. Then she sank to her knees and began to cry.

CHAPTER 6

Glitch

Marian knelt down and put her arms around Mom. "It's OK," she said. "It's all over."

It should have been me comforting her—after all, she was *my* mother—but I had no idea what to do. So I did nothing. I just stood there, digging my toes into the gravel on the water's edge while the others moved in to fill the space where I should have been.

"Don't cry," Feordin told her in a gentle voice.

"Whatever that thing was," Abbot Simon said, "it's dead now. It can't hurt anybody."

Brynhild patted her on the shoulder. "The first killing is always the hardest. But even the Sisters of the Sword would be proud of how you fought."

Nocona just stooped down near her, offering his presence as comfort.

Between sobs, Mom kept saying, "I'm sorry." And, "I'm fine." But talking seemed to make her worse.

Robin kicked a stone into the water. "It's just a stupid game," he muttered, which was a surprise to hear from any of them.

Next to me, Abbot Simon jerked as though he'd been slapped. "Game?" he repeated. But he said it softly, tonelessly, as though all his energy was focused on not losing his temper, on not going for Robin's throat. Shelton takes the game very seriously, and the abbot's reaction convinced me he *was* Shelton. To be caught up short just when he was really getting into it was bad enough. No doubt he figured Robin's calling the game "just a stupid game" was in the same category as referring to chocolate as just another candy.

Nobody else seemed to have heard them, and meanwhile Cornelius had materialized a silk hankie, which he now offered to Mom.

She took it, all the while keeping her face averted as though that would hide anything.

Thea gave me a shove. "He's all right," she told Mom. "He didn't get hurt. Tell her you're all right, Arvin."

"I'm all right," I mumbled. They'd all tried to help. All. Considering that two of them were computer generated, that didn't say much for me. And Thea'd gone and called me by my real name. Not that there could be anyone left with any doubts by now.

"I feel so stupid," Mom said. "It's just this miserable headache makes it hard for me to think straight. I'm sorry. I'm all right now."

Behind me, Abbot Simon's rage at Robin had obviously not diminished. "Game?" I heard him say again.

Mom shoved the used hankie up her sleeve and tried to smile chipperly. You could have told it was a fake even if you didn't know her.

"She's had this headache since the stable, at least," Nocona said.

"No problem," Cornelius announced. "Clerics have all sorts of healing spells. Abbot Simon?"

"Game?" Abbot Simon said, just as expressionlessly as before.

I glanced from the abbot to Robin, then back to the abbot. He had given his head the same jerk as before, but suddenly it looked less like a shocked reaction than the way a parrot will cock its head to the side when it's learning a new word. So much for my grand deduction. Chills ran up and down my arms. It had nothing to do with being wet from the stream.

"Abbot Simon?" Cornelius repeated, just the barest beginning of sounding worried.

Abbot Simon pulled himself straight. Then jerked his head to the side. "Game?" he said yet again.

"What's the matter with him?" Feordin rested his hand on the haft of his mace, as though concerned the abbot's quirkiness might take a violent turn.

For a moment we all stood there, except for Mom and Marian and Nocona, who were kneeling on the ground, and looked at each other. Then Abbot Simon cocked his head and said, "Game?"

Cornelius rubbed his arms like he'd had a sudden chill too. "Looping," he said.

Brynhild, standing next to me, shivered.

"Loopy?" Mom asked.

"Looping. A defect in the program." Cornelius rubbed his chin. "See, a program is a series of instructions. The program tells the computer, 'If such-and-such happens, do this. If thus-and-so happens, do that.' And so forth. In a loop, the program keeps telling the computer to go back to the same step, on and on, over and over again."

Brynhild shuddered, just as Abbot Simon said, "Game?"

Feordin said, "Rasmussem wouldn't have loops in their programs."

"Sure they would," Cornelius snapped. Of course he was Shelton. Plain as anything—now. Shelton knew a challenge to his hacking ability when he heard one. "Something this complicated? There's no way their programmers could anticipate every single thing the players might say or do. Real people are too variable. Every once in a while they're bound to come up with something so unexpected it never even crossed the programmers' minds."

I heard Abbot Simon say "Game?" but I wasn't watching him to see if he'd given his head that ridiculous sideways tilt. Of course he had. He always would. I wasn't watching Cornelius either. I was watching Brynhild. A moment later she gave another shudder.

"The thing with Rasmussem," Cornelius went on—and I caught just the slightest shifting in his eyes, as though he'd been distracted—"the thing with Rasmussem is that they've got people monitoring. They see a loop, and they interrupt and patch around it before the players even know what happened."

"Uh-huh," I said. "Something unexpected? Like when somebody starts talking about the game like it is a game? Or when somebody starts talking about computers and programmers and loops during a medieval adventure?"

As if on cue, Abbot Simon said, "Game?" and Brynhild did her somebody's-just-walked-on-my-grave shiver. This time I was sure Cornelius noticed it. *Everybody* noticed it.

"Wonderful," Nocona said, standing and wiping his buckskinned knees.

"It's not important," Cornelius said. What else could he say? "We don't need them."

Nocona stepped close enough that Cornelius had to lean back. "Clerics are the ones with the healing spells." Nocona threw the wizard's own words back at him. "What are we going to do if we need to raise somebody from the dead?"

"Well"—Cornelius grinned at us—"we're just going to have to be careful not to die."

Nocona gave him a disgusted look and pushed past.

Cornelius's grin lingered a moment longer, then he said, "And I've got some good spells, too, you know." He faced my mother and raised his arms. "*Sassafras Saskatchewan,*" he said—or anyway, that's what it sounded like. He lowered his arms and looked at Mom. "All better?"

"Well," she said, obviously trying hard to please, "maybe a little. Yes. I think so."

Cornelius didn't buy it, either. By his expression, he took the headache's continued presence as a personal affront.

"What did you do?" Robin asked.

"What did you *try* to do?" Marian asked, and for once I was ready to cheer her on.

"That was a Deflect Evil spell," Cornelius explained to Mom.

"Maybe you could try it again?" she asked hopefully.

"I can't do any one spell more than once in any day." Cornelius considered. ("Game?" Abbot Simon said. Brynhild shuddered.) "Got it. Maybe your headache's the result of a spell. I'll do a Ward Off Magic spell." He wiggled his fingers and held his breath until his face turned purple, all the while making this humming sound like a sick generator. "How's that?"

Mom shook her head, then winced at the movement. She looked awful, with her face all white and pinched, and her still-damp clothes clinging to her like some poor drowned creature. I wished there was something I could do: *Here comes Arvin Rizalli, ready to save the day*. I wished there was something anybody could do.

"I don't know what else to try," Cornelius admitted. "It still might be a spell, but cast by someone stronger than I am. Or whose cure we're supposed to find later on. Or sometimes there's random plague. But maybe it's just from all the excitement. Hopefully it'll go away on its own. If not, then I can try again tomorrow."

"Felice, can you travel, do you think?" Feordin asked.

Mom answered, "I think I'll be all right if we can have the horses not going too fast." She glanced at Abbot Simon just as he said, "Game?" again, then spoke in a whisper as though her own voice hurt her. "I think it'd be good to get away from here."

Brynhild shuddered.

People hovered around Mom, telling her things would be all right, helping her stand, helping her up onto her horse. I couldn't even get close.

We took the two now-extra horses with us, Abbot Simon's and Brynhild's, and headed back across the woods toward our original path. Just before the trees closed in around us, I looked back to the bank by the pool. I was just in time to see Brynhild twitch yet again, to hear Abbot Simon say, "Game?" yet again.

Looping, Cornelius had said.

Awfully touchy program, I thought.

CHAPTER 7

Lunch

"MAYBE," MARIAN SUGGESTED to Mom after we'd ridden awhile, "your head hurts because we missed lunch. It's got to be way past noon. Maybe we should stop to eat."

Girl's reasoning. And dippy girl's reasoning at that.

But after all, Mom was a girl too, and maybe Marian knew what she was talking about. Maybe a meal *would* make her feel better. Maybe.

Cornelius had already reined in. "Come to think of it," he announced, "I'm starved. This looks as likely a spot as any."

"No," Nocona said.

It wasn't that he raised his voice or sounded panicked or anything. But something about the way he said it stopped me, catching me between two breaths just as I shifted balance to dismount. "What?" I said, seeing him sitting up real straight, his eyes scanning the wooded area around us. "What is it?" I was suddenly aware how close the woods were to the road. Awfully close. I could pick no unusual sounds out of the silence. The rising and falling song of a robin. The distinctive chirps of sparrows, closer in. The background hum of insects. A hint of a breeze in the topmost branches.

Marian glanced from me to Nocona. "I don't hear anything," she announced, at the same moment Robin said, "I don't see anything."

Mom was looking like, "Oh no, not something else."

Only half paying attention to us, still scanning, Nocona said, "This would make an excellent site for an ambush."

Feordin released the breath he had been holding, a dismissive snort. "There's no way the townsfolk could have circled around and beaten us here."

Nocona didn't bother with an answer.

I said, "The townsfolk aren't the only ones we need to worry about."

"You worry too much," Cornelius said. But as soon as he dismounted, he closed his eyes and raised his hands to shoulder level. "Mmmmm," he said, sounding more constipated than anything else. "Mmmmm." Very slowly he rotated 360 degrees. He was probably supposed to look like a human radar detector. "Mmmmm." He switched directions and did another complete turnabout. "Nothing," he finally told us. "I detect no magic."

That seemed to satisfy most of the others, but Nocona said, "An ambush wouldn't have to be magic."

"Fine," Cornelius snapped. "Shall I do another spell? A Reveal Evil spell? But wait, that would only work if it were someone inherently evil who wanted to ambush us. I better cast some Wizards' Lightning too and hope I hit something lurking out there. And then maybe a Fireball, just to be sure. In fact, maybe I should make us all invisible. Maybe I should expend all my magic making sure this place is safe enough for us to sit down for twenty minutes, since you think maybe, just possibly, this spot *could* be a good place for an ambush, *if* someone wanted to ambush us."

Everybody else was already dismounted, more concerned about lunch than the possibility of attack.

I swung off my horse, the last one except Nocona to do so. "Give it a rest, Corny," I said. "Sarcasm makes wrinkles around your eyes." That's one of my mom's sayings, and I hoped it'd cheer her up to have me say it; but Marian was bustling her away to a spot under one of the trees, and she didn't hear.

Cornelius looked at me like he was considering detonating my head. Instead, he said to Nocona, "If you're so concerned about ambush, then you can stand watch for the rest of us." He turned haughtily and joined the group around the packhorse, rummaging for the field rations.

Nocona stalked away from the rest of us and flung himself down under a tree. He sat there, his back rigid, his legs crossed, his arms crossed, looking inscrutable. More probably he was just sulking.

For a few seconds, I stayed where I was. Listening. Looking. I even tried sniffing. (I smelled my own sweat, the leather breastplate, the horses, the brittle scent of greenery on which the sun has been beating all day.) Nothing amiss. Nothing dangerous. Nothing except the realization that this *was* a good place for an ambush.

So were a lot of other places, I told myself. Jumpiness could easily progress to paranoia, and then we'd be no good to the kidnapped princess or to anybody.

I stretched, pressing my hands against the stiffness

in the small of my back. Come to think of it, I was hungry myself. Come to think of it, I had to go to the . . .

Oops.

Oh yeah. They didn't have those yet. I glanced around to make sure I knew where everybody was, then crossed to the woods on the other side of the road.

Once there, I thought of my weapons, left with the horse, but didn't go back for them. I wasn't going far, no more than twenty or thirty feet. I could still glimpse my companions from between the trees and underbrush, and I could certainly hear them. Marian was laughing at something, her voice high and overly enthusiastic. That probably meant she was laughing at one of Robin's jokes. What an idiot.

I was just starting back, when I heard a twig snap behind me, from where nobody from our group could have been. *Aw no*, I thought as something very hard crashed into the back of my head. Talk about being an idiot.

CHAPTER 8

What Are Friends For?

T HE FIRST THING I noticed was the smell.

Oh nice, I thought. Now *I'm* looping.

But I wasn't back in Rasmussem's stable. The smell here was worse than that had been—kind of a combination of un-flushed toilets, musty basements, and fifty-year-old gym socks. My head had been split open by whatever had slammed into me, I was sure of it, and now my brains were spilling out onto the ground, releasing stale memories as they hit the air. How come I couldn't have my life flash in front of my eyes, like everybody else did? How come my life had to flash in front of my nose? I groaned at the unfairness of it all.

Take that back.

I *tried* to groan at the unfairness of it all. There was a gag stuffed into my mouth, and all that came out was a pathetic little noise that sounded more like the whine of an overtired five-year-old than a protest against injustice in the universe. The gag tasted dusty and greasy, and I got a mental image of the gray, stiff rags my dad keeps in the garage—the ones he uses to wipe off the garbage cans or to clean the dipstick while checking the car's oil level.

The Rasmussem program may be a marvel of technological sophistication, with cerebral stimulation instead of a dungeon master describing what we're supposed to be seeing, and with outcomes decided by instantaneous computer judgments rather than a roll of the die, but there's a lot to be said for a game that gets no rougher than pushing two-inch miniatures around on graph paper.

"Harek," a voice whispered at me.

Well, at least if I was dead, somebody else was dead right along with me.

I opened my eyes.

I was flat on my stomach, which I hadn't realized. The hard ground and the dampness had made me so stiff that it'd been impossible to tell which side was up. Another reason I was so sore was that my hands were tied behind my back. The next surprise was that I was indoors, which indicated some passage of time. In the dim, flickering light—torchlight, I knew instinctively—

I saw that there was a wall about six inches from my face: a stone wall, dark and slimy.

"Harek!" The whisper was louder, more insistent this time. It came from somewhere above me.

I raised my chin off the dirt floor and found Robin. He was chained to the wall, his feet dangling above the ground. *Oh*, I thought, finally catching on. *Dungeon*.

"Hello, Robin," I tried to say around my gag. It came out, "Huho, Huhin."

It didn't make any difference how it came out: Robin was obviously in no mood for polite conversation.

"Harek, get up." His voice never rose above a whisper, which probably meant there were guards nearby.

I decided I'd better check before saying anything incriminating. I raised my head higher and looked around the cell. The place was about as big as a small bedroom. To the right was the corner obviously used as a latrine; to the left, a heavy wooden door with a barred peephole. The guards, if any, were outside. Robin and I were alone.

"Harek." Robin was beginning to sound frantic. "Can you get up?"

"Hi hont hoe, Huhin," I said.

"What?" he asked.

"Hi hont hoe, Huhin."

"*What?*"

I tried to push the gag out of my mouth with my tongue and repeated it. How difficult was it to understand "I don't know, Robin"?

Either Robin caught on, or he'd had it with trying. From between clenched teeth he hissed, "Harek, if you don't get up by the count of five, I swear I'm going to pull loose these chains and jump up and down on your face."

My head wasn't clear enough to wonder how he could pull himself loose, but it was clear enough to know I didn't want my face jumped up and down on. I rolled onto my right side and pushed with my legs.

"One," Robin said, obviously unimpressed with my fish-out-of-water pantomime.

I gave him a dirty look. OK, so I rolled over on my back, figuring I could do a sit-up. But that was so painful on my bound arms I kept rolling until I was on my left side.

"Two," Robin said.

Cut it out, I warned him with what was meant to be a menacing narrowing of my eyes.

"Three."

I sighed and squirmed on the floor until I had my back against the dripping wall.

"Four."

Muttering under my breath, I braced my feet against the floor and slid myself up the wall. Wet and rough. It did wonders for my already sore back muscles.

"Thank you," Robin said. "Now take a look at my right boot. My *right* boot, Harek," he repeated, before I even moved.

I did my impersonation of Cornelius thinking about blowing someone's head apart, but I looked at his stupid boot. I considered making a snide remark, like maybe, "Real nice boot, Robin," but the gag was soaking up all the moisture from my mouth, and it seemed too much of an effort. Especially since he probably wouldn't understand me anyway.

"Look at the upper part of the boot," Robin said. "The other side: the outside of my leg. Do you see the fancy stitching?"

I nodded eagerly. It wasn't immediately obvious, but now that he'd pointed it out, I knew what it was, even as he said it.

"There's a secret pocket there that holds my lock pick. Do you think you can get it out?"

It was either that or wait here for another four days or until we were rescued, whichever came first. Where were the others, come to think of it? Was there anyone left *to* rescue us? I turned around and groped for Robin's boot with my hands tied behind me. The first thing I grabbed was his thigh, and he kicked me—hard—in the rear end.

"Hey!" I cried indignantly.

"Hey yourself."

We glared at each other until it suddenly occurred to me to wonder if all our noise was going to alert the guards. I pressed myself against the cell door and peered out the tiny opening. I could see a long curved hall lined with doors. To the left, the hall continued until it disappeared into darkness. To the right, there were maybe five or six doors on either side, and then the guard area. Three men were sitting there, bent over a table: cards or dice, they were too far for me to be able to tell. And having too good a time to notice a little noise from us. Apparently we were the only prisoners, or at least the only ones with a torch in our cell.

I went back to Robin, turned my back to him, and tried to grab lower on his leg.

This time I got his knee.

At least he didn't kick me, but he gave this warning growl like I was too dumb to figure out the difference between a boot and a knee.

I started to ease myself down onto my knees, but with my arms behind me, my balance was off and I dropped painfully onto the hard floor.

"There, now you've got it."

Thank you very much. I leaned back and found that my hands *were* even with his foot.

"To the right. To the right. No, to the left."

I couldn't tell which ached more, my knees or my shoulders.

"Got it! Do you feel the flap?"

I felt the flap. I felt the thin piece of metal under the flap. I couldn't get my hand turned around. Now my fingers were beginning to ache. Upside down, I got the pick between my index finger and my middle finger and lifted it out of its sheath.

The miserable thing slipped between my fingers and hit the floor.

I groaned. Robin groaned. But I was the one who had to retrieve it. I lowered myself all the way to the floor and tried to locate the pick from Robin's ridiculous directions.

"To the left. My left. Now forward. Too far. Back about three inches. Straight. Straight, Harek."

If the guards had come in then, I would have cheerfully volunteered to be on Robin's firing squad.

I rested on my right side, panting.

"Harek . . . ," Robin started.

I glared at him.

"Do you think you can pick it up with your teeth?"

With my teeth?

"Pull the gag all the way into your mouth, then bite the gag down between your teeth. Then you'll be able to get the pick with your mouth."

I couldn't think of anything else to do. And believe me, I tried. I chewed the soggy gag backward. It seemed enormous, but finally my teeth were free. I bent over and bit the pick, getting a nice mouthful of dirt floor at the same time of course.

Meanwhile Robin had used the toe of his left foot against his right heel and had kicked off his boot. "OK," he said, "now give me the pick."

Are you picturing this? Me with my poor aching body, on my knees with my hands behind my back and the pick between my teeth, and him dangling his bare foot in my face, flexing his toes?

Somehow we did it. I sat back on my heels, wondering, *Now what?* Robin swung his leg up like a dancer doing high kicks, trying to get the pick up into his right hand shackled into the wall. I was torn between the desire to get out of there and the hope he'd kick himself in the face and knock himself out. He got the leg higher and higher, finally almost reaching his hand before the pick flew out from between his toes and sailed across the room. It clinked as it hit the stone wall, then went *thunk!* against the floor.

"I'm sorry," Robin said, sounding close to whining, sounding . . . sounding . . . Well, to be honest, sounding as physically bedraggled and as emotionally exhausted as I felt. His arms had to be killing him, supporting his weight for who knows how long before I'd even come to. And those high kicks, and bouncing his heel back against the wall, and me giving him dirty looks all the time . . .

"You're doing a fine job," I said, more or less articulate now that the gag was in a manageable wad.

Robin looked amazed that I'd said it, which made me feel even wormier.

I went and got the pick between my teeth again and knelt in front of his foot again.

"I can't," he said, closing his eyes.

"Robin," I said, my teeth clamped on the pick. "Robin."

He could hear me, I was sure of it. Now I could

sympathize with how he had felt, trying to rouse me to consciousness earlier.

I nudged his leg with my shoulder.

"Leave me alone, Harek." His voice trembled with the strain of talking.

"Robin, I'll give you the pick, then you can step on my shoulders. Get the weight off your arms."

That got his eyes open.

"Go on," I said.

He clutched the pick with his right foot, and I walked to the wall on my knees, where I slid to my feet. He got his left leg up first, the one that still had a boot. It hurt like anything, but I didn't have the heart to tell him to hang on a bit longer while I pulled it off. After he stepped on with his right foot, I could hear him take several deep breaths, the last much less shaky than the first.

"OK. Tip your head to the left," he warned me.

I closed my eyes, because I wouldn't have time to dodge if his foot accidentally came flying at me, and I didn't want to see it happening.

I felt him swing his foot—could feel that he hadn't gotten very high at all. He swung again—not much better. He was too nervous about getting out of control, was worried about knocking all my teeth out on the rebound. Either that or he was too weak, which didn't bear thinking about.

"You're doing fine," I told him. "Consider me your cheering section. Consider yourself cheered on."

"Rah," Robin muttered. He kicked up. Again. And again. He inhaled sharply, and I thought he'd lost the pick, but I didn't hear it fall. I opened my eyes and didn't see it between his toes. I raised my eyes, saw that his fist was clenched. "Got it?" I asked, barely able to get the words out of my gag-dried mouth.

As though hardly daring to believe it himself, Robin nodded.

CHAPTER 9

Encounter

THE CHAINS weren't long enough for Robin to cross one hand over to the other wrist, even with the slack I provided by supporting him on my shoulders. So with the pick in his right hand he worked to unlock the shackle from the same wrist, and all I kept thinking was that if I twitched at the wrong moment, he was going to drop the stupid thing and we would have to start all over. Or if his hands were half as sweaty as mine, he'd drop it without any help from me at all.

The tremor that had started in my shoulders was traveling down my legs when I heard the faint *click* of the lock. I almost dropped Robin in my relief.

"Hey!" The chains rattled as he scrambled to grab hold.

"Sorry," I mumbled.

He pulled his right wrist free of the loosened shackle.

"Could you hurry it up?" I asked as he gingerly worked the stiffness out of his fingers, wrist, elbow, and—finally—shoulder. Sweat was running down my face, trickling into my eyes and making them sting.

Robin reached over and started picking at the lock on the left shackle. By then my knees were shaking and I was concentrating so hard on not embarrassing myself by passing out or something that I didn't hear the second lock click open. But I heard Robin's triumphant, "Ta-dah!" and I said, "Coming down," and sank to the floor.

Robin must have jumped off my shoulders—for a few seconds black shadows crowded the edges of my sight and I wasn't aware of anything—but then I was on my knees, and Robin had cut my wrists free with a blade he'd gotten from his left boot. Now he was hugging me while jagged pains shot through my shoulders and upper back, pains that flashed messages to my brain: *You thought that was pain before? THAT was numbness. THIS is pain.*

"We did it!" Robin said. "What a team!"

What a team, sure. We knelt there for about five minutes, trying to work the kinks and the soreness out of our muscles before we even got the strength to remember to keep our mouths closed while we breathed.

I untied the foul gag and threw it to the ground. The game was a lot easier the old way, with the dungeon master rolling dice to compute the amount of damage a character took.

I checked our peek-hole and saw that our guards were still engrossed in their game. "Safe for the moment," I said. "I think we should take a couple minutes to catch our breath."

Still flexing his shoulders, Robin nodded.

"What happened?" I asked. "Back in the woods, I mean."

He jerked his head up. "What happened to you?" he countered.

"I went to take a leak behind a tree, and the next thing I knew . . ." I indicated the cell.

"And they say girls are always having to go." Robin shook his head. "We were attacked. These guys came tearing out of the woods—"

"What guys?" I interrupted.

"I'll get to that."

"But they were human?" I guessed, judging from the guards I had seen down the hall. "You could see whether they were human."

"They were human," Robin agreed. "And there were a lot of them. Twenty-five, thirty of them compared to—what? eight, well, you weren't there—seven? no, but Felice was in no condition to help—six?—compared to six of us. They had us surrounded before we even knew they were there."

I rested my head against my knees. "Go on."

"The only thing that saved us was that apparently they wanted us alive."

I sat up sharply. "Why?"

He gave me that look that warned I was rushing his story again.

"Well, then, hurry it up," I said.

"Marian and I were using our swords, fighting back to back. I killed two of the attackers—well, one for certain; the other was wounded, but I don't know for sure if he died. Marian must have taken out at least four, but then we got separated. People were shooting arrows, Cornelius was shooting Wizards' Lightning. The thing is, Harek, it happened so fast." He shrugged helplessly. "Whenever we've played before, it was so orderly: people would get their turns one by one, then the dungeon master would say what the results were, then we'd take another turn . . . but this way . . ." He shook his head. "People were shouting, the horses were rearing—out of control and flailing with their hooves—and the Wizards' Lightning stank like anything and made our eyes burn, and there was all this dust and smoke so you couldn't see what was happening. Then Cornelius threw a Magic Web and caught about ten of our attackers. And me." Again he shrugged.

"They didn't stay to help you?"

"It would have only gotten more of them captured. Besides, they would have had to come back anyway for you. We figured you'd been captured already."

I was feeling pretty sorry for myself by then, and I wasn't too sure any of them would have come back for me. But Marian would see to it that a rescue attempt was launched for Robin. "So they took off without you," I prompted.

"Yeah. By then, I'd seen Nocona get hit by an arrow."

"How bad?"

"Hard to say. It got him in the leg." He indicated just above the knee.

"Bad but not horrible," I said. "Unless it severed a major artery, which would be horrible but not too horrible. Unless he passed out and the others were too busy to help, which would be—"

"Hard to say," Robin said again.

"Hard to say," I agreed.

"Thea got the creep who wounded him, and Feordin—"

"What about . . ." The name stuck in my throat. "Felice?"

Robin was sitting cross-legged, his elbows resting on his knees, his chin on his knuckles. He looked at me levelly for maybe seven, eight seconds and never said a word, and I couldn't tell what he was thinking. Then, just when I was ready to shake him, he said, "She did the best she could. She picked up a sword from one of the dead attackers, but that's not her specialty. And she's not well."

What was this, Noah Avila defending my mom to me? "Look—" I started, but he cut me off. "We all did our best. But we were outnumbered."

I held my open hands out, indication that I wasn't looking for a fight.

Robin didn't look convinced, but he nodded.

I said, "So Nocona was injured, you were captured, and the others . . ." I didn't want him to accuse me of being judgmental; what was another word for "lit out"?

"Left without me," Robin supplied.

"Left without you. Any of the bad guys follow them?"

Robin shook his head. "No, those who were left worked at freeing their friends in the Web. Course, once they got me free, they tied me right back up again. Then they threw me facedown across a horse. I saw them carry you out from the woods, and you looked like you were dead, but I figured they wouldn't've bothered with you if you were."

"I wonder why they bothered at all?"

"They're slavers. I overheard them talking. They're collecting for a ship that's coming in next week."

It made sense. A local robber baron turning his gang to commerce during hard times. "Do they have the princess?" I asked.

"Didn't sound like it."

"All right. Think you can unlock that door? Without the guards hearing?"

"Sure as my name's Robin Hood," Robin said.

"Wonderful."

He took his lock pick and started fiddling with the mechanism on the door.

"Ah, Robin?"

"What?"

"Maybe you better give me the dagger."

He hesitated, and I sure hoped he wouldn't argue with me, because I didn't know how he'd take to my pointing out that I was a warrior while he was only a thief. On the other hand, I was just thinking how I'd messed up everything I'd started this campaign, and that maybe I'd be better off letting him handle things, when he pulled the blade out of its secret compartment and passed it to me.

"Thanks." *Small, but a clean edge. Good balance.* Lucky for me, the thing wasn't iron but some lightweight alloy—made for hiding. I tried to get the feel of it in my hand, tried to let my mind go blank, to let Harek the professional elf warrior in, and Arvin— who-knew-how-to-cut-his-meat-with-a-knife-but- that-was-about-it—out. I'd have to act instinctively. If I stopped to figure things out, that'd be the end of all of us: Harek, Arvin, and Robin.

I stood out of Robin's way but close enough to see through the little barred window. I was watching the guards when the lock clicked open, and was sure they hadn't heard.

"I'll go closer," I whispered, indicating the darkened doorways to the other cells. "You stay here and create a diversion."

I slipped past him and into the hallway. *Don't look up*, I mentally begged the guards. On tiptoe I ran to the first alcove, the doorway of the cell closest to us. I leaned against the door, sure my heart was beating loud enough to alert the guards. When they didn't look up, I took a deep breath and ran to the next doorway, shrinking as far back into the shadows as I could, out of the puddle of light where the guards were playing cards.

I glanced back to where Robin was waiting. No sign of him, but, assuming he was where he was supposed to be, I waved for him to get going.

Robin gave me an instant to flatten myself into the shadows again, then went into action. He stepped out into the middle of the hall where he was illuminated by the torchlight from our cell, and pulled the door closed behind him with a rattle loud enough that the guards *had* to hear it.

"Hey!" one of them yelled.

For the briefest moment Robin froze, looking like a headlight-startled rabbit. Then he took off down the hall.

The guards jumped up from their game, upsetting one of the benches. I heard the scraping sound of swords leaving scabbards, and then the pounding of feet down the hall, toward the fleeing Robin. And, thanks to my own plan, toward me, too.

The shadows preceded the guards as they left the

well-lighted area. I held my breath and shrank as far into the alcove as I could while they came closer, closer. The one in the lead passed, never seeing me. I let him go. The second passed. Almost. My foot caught him totally unawares, and he went sprawling, his sword skittering down the hall without him. I stepped out into the hall, and the third guard ran straight into my outstretched dagger. Conditioning kicked in totally. I didn't even flinch as the guy doubled over—I braced my free hand against his helmet and shoved him away from me as though I'd been killing people all my life.

The first guard had skidded to a stop and rounded back on me. Beyond him, Robin had realized the trap had been sprung, and headed back, but there was no way he'd get here in time to be any help at all. I kicked the guy I'd tripped just to keep him off balance a bit longer, then thought, *Who am I trying to kid?* There I was with a five-inch knife, facing a guy with a three-foot-long broadsword, and I was closing in for hand-to-hand combat? I threw the knife. It hit the first guard in the throat and he keeled over backward with an awful gurgling sound.

The second guard started to get up and I kicked him yet again. Now what? Suddenly all the instinct was gone, and here I was without a weapon and burdened with this man who refused to lie still and surrender. I put my foot down on the small of his back, but I could tell that wasn't going to keep him long. "Surrender or die," I told him.

His hand whipped behind his back and grabbed my ankle. I hit the floor hard and rolled, half expecting to find him on me.

I found him dead.

"What a team!" Robin said. He was holding the sword with which he had just killed the guard, the man's own blade.

"What a team," I answered.

Robin retrieved his knife from the guard's throat and returned it to me. "You all right?"

"Yeah."

This was, I reminded myself, just a game. And Harek was a trained warrior who had killed many times before.

It didn't help.

CHAPTER 10

Disappearing Act

ROBIN LOOKED UP from riffling through the pockets of the dead guards. "Half of this is yours."

"Ahhh . . . ," I said, unenthusiastic but worried about getting the reputation for being a killjoy. I just wanted to get out of there.

Robin stuffed some copper coins and a small throwing knife into various hidden compartments about his person, then buckled on the dead guard's sword belt. After all, his inclination was to be a thief, and he certainly wasn't going to twist my arm to force this booty on me. "Let's explore," he said.

"Ahhh . . . ," I hedged.

"Harek, look around you. This is a dungeon. We're supposed to explore dungeons."

"Ahhh . . ."

"There might be treasure here. There might be magic items that we'll need for later on in the quest."

He was right, of course. Not that it seemed likely. Still. There was no use getting all weird on him just because I was grossed out by our having killed the guards.

"But we'd better make it quick," I said. "We don't know how long till the next shift of guards comes on."

Robin saluted to show he understood and jangled the ring of keys he'd filched from one of the guards.

I went and got the torch from our cell. It stank— something like burned hair—and sputtered and threw distracting shadows on the walls so that I kept jumping, sure that someone was coming out at us. But Robin had already opened the door of the next cell and was waiting for me.

The room looked pretty much like the one in which we had been locked: chains dangling from the wall, cesspit in the corner. "Nothing here," I said, pulling back.

Robin gave me a you're-not-getting-off-that-easy look and stepped forward. "Something written on that far wall?" he asked.

It looked like a four-lines-and-slash accounting, where someone had been keeping track of days—a lot of days. But I held the torch higher and Robin took another step forward.

And disappeared.

There was no shimmering, no fading out, no flash of smoke or crackle of electricity in the air. But no Robin either.

"Robin?" Gingerly, I held out my hand. Being an elf, I should have been sensitive to the presence of magic. But I felt nothing. "Robin?" My voice was shaking, though Noah Avila had certainly never been a special friend. I took a step away.

Suddenly Robin was there again, stepping backward from . . . wherever. He swore, using the kind of language that lands kids in principals' offices. Finally he asked, "Where was I?"

"I don't know," I fairly screamed at him. "You tell me."

"I don't know." He rubbed his arms, looking at the air before him warily. "Nowhere," he said. "I was nowhere."

"Don't give me that. You were gone. You weren't here."

"But I was nowhere," he insisted. He shivered. "There was nothing there, Harek. Nothing."

"What do you mean, nothing? Do you mean it was dark? You couldn't see anything because it was dark?"

"I don't know."

"What's that supposed to mean? Either it was dark or it wasn't."

"No."

"Robin." I was ready to shake him: it seemed such a basic question, but I switched tactics. "Could you hear me call you?"

He shook his head.

I lowered my voice. I'd been close to yelling, and I suddenly remembered where we were. "Some kind of magic?" I asked. A powerful enough wizard could have put warding spells around an area, to hide it from detection. "Some place we have to pass through?" Now, there was a thought.

Robin was shaking his head. "I don't think so. You try it."

"What if I get stuck?"

He shouted at me: "There's nothing there."

"I know there's nothing there," I shouted back. "You keep telling me there's nothing there. All right, I get it: there's nothing there."

We stood nose-to-nose, glaring at each other, both breathing hard. We were being stupid—loud enough to attract unwanted attention. All of a sudden I could feel every ache from being whacked on the head and tied up and thrown into a cold, damp dungeon.

I looked beyond him to the perfectly harmless-seeming air into which he had disappeared. "How did you get back?" I asked.

"Just stepped back," he told me.

I took a steadying breath. I flexed my hand on the handle of the torch. I was taking it with me, to light up Robin's nothingness. I started to take a step forward.

In the half moment as my center of balance shifted, Robin said, "It's just a matter of finding your body so that you *can* step back."

I finished the step.

And I was nowhere.

No walls around me. No floor under my feet.

No feet, come to think of it.

I was slightly dizzy, though I wasn't aware of having a body, as though my head—if I still had one—was stuffed with cotton.

Was it dark?

I don't know.

Not, I don't remember. Just, *I don't know.* I didn't have eyes to see with, or a brain to think with. Dark or light? The question was meaningless, like asking, Is the sky afraid?

I wondered if this was death. Or rather the computer equivalent of death. But Robin had come back from it. And only a cleric can bring people back from the dead. Game rules.

I wanted to step back, but I couldn't.

I didn't know how.

Just like I don't know how to wiggle my ears, can't find the right muscles to spread out my toes, couldn't begin to flex my appendix.

I couldn't see.

Couldn't hear.

Couldn't feel.

Couldn't scream.

Couldn't move.

I was beginning to dissolve, to spread out, to lose track of who *I* was. In my head (I think) I formed a picture of myself. I made that image step backward.

Nothing.

I remembered that I wasn't Harek Longbow of the Silver Mountains Clan, tall and fair and muscular and self-possessed. I was Arvin Rizalli. And while I couldn't remember exactly what that meant, I knew it was the opposite of Harek. I got a vague image in my head (I think) then gave *it* a mental shove backward.

I stepped back into the cell.

Robin had the decency not to ask me whether it had been dark.

I grabbed hold of his arm to steady myself. "Something's wrong, Robin," I gasped.

"Yeah, tell me about it. Let's get out of here."

We stumbled out of the cell, down the hall past the dead guards, through the guard area with the tipped-over bench. Robin snatched up the abandoned playing cards. I didn't wait, but he was only two steps behind me when I reached the stairs.

The stairs were carved out of the ground and slanted first one way then the other. They were worn lower in the middle than at the edges, so that I continually felt off balance as though I were about to fall.

At the top was a foyer. In one direction a door led outside, guarded by one of the bandits, who had his back to us. It was night already. I could see the not-quite-full moon low in the sky, and bright pinpricks of stars.

To the left of the stairs was a hallway leading farther into the bandits' hideout; but when I looked in that direction, my eyes watered and I lost track of where my feet were. It must have had a similar effect on Robin, for he never suggested exploring. He indicated my dagger—his dagger—tucked into my belt.

This wasn't like a bloodless miniatures-and-graph-paper game, nor like a video game with cartoonish graphics; so instead of challenging the guard, I sneaked up behind him and whacked him on the back of the head with the pommel of the knife.

He'd barely stopped twitching when Robin started searching his pockets.

"Would you cut that out?" I demanded between clenched teeth. "What if he comes to?" But I picked up the crossbow that had clattered to the ground beside the guard.

There was a courtyard ahead of us, a stretch of maybe ten yards, unoccupied land between the bandits' rather shabby fortress and the outer wall. The wall was stone, but it had a wooden door with a crossbeam lowered into a slot for a lock. I'd taken about two steps in that direction when another guard came strolling around the corner, unenthusiastically checking the perimeter. He was obviously as surprised to see me as I was to see him, but I had the crossbow.

I killed him before he had a chance to make an outcry.

For once Robin refrained from looting the body. Instead he ran ahead and pulled on the rope that eased the beam out of its slot.

We inched the door open and peeked outside. There was a clear area between us and the forest, and no obvious guards. But there were an awful lot of trees. An *awful* lot of shadows.

"We're sitting ducks here," Robin said. "Our best bet's to go fast."

He was right. If the trees could hide guards, they could hide us too. It was just a matter of hoping there weren't any guards, and of getting from the doorway to the forest. At a run, it should take us about five seconds. I nodded and told him, "On the count of three."

"Onetwothree," Robin said, taking all of about a quarter second to say it and to fling open the door and to start without me. I sprinted across the packed dirt toward the edge of the forest, counting off the five seconds I had estimated till safety. *One* . . . no sign of movement; . . . *two* . . . no shouts to stop, no clang of metal weapons, only my pounding heart; . . . *three* . . . I scanned the shadows ahead of us, aware at the same time that there might be guards behind us; . . . *four* . . . surely if there was someone there, he would have reacted by now; . . . *five* . . . the trees loomed, menacing or friendly, I couldn't be sure; . . . *six* . . . OK, so I'm a lousy estimator of distance; . . . *seven*. The branches whipped my arms as I pushed through them.

I took several steps more, but there was too much underbrush for mad dashing.

"Whew!" Robin leaned against my shoulder for a moment, his face sweaty but exultant.

Just off to his right, a hand pushed away a branch. Just as that registered in my race-numbed brain, a voice said, "Nice work, boys."

CHAPTER 11

Reappearing Act

HUMAN-SHAPED SHADOWS separated themselves from forest-shaped shadows. Two of them grappled with Robin, to keep his sword sheathed. Somebody seized my wrist also, even though I hadn't moved.

"Easy, easy." Our wizard, Cornelius, stepped closer to Robin, making sure we could see his face. "Don't you know your friends when you see them?"

"*When* I see them," Robin said. He pulled free from Marian, who was one of the people holding him. The other was Thea Greenleaf, and she continued to grip his arm for a couple more seconds, as though to make sure he knew that she wasn't letting go till she was good and ready to let go.

The stocky shadow by me, Feordin, had released me already. The others, Mom and Nocona, weren't there.

"What's your problem?" Cornelius demanded of us. "We came here to rescue you."

Robin glared at him. "You. You're our problem. Harek and I don't need rescuing. We're perfectly capable of taking care of ourselves, *and*"—he cut off any possible rebuttal—"*and* you might be a second-rate wizard, but you're a complete failure as a hacker."

Cornelius sputtered in angry amazement that anyone could say such a thing.

"Stop it," Thea demanded in an urgent whisper—a reminder that we might not be alone in the woods. "Just stop it."

Cornelius and Robin stood glaring at each other, both breathing hard. I stepped into the breach. "We ran into a problem—a serious problem."

"Yeah?" Feordin asked, not willing to commit himself yet. For all he knew—for all any of them knew—we'd had a rough encounter and were taking out our frustrations on them.

"We got away from the guards no problem. But we found a hole in the program."

"What do you mean—*hole?*" Cornelius asked.

Feordin elbowed him aside. "Let me handle this. What do you mean—hole?"

"We went exploring in the dungeon," I said. "We walked into this one cell, and there was nothing there."

"Nothing," Robin repeated for emphasis.

I paused to let that sink in.

Feordin looked from me, to Robin, to Cornelius.

"Nothing," Robin said yet again.

Cornelius shrugged. "Some kind of . . . optical illusion—"

"No," Robin and I chorused.

"Or a spell—"

"No." We got it in unison again.

"Or a . . ." Obviously Cornelius couldn't think of any other explanation.

"Hole," I suggested.

"Hole," Robin said.

Cornelius sighed.

"You're missing a level," Robin told him. "You copied the program and you missed a whole stinking level. We're stuck here for what's going to feel like five days, and there's non-player characters looping, and gaping holes in the program, and . . . and who knows what will go wrong next." He threw his arms up in disgust.

"Shhh, keep it down," I warned, Thea's anxious face reminding me that we were in hostile territory. "I don't think it's *that* bad."

Robin gave this highly betrayed, I-can't-believe-you're-on-his-side glare.

"Listen. How did we end up in that dungeon? Inept playing." Now they all looked ticked-off at me. "I mean, think about it: we were captured because we didn't fight off the ambush well enough—"

"Well, excuse me," Marian cut in.

I ignored her. I was already saying "we" to be polite. What more did she want? "Why didn't we fight off the ambush? Well, for one thing, we declared ourselves to be at much higher experience levels than we really are."

"*That*—" Cornelius started.

"And secondly," I talked over his objection, "we were short two players because we inadvertently got them looping."

"Does all this have a point?" Robin asked me. Boy, he was OK alone, but get him near Marian and he turned into a real pain.

"The point is, in normal circumstances we wouldn't even be here. There was nothing in that cell because Rasmussem didn't think we'd even see the fortress, much less go exploring in the lower levels. If—*if*—this were a regulation game"—I paused to let that sink in—"there'd have been someone monitoring, someone who would have switched us over to some subroutine."

It took a moment for that to settle. Then Marian said, "But we are on our own, children." Tenth-graders. But she was right.

We all looked at Cornelius. "Oops," he said. Then he grinned. "But think of all the money you saved."

Everyone groaned.

"Come on, let's get out of here," Thea said. "Before those creeps find us and drag us all in there and we all get to spend four days doing nothing."

"What about," Feordin said, "my mace?"

What was this, Riddle Time? "Ahh, I don't know," I said. "What about your mace?"

Feordin gave me a dirty look. "I was using it back there, during the battle where we stopped for lunch. I killed three of our attackers, and then one of the miserable dogs knocked it out of my hand."

"One of the ones you'd killed?" I asked.

"Funny, Harek. For someone who wasn't even there. Where were you, by the way?" He gave me about half a second. "Never mind, tell me later. Anyway, we had to make a temporary retreat. Then, when we came back, my mace was gone. One of those louts must have taken it," He nodded toward the bandits' fortress. "It's got to be here."

We all gave each other anxious looks.

"We're not going back in there, Feordin," I said. "For all we know, that part of the program may dissolve while we're in there." All around me, our companions nodded.

"That's my mace," Feordin cried.

"Yes," I said.

"Don't you remember my name?"

"Ahh—"

"I'm Feordin Macewielder—"

"Yes, but—"

"—son of Feordan Sturdyaxe"—Oh, no, he'd gone and started—"grandson of Feordane Boldheart, brother to Feordone the Fearless, great-grandson of Feordine Stoutarm who served under Graggaman Maximus."

"Yes," I said, "but—"

"Feordin *Mace*wielder," he repeated. *Not again*, I thought, but he left it at that. "*Mace*wielder. I'm Feordin Macewielder, and now I don't have a mace."

"Well," I said hopefully, "maybe you can get another."

He growled at me, and for a moment I actually thought he was going to bite me. "Cowards. Then I'll go alone."

"No, Feordin. This has nothing to do with fighting the campaign. This is the program's seams showing."

Of all people, it was Marian who came to my rescue. "Feordin, you've got to think of the good of the company. You go in that fortress and you may not come out again. We're already two people short."

He was considering trying it anyway—you could tell by his expression. But finally he relented. "All right," he mumbled.

"Good," Cornelius said. "Let's get back to the camp."

"Is that where the others are?" I asked. "Nocona and . . . Felice?"

"Yes," Thea said. "Felice was feeling so wretched, we decided it'd be best if she stayed behind. Nocona stayed with her in case there was any trouble."

Nocona? They'd left a wounded man to protect my mother? I was furious, but I only said, "Still has her headache, huh?"

Thea gave me a sharp look, then nodded without saying whatever was on her mind.

Darn, I thought. Somehow I'd hoped that in the hours Robin and I had been held captive things would have changed, improved—would have worked themselves out for the best.

All things considered, I should have known better.

CHAPTER 12

Day Two

AT THE CAMP, Robin, who hadn't had anything to eat since lunch, and I, who hadn't had anything to eat at all, got a cold dinner of everybody else's leftovers. The only good thing was that the group decided that I—along with Robin, Mom, and Nocona—needed to rest to regain our strength. So the others divided up the night watches among themselves, and I got to sleep.

In the morning I awoke to Feordin muttering to himself as he went along, scuffing his feet and bumping into people and pushing them out of his way.

"*Mumble, mumble* mace," was the first I caught. "How do they expect me to do my job without a mace?" I missed part of the next, but then heard the names Feordan Sturdyaxe and Feordane Boldheart. Then he called someone—probably me—a lazy, stupid wimp. "*Mumble, mumble* sword or bow." And then he said something about the good old days of Graggaman Maximus, but by then he was loading up his horse, too far away for me to hear clearly. In any case I was less interested in listening to Feordin complain than in finding out how my mom was doing.

But as soon as I saw her, I could tell that her headache hadn't gone away.

She was sitting up, with her blanket wrapped tight around her, her knees drawn up to her chest, resting her head in her hands. Marian hovered over her, trying to get her to drink from a tin cup.

"Harek!" Mom called as soon as she spotted me. But the effort, or the noise, must have hurt, because she winced and pressed her hands tighter to her head.

"Here, let me make a fire," Cornelius offered, "then we can have some nice hot —"

"No!" Nocona and Thea said together. Thea added, "We can't risk a fire being seen. We'll have to have a cold breakfast."

By then I'd made it to Mom's side, and she reached up to take my hand. "Are you all right?" she demanded in a quivery whisper-voice. "I woke up during the night, and Cornelius told me you were all right."

"Yeah, I'm fine." Considering how she looked, it

seemed pretty stupid to ask how she was, and I didn't know what else to say. "What's the plan?" I asked Cornelius.

"No fire."

"Yeah," I said, "no fire. What else?"

He shrugged.

"You going to try some magic on her headache, or what?" I was fast losing my patience and I still couldn't bring myself to call Mom Felice.

"I tried already," our wizard said. "While you were busy snoring away."

How come I always ended up looking like a fool, no matter what?

"I tried the Deflect Evil spell, and I tried the Ward Off Magic spell."

"No effect at all?" I asked, though I could see for myself. Something was wrong. Seriously wrong.

"I'll be all right," Mom said. "Only . . . what? Four more days of this? That comes to . . . ninety-something hours." She groaned. "How many minutes does that make?"

Who knows? I thought. She was always the one who was good at doing math without a calculator.

"Can we get out early?" she asked. "Can *I* get out early? I'm sorry to be spoiling everybody's fun, but if you can't make this headache go away, I don't think I can stand four more days of it."

We all looked at each other hopelessly. Even Feordin, who was mad at us, was clearly upset.

"I'm sorry," Cornelius said.

"There's no way to get out?" Mom demanded, sounding somewhere between wanting to cry and wanting to shake him.

"Well, if we were at Rasmussem—"

Almost everybody groaned. We *all* glared.

"Well, now we know for next time. If we just leave someone by the equipment to—"

"Quit while you're ahead," Nocona warned.

"Sorry," Cornelius said again.

"Well, *I* think," Marian said, "that we missed something."

"What's that supposed to mean?" I asked.

"Obviously"—how come, I wondered, girls always have to talk in that irritatingly superior tone of voice whenever they're explaining something?—*"obviously* Felice wasn't meant to have this headache for two days. *Obviously* we were supposed to pick something up at the town and missed it."

And how come, even though she kept saying "we," I kept hearing "you bozos"?

"What sort of something, Marian?" Thea asked.

"Well, I don't know. Probably something magic."

Robin said, "That's pretty lame, Marian."

"Well, I'm not hearing anybody else come up with something better," she snapped.

Oh-oh. Trouble in Love City.

"Listen," Robin said. "Like Harek pointed out last night, we took one long side trip yesterday. I think we were supposed to find the cure yesterday afternoon, beyond where the bandits attacked us. If we get back on the road, we'll find what we need by noon today."

"Yeah," Marian said, her voice getting louder and shriller. "Fine. But what if it's behind us?"

"There was nothing in the town," Robin said, his snotty tone matching hers exactly.

"But if there was, we'll be pretty darn far from it by noon today."

The two of them stood glaring at each other.

Cornelius started, "I think—"

"*What?*" Both turned on him and he took a quick step back.

"I think," he suggested meekly, "it'd be best to cover both options."

"Separate?" Thea asked, her voice an incredulous squeak.

"Well," he said. "Yes."

We all thought about that for a while.

"I'm so sorry," Mom said.

"Shh, it's OK," Marian said. Pain that she was, I was glad she was there. Boys aren't good at comforting girls, and Mom needed all the comforting she could get. Marian stooped down to take Mom's hand, but what she said was for all of us. "I'll go back."

I figured Robin was probably right, that the answer lay ahead of us, not behind. Still—just in case—I was glad when Nocona told her, "I'll go with you."

"But you've been hurt," Mom protested. "What about your poor leg?"

"Almost all better." Nocona flexed his leg to show her. "Injuries here heal real fast, or the game would drag." He seemed suddenly to realize what he had said. "Generally," he mumbled.

"I'll go too," Feordin said in the uncomfortable silence. He glared at Marian and Nocona. "Keep them out of trouble." He glared at the rest of us. "Maybe find a replacement mace."

Robin looked at me and Thea and Cornelius.

"I'll go on," I said.

"Me too," Thea said.

Cornelius nodded.

"Then we should go as quickly as possible," Robin said.

I half expected Marian to back down, once she saw that Robin was going to be stubborn about it. But she didn't. We divided our provisions, gulped down another cold meal, packed the horses, then Marian, Nocona, and Feordin rode one way, and Thea, Robin, Cornelius, Mom, and I rode the other. And the worst part was my nagging fear that neither group was right.

We backtracked over a part of the forest through which we'd already traveled—even though *I*'d been unconscious for the trip—and we were fairly certain that the whole bandits' fortress had been one enormous dead end. So—assuming there'd be no new dangers, no clues, nor objects we'd need for later on in our quest—we pushed the horses to the limit.

No, take that back.

We pushed Mom to her limit. She ended up riding double with Thea, afraid she'd pass out or get jostled off.

We slowed when we got back to the road, to the previous day's ambush site. Cornelius's Wizards' Lightning had taken down branches and gouged trees and scorched the ground. The air was still smoky from it. Smoky and . . . more. The bandits had abandoned their dead companions. An afternoon and a morning out there, and already the bodies gave off the stink of meat gone bad. Combined with the smoke, the effect was of a particularly sinister barbecue.

Robin was eyeing a body that was lying half on the road, like he was wondering what was in the guy's pockets.

"Don't even think of it," I warned. I didn't want to look at some one-day-dead guy's face.

Mom went back to her own horse. Now that we were on unfamiliar ground, we traveled more slowly. Besides, if anything happened that we had to try to outrun somebody—or something—any horse carrying double would be the first to falter. That's how come Mom had ended up with Thea anyway. Thea was the smallest and the least burden to her mount to begin with. Being an elf, I was the smallest of the men, and I'd been just about to offer to have Mom come over with me, when she announced she was well enough to go on her own.

Sure, I thought, as long as we kept the horses to a slow walk.

Midafternoon Thea suddenly said, "What's that up ahead?"

I sniffed the air. "Smoke."

She gave me a dirty look.

A small fire, I judged by the smell of it, and by the tiny gray wisp I could see between the treetops. The clean smell of nothing more than wood burning.

"Probably a campfire," Robin said. My thought exactly. I got out my new crossbow anyway.

We advanced cautiously.

The trees thinned. We came to a clearing and found a wooden cottage. The smoke was coming from a chimney. Nobody in sight.

Robin dismounted, taking his bow and quiver with him.

"Harek, maybe you better stay here," Thea said in a whisper. She glanced from my mother to me. Obviously Mom would be no good to anybody if we had to fight. Just as obviously she shouldn't be left on her own. I was going to stay, but Mom said, "We can't keep fragmenting." Swaying slightly, she got off her horse. She even brought out her slingshot.

We left the horses under cover of the trees and approached the cottage. Thea and I were first, then Cornelius, then Mom, Robin in the rear.

I pressed my ear to the door but could hear nothing. I held up three fingers to Thea. She was better about it than Robin had been. She waited for me to mouth the words *One, two, three,* then the two of us kicked in the door.

CHAPTER 13

The Statue

THE DOOR BURST INWARD with a splintering sound. I had my crossbow leveled and cocked. Next to me, Thea held her broadsword ready. Cornelius had his arms raised, positioned to let fly with Wizards' Lightning. Mom was crouched behind him with her slingshot, her lips thin and pale, her dark eyes sparkling feverishly. She'd been in no state to care about her appearance over the last two days, and her gypsy hair had become a wild halo of frizzy curls. If you hadn't known her, she might have passed as grim—fanatical even. Behind her, Robin had his longbow drawn, a green-fletched arrow notched.

Facing us, a little old man sat at a table, He paused, his spoon halfway between his bowl and his open mouth. A nasty grayish brown broth dripped off his chin *splat! splat!* back into the bowl as he gaped at us.

I checked around the room. It was dark, since

there was only one window, but so bare—fireplace by the far wall, bedding in one corner, a storage chest, the table—that it was immediately obvious the old man was alone.

"You broke my door," he said. He was hard to understand because he only had two, maybe three teeth, and he still had a mouthful of soup. Beans and onions by the smell of it.

"Ahhhmmm," I said, glancing to the others for help.

He wiped his mouth with his sleeve. "You broke my door," he repeated as though I hadn't said anything. Which I guess I hadn't. He shoved his chair back and approached. "Why are people like you always pushing in here, busting my door?" He poked a dirty finger at my chest. He was short enough that I could see the top of his head, bald except for a few tufts of age-yellowed hair. "Well?" He poked me again. "What do you have to say for yourself?"

Mom saved me. She said, "We're sorry."

He thought that over. "Hmph," he said finally. "Fat lot of good that does me." But he turned away from us and returned to the table.

Cornelius stepped forward. "We were wondering—"

"I ain't saying nothing," the old man said, sounding as though he meant it, "till you wild ruffians fix yonder door." He sat down and resumed slurping his soup. Then he added, " 'Cept you. The polite one. You better sit down. You don't look so good." So much for my evaluation that Mom looked grim and fanatical.

Mom stayed where she was.

I don't know about the others, but I seriously considered just leaving. We were on the road to Sannatia, what more did we need to know? We didn't have time to waste. But there was the nagging suspicion that Rasmussem wouldn't have put the old man here if he didn't serve a purpose. Maybe he could even cure my mother's headache.

I asked Cornelius, "Any spells you can think of that might help?"

The old man interrupted. "Spells! Unravel at the first full moon. You fix that door proper with hammer and nails."

Cornelius smiled at me. "You and Thea are the ones who kicked it in."

Thea cut me off before I could come up with a suitable reply. "And the rest of you are the ones who'll have to wait if we have to do it on our own."

"We can help," Robin told Cornelius. "Aren't we supposed to be in this thing together?"

"Hmm." Cornelius turned to the old man. "We'd be happy to fix your door if we could, but we don't have a hammer."

The old man sighed. He set his spoon down and went to the chest. After rummaging around in there for what seemed like half the afternoon, he brought out a hammer. "Here," he said, putting it into Cornelius's hand. He shuffled back to the table and sat down.

Cornelius looked at the hammer. He looked at the old man. He said, "We don't have nails."

The old man slammed down his spoon and returned to the chest. Finally he brought out an old piece of cloth, which he unwrapped to reveal three nails. They were all rusty and bent, obviously secondhand.

We had to bang them straight with the hammer before we could even use them. Then we had to decide where three nails would do the most good. We reinforced the crossbeam and got the wretched door hanging straight. By the time we were done, the thing looked better than before we'd kicked it in.

"There," Cornelius said, "now—"

The old man held up a bony finger, indicating for us to wait. He wiped a piece of bread around the inside of his bowl to get the last of the soup, then stuffed the bread into his mouth and chewed. With the small number of teeth he had, chewing was a major job.

Finally he placed his bowl on a shelf over the fireplace. "So," he said, "you must be here to see the statue."

We all looked at one another.

"Statue?" I said.

"Four silver pieces." He held his hand outstretched.

"What makes you think we want to see some stupid statue?"

He narrowed his eyes at me. "I wouldn't imagine you'd want to see a *stupid* statue," he said. "I imagine you'd want to see a *magic* statue."

That got us all listening.

"What kind of magic?"

"What's it a statue of?"

"What does it do?"

"Where is it?"

The old man waited for us to peter out, then explained: "Good luck just to rub it; magic for the taking. Five silver pieces before I tell you any more."

"You said four a minute ago," I said.

"That was before you insulted it."

Robin had obviously taken as much as he was going to. "Maybe we could go and look for it on our own."

"Maybe you could," the old man said. "Maybe you could even slit my throat and steal my money. But maybe you couldn't find the statue on your own. And maybe the bad luck of harming the statue's guardian would follow you to wherever you're going. Six silver pieces."

Thea, who had our money from the town, handed over six silver pieces before he could raise the price any more, "How far is this magic statue?" she asked.

"Follow me." He led us outside the cottage and around the back. The statue was about six feet away from his back wall, still in the clearing.

"Gee, that *would* have been hard to find," I said.

Mom stuck her elbow in my side.

The thing was weird.

It was chiseled out of rock, real rough like it'd been done by an amateur, or by someone who hadn't quite finished. Basically it was human shaped, slightly bigger than life-size, and lying flat on its back. The face was all knobby and gnarled, but the expression was clearly recognizable. It was an expression like you'd expect to see on the face of a kid who's just called his teacher a hairy, sweaty grub then suddenly realized the teacher is standing right behind him. It was the expression of unavoidable doom. I'd expected some sort of saint or hero. This was strange workmanship, a strange pose, a strange face. It sort of looked like, almost looked like . . .

"It's a troll," Thea said. "It's not a statue at all; it's a troll that turned to stone when it was caught in the sunlight."

"Yes," the old man said. He swiped away a spider that was casting a web from the troll's chin to its shoulder.

"This is supposed to bring us luck?" Robin asked. "It doesn't look like *he* was very lucky."

But I could see where there was a worn spot on the thing's forehead, where countless pilgrims before us had rubbed for luck. This thing had been here for a long time, and *somebody* believed. A lot of somebodies. I reached my hand out and got a very faint tingle.

"Magic," I said uncertainly.

"For the taking," the old man declared.

"Yeah. So you said." Cornelius ran his hand across the figure's face also. He wasn't an elf, so he'd have to do a Reveal Magic spell to know for sure, and he

112

wouldn't waste a spell that way. "What's that supposed to mean?"

"The boots," the old man said. "The sword. The crystal."

I looked in the same order the old man said it, starting with the feet. The troll was indeed wearing boots, and suddenly I realized that they weren't stone but leather. My gaze shifted upward. The sheath strapped to the troll's belt was stone, but the sword handle that stuck out of it was metal. And around the creature's stubby neck was a delicate gold chain from which hung a clear piece of glass, no bigger than a baby's fingernail, teardrop shaped.

I rested my hand on the crystal and got what felt like an electric shock. "Yow! It's magic all right."

Thea passed her hand over the sword, then the boots, and nodded.

Cornelius raised his arms and spat out some of his hocus-pocus, no doubt his Reveal Evil spell. He must have gotten a negative, for he only said, "Magic for the taking?"

"Take them," the old man offered.

Cornelius folded his arms with a what-do-you-take-me-for? expression. "Surely we're not the first to come by?"

"Most comers take just the luck. But you're right. Others before you have taken the magic objects."

"Well?" Cornelius demanded.

The old man shrugged. "Eventually they come back."

"Eventually?" Mom asked. I turned and saw she was sitting on the grass. She seemed worn out. "Do we have to return them by a set time?"

The old man shook his head.

"Then why do people bring them back?" Robin asked. "*I* wouldn't bring them back."

The old man shrugged. "I don't know why. I don't know what the magic is. I never ask. Nobody ever tells me. They just pay me four silver pieces and I bring them here."

"You don't know what the magic is?" I cried indignantly. "You mean there isn't a healing spell?" I'd been so sure, I'd convinced myself.

"Not that I ever heard. You need healing, go find a cleric. I'm going back in the cottage. Either take the things or not, *but don't . . .*"—he looked each of us in the eye like he was about to say something very important—"don't you dare write any nasty words on that statue."

"Wonderful." I watched him hobble back around the side of the house. "All that time wasted, and we don't even know what for."

Thea whacked my arm. "Stop complaining, Harek. Let's get the magic objects and see what happens."

CHAPTER 14

Boots, Sword, Crystal

CORNELIUS WENT FOR ONE BOOT, Robin the other. Thea pulled the sword out of its stone scabbard. Mom was sitting on the grass looking like nothing short of a major explosion was going to move her. That left me to get the crystal pendant.

The chain was made of tiny gold links. There was no sign of a clasp, so I figured it must be in the back. Still, I was afraid that if I just tugged the delicate chain around, it might snag on the rough surface of the stone troll and break. I knelt down for a closer look.

With one hand on the creature's chest, I reached the other around the back of its neck. Something tickled the back of my hand, and I jerked away a moment before I realized it was just a blade of grass. Maybe.

I figured I shouldn't be sticking such an important part of me where I couldn't see. I bent over. Sweat prickled on my back, from the heat, but also from the uncomfortable position and from the tension.

The grass I'd already felt blocked my sight. I blew, and the blades bent away from me, but I still couldn't see any clasp. I blew again, a longer breath this time.

Behind me, Robin said, "Harek?"

I rested my forehead on the ground and wished I'd die before I had to look up.

"Harek, why are you blowing in that troll's ear?"

Better still, I wished Robin would die.

"Ha-ha," I said. I brushed my knees off and stood. "You're so clever, you unclasp the chain." I turned my back to him in time to see my mother cover a smile with her hand. "Ha-ha," I retorted again, unable to think of anything better.

She burst into laughter, then put her hand to her head. "Don't make me laugh, Arvin," she begged. "I finally understand what all those cartoon characters mean when they say, 'It only hurts when I laugh.'"

"Hmph," I said, tapping my foot. But it was good to see her smile.

"What's the problem here?" Cornelius asked. I saw that he'd put on the troll's boots, which seemed dangerously presumptuous to me, but that's Shelton for you.

I explained my reasoning about the chain.

"Hmmm," Cornelius said. "When were necklace clasps invented?"

We all shrugged.

"Probably it just slips off over the head."

"If it does, we're in trouble," I said. "I don't know how much a petrified troll weighs, but I'm willing to bet it's more than I can lift."

"Stand back, everyone." Cornelius rolled his sleeves back from his hands. "Cornelius the Magnificent comes to the rescue yet again."

"*That's* all we need," Thea muttered.

Cornelius ignored her.

"Nothing up this sleeve—" he began, demonstrating.

"Get on with it," we chorused.

Cornelius gave us a well-it's-your-loss look and began a spell that sounded like a spastic snake giving birth.

But slowly and steadily the stone troll began to rise from the ground. Cornelius brought the thing to about shoulder level, then reached over and gently lifted the chain up over the troll's head. "Shall I make the statue somersault?" he asked.

"No," I said. I could just imagine the old guardian dropping dead of a heart attack.

Cornelius lowered the troll back to its original resting place. "Three-point landing," he announced.

Robin clapped his hands, slowly.

Ignoring, or not noticing, the obvious sarcasm, Cornelius bowed. And placed the necklace around his own neck.

"How come you get all the goodies?" I asked, though Thea still held the sword.

"As I explained to Robin while you were busy cuddling with the troll, since these objects are magic, who better to look after them than a magic-user?"

"Well, I'm keeping the sword," Thea said. "An elf warrior could make better use of it than a wizard."

"Perhaps," Cornelius said smugly. "Perhaps not."

Thea gave the thing a fancy flip. I half expected that she'd had enough and was finally going to chop off Cornelius's head, but the flip ended with her holding the sword broadside-up about two inches from his nose. "Orc Slayer," she said and her tone hinted that she *had* thought of her other options. "It says its name is Orc Slayer."

Cornelius ran his finger across the engraved script.

The words were written in Common Tongue, the language we were using. I couldn't tell what metal the thing was made of—not iron, which Thea wouldn't have been able to handle, nor bronze.

"This wasn't made by trolls," Cornelius said.

Thea snatched the weapon away as though afraid he'd try to talk her out of it, and tucked it into her belt.

"The boots have writing on them, too," Robin said in the uncomfortable silence. "Show them, Cornelius."

Cornelius sat down on the ground and crossed his legs, holding one foot up by the ankle so that we could see the sole of the boot. Probably he didn't trust us enough to take the boot off.

Etched into the bottom of each boot were these words:

Northward, Southward, Eastward, Westward,
Inward, Outward,
Always Homeward,
That is the Magic Word.

"Nice boots," Robin said. "Lousy poetry."

"How come the boots fit you?" I asked Cornelius. "The troll's feet are a lot bigger."

He shrugged. "As soon as I put them on, they just

kind of . . . molded themselves to my size. As a matter of fact, I put them on over my regular boots."

"That's the magic," Robin said. "They fit whoever wears them. There are Nike salesmen who would kill for that spell."

"There's more to it than that," Thea said, sounding as though Cornelius's self-confidence and Robin's flippancy were beginning to get to her. "If you read the poem—"

"I read the poem," Cornelius snapped. "It doesn't make any sense."

She turned her back on him.

"Well, *I* think," Robin announced, "you should give the crystal to Felice."

"Why?" Cornelius asked.

"Why?" I echoed.

"Just in case it has healing powers."

"The old man said no," I reminded Robin.

"The old man said he didn't know."

Sulkily Cornelius handed the crystal over to my mother.

"You don't know what that does," I told her as she slipped it over her neck.

"Oh, Harek," she said as she adjusted it, "you worry too much. This is just a game."

Oh yeah? I thought. *Since when?*

I waited two seconds. Then I asked, "Well, does it work?" Silly question. One look at Mom's face had already told me it didn't.

"Maybe you have to wish on it," Thea suggested.

Mom clutched the tiny crystal fervently.

"Maybe you have to wish out loud," Cornelius said.

Mom clutched the tiny crystal and said, "I wish my headache would go away."

"Maybe you have to wear the necklace, walk in the boots, and kill an orc with the sword, all at the same time," Robin said.

"Maybe the thing is worthless," I snapped.

Robin spared a dirty look for me before he turned back to Mom. "Well, keep it for a while and see what happens."

"Yeah," I added. "If you start to develop warts and leathery skin, let us know." A moment later I realized how bad that sounded, but by then it was too late.

"Let's get going," Thea said. "The afternoon's already half gone."

And how are Marian and her group doing? I wondered.

Heading back to the horses, I heard Cornelius muttering under his breath.

I gave him a shove and told him, "You have something to say to me, you say it to my face."

"I didn't say anything," he protested. "I mean, I was just repeating the poem from the boots, trying to figure it out." He looked for support from Robin, Thea, and Mom, all of whom had heard my outburst and were watching me warily.

My face went all hot. "Sorry," I muttered. They were ganging up on me even when they weren't ganging up on me.

"'Northward, Southward ... ,'" Cornelius repeated as we tightened our saddles, checked the bindings on our provisions. He shook his head. "*What* is the magic word?"

"The whole rhyme?" Robin suggested.

"I've said the whole rhyme," Cornelius told him.

Thea said, "The poem is written twice, once on each boot. Maybe you have to say it twice."

Cornelius took a deep breath. "'Northward, Southward, Eastward, Westward, Inward, Outward, Always Homeward. Northward, Southward, Eastward, Westward, Inward, Outward, Always Homeward.'"

"Kind of catchy, huh?" Robin asked.

"No." I was watching Mom, who looked all tired out and not very steady. "Maybe you should find out what the spell *does* before you try to figure out how to do it," I suggested.

"It's a traveling spell," Cornelius said. "Obviously. 'Northward, Southward . . .'"

Thea said, "The boots said, 'That is the magic word.' Not 'Those are.' It must be a one-word spell."

You could see the light bulb go on over Cornelius's head. "You say where you want to go," he cried. "And you get transported there." Then, before anyone could warn him to be careful, "Sannatia!" he said.

Nothing happened.

"Rasmussem!" he said.

Still nothing.

"Princess Dorinda!"

"That's two words," I told him.

"You're no help at all, Harek."

"Maybe you're not getting the poem right," I said. "Maybe you're leaving out a word."

"Harek," Cornelius said, "the poem is not so very hard to remember. It's only eight words long."

"Look, to be sure," Thea said.

Cornelius sighed. Angrily he flung himself down

onto the dusty road and picked up one foot. "'North-wardSouthwardEastwardWestward,'" he read in a rush. "'InwardOutwardAlwaysHomewardThat—'"

He wasn't there anymore.

The air shimmered the way it sometimes does over the road on a real hot day, or when you look directly at a fire. But then the air unwrinkled, and all that was left was the dust settling slowly back to the road.

Thea yelped, "My sword!" and indicated her sword belt, where there was nothing. Mom touched her neck, where there was no necklace.

"*That*," I moaned. "*That* is the magic word."

Everyone groaned.

"Stupid thing," Robin mumbled.

We went back around the cottage and found Cornelius pulling the boots off the troll again.

"*That*," I said, just in case he hadn't caught on. "Don't use the word *that*."

"I'm not an idiot," he said.

I didn't argue. I only told him, "You better not put those boots back on. There's no telling when and where you might unexpectedly end up back here again."

"Well, now I know," he said, handing the sword back to Thea, the crystal back to Mom. He'd snapped the chain, then tied a knot in it. "I'll be careful."

"You'll never be that careful," I said.

He winked and pointed, to indicate he'd caught me using the magic word, which he'd be too clever to do accidentally.

Thea bundled her sword away, but said, "We're not coming back for you again."

For once she was on my side.

CHAPTER 15

Nonplayer Character

LATE IN THE AFTERNOON we rode around a curve in the road and found dead bodies.

Two men. Two horses. Their deaths were recent enough that the bodies hadn't yet begun to smell, but something had gotten to them already. Something that had eaten major portions. Mom was looking anywhere but at the bodies. The others seemed excited at the prospect of a new adventure, gruesome or not. I felt the reverse: this was gruesome, adventure or not.

Cornelius went into his Reveal Evil routine, before he remembered he'd already used that spell up for that day.

"Eventually," Thea pointed out, "we're going to have to go past them."

I was determined not to let her show me up, so I dismounted and examined the tracks in the road.

"Wolves." I pointed at the tracks. "A lot of them.

And it looks like when they finished here, they headed off in the same direction we're going."

"Did the wolves kill these guys," Cornelius asked, "or were they dead before?"

That was exactly the kind of thing I'd been doing my best to avoid seeing. "Ahh, no sign of arrows," I said, though I certainly hadn't examined enough to go around making pronouncements like that.

Mom said, "Wolves don't attack people."

"Maybe not at home," Robin told her. "But things are different here."

I searched the ground for more clues.

With a sigh, Thea brushed past me and moved in closer to the bodies. She turned one over on its back and stooped for a closer look. "Still warm," she said.

I had difficulty with my next swallow.

Then she got up and strolled around the area, seeming pretty nonchalant about the situation. "I don't know," she announced. "It's impossible to tell whether they had sword wounds before the wolves came."

"So what does that mean?" Mom asked.

"Nothing." Thea wiped her hands on her pants, though I hadn't seen that she'd gotten any blood on them, and swung back up on her horse. "Either they were killed by a pack of wild wolves, or they were killed by something or somebody first and then scavenged by wolves right after. But in any case, they were killed just a few minutes ago. That means we have wolves, and possibly something or somebody else, uncomfortably close to us. And it's going to be dark soon." She suddenly turned on me. "Come on, Harek, let's go. Stop being such a ghoul."

Me? I wasn't the one going around touching dead people to find out corpse temperatures. But I remounted without saying anything and we rode on. It was my turn up front, and I slowed our already slow pace. I jumped at every rustle of leaves, nearly had a coronary each time a bird or a squirrel decided to shift position.

After about the fourth time I'd motioned for the others to stop talking so loud, Cornelius rode up to me and said, "Would you knock it off, Harek? You're making everyone crazy. What do you think you—"

From just ahead, a wolf howled.

Cornelius almost fell off his horse. But while I sat there like a lump of cold oatmeal, he recovered immediately and spurred his horse ahead. Thea and Robin tore in right behind him. I came to my senses enough to get going before my mother left me in the dust.

We burst into a clearing. It was about as big as the

parking lot at school. And like the parking lot after a rain, there was a small lake at the far end. Running along the edge of that lake were about two dozen large wolves. Running maybe two seconds ahead of the lead wolf was a man.

Cornelius raised his hands and flung out Wizards' Lightning. There was a *crackle!* then the two front-running wolves disappeared into a fuzzy blue explosion of burnt fur and sulfur.

Still running, the man turned his head toward us. Despite the distance, I could read the fear and horror on his face. I didn't blame him. Five of us, more than twenty wolves. And they were about five feet behind him, while we were the entire length of the clearing away.

Thea and Robin had already fitted arrows to their bows, and I reached behind for my quiver as they released. Mom, who didn't have a bow but only a slingshot, was bouncing up and down in her saddle, waving for the man to run toward us.

But whether he was reluctant to bring the wolves on us, or was afraid to put himself between our weapons and the wolves, or was just too confused to know what he was doing, he continued to run along the shore of the little lake. He was about halfway down its length. If he didn't change direction soon, he'd reenter the forest on the far side and there'd be nothing we could do to help him then.

Robin's arrow hit one of the wolves. Thea, using a shorter bow, didn't have the distance. But the wolves seemed aware of us now and were beginning to slow down just the tiniest bit. I'd finally gotten my crossbow ready and fired a bolt. It hit the new lead wolf, who collapsed and disappeared in a flurry of gray-and-white wolf bodies moving too fast to avoid trampling him.

Next to me, Cornelius shot another round of Wizards' Lightning, and two more wolves disappeared.

Mom had started yelling for the man, "Come here! Come to us!" despite her aching head.

Finally he seemed to catch on. By then the wolves had had it, and once he headed toward us, they dropped way behind.

Robin and I each got off another arrow, although we ended up shooting the same wolf. Cornelius, who could only use his Wizards' Lightning a limited number of times each day—depending on how much energy he put into each one—held back when he saw the wolves had given up the chase. As though on a command, they wheeled around from watching the man they'd been pursuing, from watching us, and disappeared into the forest.

The man we'd rescued kept looking over his shoulder. Once the wolves were gone, he slowed to an unsteady walk. He had his hand pressed to his side. As we approached, he dropped to his knees, looking exhausted. Then he coughed, and spat up blood.

"Thank you," he said with what little breath he had left. "Thank you. Friends. You saved my life."

"Don't try to talk," Mom warned him. She didn't look like she should be talking either. Now that the excitement was over, she looked like she might fall out of her saddle. Suddenly I thought she *was* falling and reached out to grab her, but then realized she was simply dismounting. I hid my movement by getting down also.

Mom knelt by the man. He had the look of someone who'd been around. Our kind of people perhaps, a mercenary, an adventurer. His hair was that color people call salt-and-pepper: the same amount of white as dark, which put him at about Mom's age—her real age, not Felice's. But he looked strong—at least a head taller than Robin, the tallest of our group, and his shoulders were about as wide as any two of us put together. He wore a leather breastplate which had seen better days, and he had on a wolfskin vest. Maybe the wolves had recognized it for what it was. Maybe that was why they'd pursued him so intently.

"Your arm," Mom said. "You've been hurt." She tried to push his bloody sleeve up his arm, but he pulled away from her, pressing his arm against himself. He wiped his other arm across his face, smearing the trickle of blood that came from the corner of his mouth.

"I'm all right," he assured us. "If you hadn't come when you did . . ." He shook his head and didn't finish his thought. He didn't need to.

Cornelius said, "What happened? Were those your companions?"

The man looked up sharply.

"Cornelius," Thea said in a warning tone. Then to the man, "Sorry. Sometimes he doesn't stop to think before he talks. I'm Thea Greenleaf, of the Greenmeadow Clan. This model of discretion is Cornelius. This—"

"The Magnificent," Cornelius interrupted.

"The Magnificent," Thea added. "This is Robin. Felice. Harek Longbow."

Each of us bowed or smiled in turn.

The man looked at us somewhat warily. "My name is Wolstan," he said, just when I was beginning to suspect he had no name. Slow-witted or in shock? In shock, I hoped.

Thea licked her lips, no doubt wondering how to broach the subject delicately. Good old Cornelius took over for her. "So, were those your friends up there on the road?" At least he didn't add, "Mangled and lunched on by the wolves."

Wolstan gulped. "Yes," he said slowly. "The wolves . . ." He glanced away.

"The wolves killed them?" Thea asked gently. "Or did something else?"

"The wolves. It happened so fast. One of the wolves jumped—landed right on my horse's rump. The horse panicked, bolted. *I* panicked," he admitted with another quick glance at us. "I could hear my brothers screaming . . . There was nothing I could do . . ." He buried his face in his hands.

"Your brothers?" Mom asked, her voice hardly more than a breath.

"How terrible," Thea said.

"Then my horse threw me, and I started to run." He shook his head and looked up. "It's all my fault," he said. "If I'd handled things better, been braver and quicker, my brothers might still be alive."

I could sympathize with that feeling. I patted his shoulder but didn't know what to say. For a moment I even wished that pain-in-the-buns Marian was still with us: she seemed to have a knack for comforting people.

Not like Robin who, somewhat callously I thought, brought everyone back to our business. "We were headed for Sannatia," he announced.

Wolstan started, as though he'd been slapped.

"We're on a quest," Robin explained, ignoring my dirty looks for his timing. "To rescue the Princess Dorinda."

Wolstan's dark eyes widened in amazement. "To rescue . . . ," he repeated, "the Princess Dorinda . . . ?"

"She's been kidnapped," Robin said. "Disappeared. Members of the Grand Guard killed. She appears to have been taken to Sannatia."

"Yes," Wolstan said. "I know. We—my brothers and I—we'd heard the same story." His eyes shied away from ours again. He stared at his hands, clasped in his lap. "We too . . . wanted . . . to rescue the princess."

Robin flashed me a self-satisfied grin to show his had been the right approach all along. "Would you like to come with us, then?"

Wolstan's gaze went to each of us in turn. "Yes," he said. "If you'll have me."

"Of course," we all said.

We sat down on the grass while Wolstan went to the lake to clean off the wound on his forearm ("You don't have a cleric with you?" he'd asked) and to wrap it with a makeshift bandage ripped off the bottom of his shirt. Mom offered to help, but he wanted to do it himself. Maybe to prove he was a tough guy. OK with me. His sleeve was soaked with blood and the arm must have been a mess, though he acted like it was nothing.

"Think he's a coward?" I asked. "Is he going to be a liability?"

"Arvin!" Mom started, obviously shocked. But it must have hurt her head to talk, for she didn't say anything else.

Cornelius, however, was never at a loss for words. "What a terrible thing to say, Harek. The poor man's been through a lot."

"Yeah," I said. "And he ran away from it."

"Think you would have done better?" Thea asked.

Ouch, that hurt. I nibbled on a blade of grass. "The point is, the way this game is going, I'm not expecting much help from Rasmussem."

Robin reached over and whacked my arm. "You worry too much," he said.

I'd strangle the next person who said that, I decided.

"Now quiet," Robin said. "He's coming back."

Wolstan approached, the bandage around his arm already bloodied.

"You sure you'll be all right?" Thea asked.

In answer, he bent his arm and straightened it several times.

Thea said, "Then we'd better get going, or we'll be caught out here by dark."

"But," Wolstan said, "surely we should camp here for the night?"

"With all those wolves hanging around?" Cornelius asked.

"Better them than the caves," Wolstan said.

We looked at each other. "What caves?" I asked.

"The Shadow Caves." Wolstan was obviously amazed that we didn't know. "They're just ahead. That's the way to Sannatia. They'll bring you almost to the desert's edge. Unless you go around the long way, which takes two days instead of half."

"Wolstan," Robin said, "why is that bad?"

"It's not—during the day. But at night, orcs come

out of the side tunnels." He shuddered. In a quiet voice he added, "I hate orcs."

Robin wiggled his eyebrows at me.

Thea looked excited about the prospect, but she only said, "Yes but, Wolstan, if we stop now and wait till dawn, think of all the time we'll lose."

"If you don't want to come with us," Cornelius said, glancing at us for approval, "we could still give you a horse."

We told him about the extra horse we had now that Brynhild was gone. We didn't, of course, tell him *where* Brynhild had gone.

"But you're going on?" Wolstan asked.

"We have to," Cornelius said.

Wolstan sighed. "Personally, I'd rather deal with the wolves." He shook his head. "But I'll come with you."

We gave him Brynhild's sword, which she'd kept wrapped in her saddle roll. It was a bit short for him, since she'd been a halfling. But we were glad of his company. If we were going to be meeting a horde of orcs—on their own ground, no less—we could use any help we could get.

CHAPTER 16

The Shadow Caves

THE CAVES WERE ONLY a few miles' journey from the clearing. The entrance dipped into the ground, looking less like a hill than a big bump.

"It looks like a burial mound," I said.

Everyone glared in my direction.

Disconcertingly near, a wolf howled.

Wolstan nearly jumped out of his skin.

Cornelius said something that sounded like "*Turgid hostage FORTRAN*," and a little ball of light appeared in his cupped hand.

"Ah! Tinkerbell!" I said.

With a condescending smile, Cornelius motioned for me to take the lead, since it was still my turn.

I took a deep breath and stepped into the darkness. Behind me, muffled by the stone walls, once again came the eerie cry of the wolf.

Cornelius and his horse crowded in behind me. The light he held let us see about as far ahead as you might at night with a car's high-beam headlights, except it was a circle of light, not a beam, so we could see the sides and behind too.

The cave dipped sharply downward and widened. Cornelius moved in next to me, and we started walking right away, leading our horses behind us to make room for the rest of the group. Above the clatter the horses' hooves made on the stone floor, I called back to Wolstan, "Who carved this out? Orcs?" for the passage obviously hadn't been chipped out by nature.

"Dwarfs," he answered. "Mining for copper. Some of the smaller tunnels interconnect, some are dead ends, some are filled with water. Once the dwarfs moved out, the orcs moved in."

It was a natural orc habitat: dark, damp, smelling of mildew and worms. They'd love the mazelike construction of the place, too, which would make it impossible ever to ferret them out.

We passed countless offshoots, smaller tunnels that branched away into darkness. The main tunnel dipped, curved, climbed repeatedly. Sometimes it would open up into a huge cavern, though mostly the ceiling was too low for us to ride horseback. Once we skirted an underground pool. Its black surface reflected back Cornelius's light, showing nothing of what was underneath. Ripples gently lapped the stone basin, though there was no breeze. When we spoke, our voices echoed back in sinister whispers. Our road was smooth, constructed that way by dwarfs with wheelbarrows full of copper, or worn by the feet of countless travelers.

And all the while we watched and listened, alert for orcs.

I was used to a game moving faster. "You have entered the Shadow Caves," a dungeon master might say. "After walking for two hours, you come to a door." Or, "Several furlongs later, you hear the rattle of loose pebbles from a corridor off to your right." Instead, I was in a constant state of expectancy, the surging of my own adrenaline wearing me out, the tense waiting dulling my warrior's edge. Already I knew that if orcs attacked *now*, I wouldn't be able to fight them off as well as I could have an hour ago. But the alternative was to give in to boredom, to deaden the instinct to strain my senses outward, to depend on the others to catch any telltale clue that we were being followed or were approaching danger.

Something skittered in the tunnel behind us. We

all whirled around, flashing swords, daggers, bows: ready to battle for our survival.

It was only a red-eyed rat, its sharp claws clicking on the stone path before it disappeared into a crack in the wall.

Cornelius released a breath. "How about we break for supper?" he suggested.

I didn't point out that his timing was disgusting. Instead I said, "Sounds good to me." I stretched, trying to work the beginnings of stiffness from my muscles.

Cornelius went to unload Phoenix, while Robin watched the rear. It was Thea's turn to be up front; and as for Mom, she just sat down where she was, looking exhausted.

"How about you, Wolstan?" I asked. Nobody was talking to the poor guy. That was a situation I would have hated, but I was never good at small talk. "You hungry?"

He shook his head. He had a way of always avoiding people's eyes. "My brothers and I, we'd just eaten. You know. Before."

There I went, trying to be helpful, dragging up painful memories. I sniffed at an unpleasant odor. "Lucky," I told him. Then, to Cornelius: "What *is* that?"

"Smells rancid," Thea said. "Something go bad?"

Cornelius sniffed at the various containers of food and shook his head.

Robin called up, "I don't smell anything."

"Good," Thea said. "You can eat first and we'll watch to see how sick you get." She swept her scabbard to one side and sat down, still facing outward. Resting her chin on her knee, she buried her nose into the crook of her arm.

I approached Cornelius. "What have you got?"

"Smoked mutton." He held out the strip of oiled leather in which the meat had been wrapped.

"Yeah?" Thea said. "How long's it been dead?"

The pieces of meat looked hard and dry and salty, but when I sniffed them, they smelled more smoky than anything else.

"Stop making such a fuss," Robin called from his position. "Next time, take your vacation at the Hyatt Regency."

"Hmph." Thea pulled the scabbard onto her lap and began to polish the pommel of her troll-acquired sword with her sleeve.

She *wasn't* making a fuss though. The smell wasn't so bad back where Robin was, but up by Cornelius and the packhorse it was foul. And beyond him . . . it was even worse. I sniffed like a bloodhound following a track, approaching Thea.

She'd unsheathed her sword to polish the blade. Just as I reached her, she swung the sword at me.

I yelped, falling backward.

"Harek!" she cried.

"What?"

Again she shoved the sword in the direction of my face, but now I realized she wasn't trying to give me a nose job; she was trying to have me look at the sword.

It was glowing, and the words etched in its surface, ORC SLAYER, appeared to be written in red.

I raised my eyebrows.

Then I sniffed the sword, to see if the awful smell came from it.

Nothing.

I sniffed beyond Thea, where the tunnel stretched before us.

No.

I tipped my face up. Directly above, about seven feet off the floor, was a hole—a huge hole: another tunnel high up. And from the darkness within, a stench as bad as the time I'd opened my locker the first day of school and found a salami sandwich someone had left from the previous year.

And glowing amber eyes, which blinked in recognition of having been discovered.

"Orcs!" I screamed.

Three of the creatures leapt out. I threw myself to the side to keep them from falling on me. At the same time I scrambled to get my sword out of its sheath, calling myself an idiot for having left the crossbow hooked to my saddle.

I only had my sword maybe a quarter of the way out when something slammed into my chest. I saw the glint of a dagger hilt, and remember thinking, *Aw nuts. Just when things are getting exciting, I have to go and get myself stabbed to death by an orc.* A half second later, the orc's momentum hurtled us both to the ground. Concussion on top of everything else, I thought. And here was this stupid orc who didn't even realize he'd already killed me, with his greasy little hands around my neck, trying to strangle me.

I was vaguely aware that the other two orcs had missed entirely and landed face first on the floor, but that was small consolation for being dead.

On the other hand, like a snake that's too dumb

to know it's dead, my body could still move. And come to think of it, the pain in my chest wasn't actually that much worse than getting hit by my cousin Tom's fastball, something he manages to accomplish just about every family reunion picnic.

The orc had my right arm pinned across my chest, since I'd been reaching for my sword, but I was able to slam the heel of my left hand into the creature's face. Then, since I hadn't quite died yet, I forced him farther back with my left forearm against his throat. That finally gave me enough room to tug my sword out of its sheath, and without stopping to think, I simultaneously shoved it into him and rolled him off. His dagger was still in my chest, and it only seemed reasonable to pull it out. Only then did I realize that just the tip had penetrated my thick leather breastplate. The pain was from the force of the blow and the fact that the blade was iron. Apparently I wasn't dead after all.

Which was a relief no matter how you look at it.

Orcs were still dropping out of the upper tunnel. They were about human shaped, though short and stocky and hairy in all the wrong places. And they had pointy yellow teeth. There were a couple dozen out already, and more crowding the hole. I killed two of them before I got a chance to take a breath, to look around and see how the others were doing.

Thea was swinging her sword, which now glowed as bright as Cornelius's magical light. Good thing, for Cornelius had had to drop that spell to use his Wizards' Lightning. Mom looked like she was just barely holding on, but Wolstan was by her side, and you could tell he was an old pro at this. Robin was using his sword too, although thieves prefer bows or slingshots. This was too close-quarters for that.

An orc swung a broadsword at my head. I ducked and his blade swept off the head of another orc who'd been coming up behind me. Like I said, orcs aren't too bright. I stabbed the first one, even though I did probably owe him my life. "It's just a game," I murmured.

"Back off!" Cornelius yelled to me and Thea.

We were badly positioned: Cornelius didn't dare use Wizards' Lightning on the remaining orcs for fear of hitting us.

We slashed our way to his side, whereupon he raised his hands and shouted something like *"Piccadilly Circus!"*

No sooner were the words out of his mouth than a huge fireball appeared, which spun down the corridor like a giant lethal bowling ball.

There were yowls and the smell of charred flesh, but meanwhile the way toward Sannatia was blocked, and we had to back up the way we'd come.

"The horses," Mom said, grabbing at Phoenix's bridle. "Our supplies."

"Leave them." With one hand I dragged on her arm, with the other fought off another orc. From the new direction we were heading came the sound of running footsteps: more orcs coming from the rear, surrounding us.

She let go of the bridle and came.

"This way." Thea sprinted down one of the side tunnels.

"What if that's a dead end?" Robin asked.

"That's the dead end," Thea said, indicating the direction from which the orcs were coming.

A short way later, the tunnel forked.

"Which way?" Thea asked Wolstan.

"Who knows?" Wolstan indicated Mom. "She doesn't look like she's going to make it much farther whichever way we go."

It was true, but I hated him for saying it.

Thea chose left.

At first the path dipped down, then it curved to

the right. We passed one secondary passage, turned right at the next.

And still every time we stopped for a breath the orcs' footsteps echoed hollowly behind us.

"They can see the light from your sword," Cornelius told Thea.

"Cannot," she said. "We're too far ahead."

"Orcs can see real good in the dark," Wolstan said. He gave a shudder. "I hate orcs."

We found another tunnel to the left. Took that. Bypassed two more to the left and one to the right, took the third one that opened to the left.

"Slow down," I said. "She can't keep up." By "she" I meant Mom.

"Here." Wolstan hooked his sword onto his belt. "I'll carry her."

"You will not," Mom said, but Wolstan grabbed her and flung her over his shoulder.

"Anybody keeping track of how we've come?" he asked.

"Ahmm," we all said.

And still the footsteps trailed us.

"It's your miserable sword," Cornelius told Thea.

"You've wanted this sword all along," Thea said.

"And if you can't have it, you don't want anybody else to have it."

"The sword can sense the orcs," Cornelius said, "which is why it glows. The orcs can sense the sword, which is why they can follow us."

"I think he may be right," I said.

"My other sword's with the horses," Thea said angrily. "And without this, we'll be totally in the dark. And—and . . ." She gave a cry of disgust and flung the sword down the tunnel away from her.

For a short while, the faint glow from behind us lit the walls. But then we were in the dark.

CHAPTER 17

In the Dark

"I'LL BET, CORNELIUS," said Mom, still slung over Wolstan's shoulder, "that you can't make another light for us until tomorrow."

"Ahm," our wizard said, "no. Sorry."

"Then, Wolstan, I really appreciate your carrying me, but could you please set me down before you accidentally walk into a wall, or before I throw up?"

I could hear the faint scuffling of her shoes as Wolstan set her upright, but I could see absolutely nothing. And elves have better night vision than humans.

Cornelius said, "I do, however, have an idea." He started muttering, and the nonsense words were vaguely familiar. His Illusion spell, I realized.

There came just the faintest hint of light.

Take that back.

To use the word *light* at all would be an exaggeration. But suddenly I could make out patterns: black designs on black background. "Oh, very nice," I told him. "What's that supposed to be?"

"It's a torch." Cornelius sounded hurt that I'd had to ask.

"Why's it so dim?"

"Because, Harek," he explained too patiently for it to be patience, "it's not a real torch. It's just the illusion of a torch."

"Give your eyes a moment to adjust," Thea advised.

It got a little better. A little.

"We better hold hands," Robin said. "So nobody gets lost."

"Lost?" I said. "At this rate we could all fall into a chasm and not know it till we hit bottom."

"There haven't been any chasms so far," Thea said.

"So far," I pointed out, "we were in the main tunnel."

Slowly we made our way forward, bumping into walls and each other, stepping on people's feet.

At last the company began to unwind, to feel proud of themselves. "Did you see that big one?" Thea asked. "The one with the bear-head helmet? Did you see how long he twitched after I cut his head off?"

"Yeah," Robin said. "And how about the one I got with his own pike?"

"Did you smell them fry?" Cornelius asked.

And on and on. Wolstan didn't say much. He occasionally muttered, "I hate orcs," but that was about it. Mom didn't say anything at all. Neither did I. They were only orcs, I told myself. It wasn't like they were *people*. It wasn't like they were *real*. But I just couldn't get up any enthusiasm. Nobody seemed to notice.

After what seemed like a couple days, the passage narrowed and we had to readjust ourselves single file. Cornelius ended up in the lead, with me right behind. At that point, we were going downward.

"Corny, we're never going to find our way out of here," I muttered.

"Don't call me Corny," he snarled.

Mom squeezed my shoulder and I patted her hand.

We found another passage, but it smelled so damp and nasty, we bypassed it. We took the next one, though it was just as bad.

Suddenly Cornelius took a step backward, coming down hard on my foot. Mom slammed into my back. I could feel Thea walk into her, Wolstan into her, and Robin into him.

"Now what?" I asked.

"Water."

I peered around him into the dark. Ahead our path was blocked by a body of water several yards long. Beyond that, the tunnel widened and slanted upward. But of course there was no way to judge how deep the water was, nor even, for that matter, if it was plain, harmless water.

Cornelius picked up a pebble and tossed it into the water. "Doesn't sound deep," he said.

"What does deep water sound like?" Wolstan asked.

Cornelius hiked his robe up over his knees and stepped in. He took another step. Another. The water was up about midcalf. "Cold," he said, still moving forward cautiously. "Bottom's slippery." Almost halfway across, he pitched forward.

"Cornelius!" Thea cried.

"It's all right. It's all right," he assured us. The torch had fallen into the pool, but since it was only the image of a torch, the water hadn't extinguished it. Cornelius picked it up, but didn't stand right away. "Something's here." He felt around in the water.

"Something alive?" I asked.

Cornelius held up a metal box, about the size of a shoe box.

"Oooo, treasure," we all said. Except for Mom, who was sitting on the ground and didn't seem to care about anything. And Wolstan, who was only a non-player character and had his own reasons for whatever he did.

Cornelius waded the rest of the way across the pool. "Seems safe to me," he called back.

We assumed that if nothing had grabbed him, nothing would grab us and made it safely across, joining him on the other side.

"Should we open it?" Robin asked, eyeing the box.

"Sure," Cornelius said. "Why not?"

"Because we've got orcs breathing down our necks," Wolstan said.

"We've got a moment or two." Robin looked at Mom. "Care to try the lock? That's one of a thief's specialties."

"Go ahead," she told him.

Robin fiddled with the mechanism and the lid sprang open.

"Oooo," we all said again. Except Mom and Wolstan. Even in the terrible light, diamonds, rubies, emeralds, and assorted other goodies glittered brightly.

Cornelius closed the lid before we were ready to stop ogling. "I'll hold this until we have a chance to divide it properly," he told us, and tucked the box under his arm.

Robin glanced at me with raised eyebrows but didn't say anything.

CHAPTER 18

Lost

IN THEORY we wanted to head upward. But it was impossible to guess from the direction a tunnel started where it would go. Up, down, around, dead ends. More and more frequently we stopped to rest, worn out by anxiety and frustration. There was no way to judge how far we'd gone, how long we'd been at it.

"How are you doing?" I asked Mom during one of our stops. Wolstan had been carrying her again, and she was no longer complaining.

"I wonder if I'd feel better if I died," she said. She was sitting with her knees drawn tight up to her chest, her face buried in her arms.

I glanced around for help, but none of the others seemed to have heard. The thought was scary, even in the context of the game.

"I—" I started, having no idea how I was going to end.

"Shhh," hissed Robin, and a moment later I heard it too, the clump of heavy booted feet, the jangle of armor.

I jumped to my feet. "Let's get out of here."

"No," Thea argued. "The only way we'll ever escape is to find someone who knows his way around. Let's move down to that corridor entrance and hide. See what comes."

"What if whatever comes, comes down that corridor?" I asked, disoriented by the echoes.

"*You've* got a sword," she pointed out. "I don't know what you're worried about."

Ouch. A slam against my valor. I pulled the dagger from my belt and held it out to her. All the others had iron weapons, which we elves couldn't use; I was the only one with bronze. But it galled her to have to take charity from a Silver Mountains elf, I could tell. And I had to fight my inclination to hoard both weapons, just in case.

She snatched the knife. "Cover that torch," she warned Cornelius.

Cornelius, not willing to trust any of us with the treasure box, juggled both items and couldn't manage.

I took the torch, put it on the ground, and sat on it—one advantage to an illusionary light.

Seconds later someone from our group sniffed, very softly.

Carefully I inhaled. It was either two-week-old bacon, or orcs.

They didn't carry torches, since orcs can see perfectly in the dark, but when I glanced out from our side passage, I could see the glint of their eyes. Twelve glowing amber buttons, indicating six orcs. One for each of us. We could handle that. (Or twelve one-eyed orcs walking in pairs. We could handle that too, just not as easily.) Either way, I'd be fast, so I could help my mother with hers.

So softly she could barely be heard, Thea said, "Ready?"

I put my left hand on the shaft of the torch. Somebody had to bring it, or we wouldn't be able to find the orcs when they blinked. My right hand already held my sword.

"Go!"

We leapt out of our hiding spot. Holding the torch, I could see the surprise on the faces of the orcs before we bowled into them.

The trouble with orcs is, even though they're stupid, they're born fighters. I mean, that's an orc's idea of a good time—battle, pillage, and burn. You can surprise them, but the advantage doesn't last more than two seconds.

I found myself faced up against an old veteran of an orc who was missing one ear. Instead of a sword, he had this enormous club, about as big around as my waist, with metal spikes sticking out of it. When the orc saw me, he grinned, displaying many sharp teeth.

"Heh, heh, heh, warrior elf," he said, though it sounded like what he meant was: *Oh, nice—white meat for a change.*

Thea may have wanted someone to lead us out of the caves, but I certainly wasn't going to mess around trying to convince this guy to play tour guide.

I tried for a quick jab, but the orc skipped back out of my way, faster than you'd have expected from such a stumpy, twisted body.

"Heh, heh, heh, warrior elf," he said again.

I feinted to the right, then swung my sword to the left.

He blocked with his club. My sword hit it, whatever the wood was, and bounced off without even putting a dent in it. Meanwhile, my arm went numb right up to my elbow.

"Heh, heh, heh, warrior elf."

He was beginning to get on my nerves.

I pretended that I was going to feint to the right again: feinting a feint, I guess, to be technical. I leaned to my right, jabbed at his face with the torch in my left hand, but still followed through with the sword in my right.

The blade cut deep into the orc's side. His eyes widened in surprise. He didn't fall, but at least he stopped laughing. I yanked on the sword, but it wouldn't pull free. The orc wobbled a bit on his feet then lifted his club, aiming somewhere between my eyes and the top of my head.

I abandoned my sword, still in the creature, and took a step back.

He took a step forward.

I took a step to the side.

He took another step forward.

OK . . . I took another step to the side.

He took another step forward. By then he had stepped beyond me, but didn't seem aware of it. His eyes were still wide open as slowly he began to tip; then he dropped, like a tree coming down.

I retrieved my sword by bracing my foot against his ribs and tried not to think about it.

Four of the other orcs were dead. Wolstan had the last one pinned to the wall, his arm pressing against the orc's windpipe, and his dagger against the orc's belly. Thea was dragging on the arm of the hand that held the blade. "No!" she demanded, and her tone indicated she'd said it before and I hadn't heard because I was so caught up in my own battle. "No, Wolstan. Don't. Don't!"

Wolstan had what could only be described as a feral glint in his eyes—like an animal gone wild. Low and throaty he said, "I hate orcs."

"Yes," Thea said, not letting go. She shook at his arm. "But we need him, Wolstan."

He took a couple steadying breaths. The unnatural gleam became the reflection of my torch in his pupils. "Do you want to help us?" Wolstan asked the orc. "Or do you want me to cut you open and strangle you with your own insides?"

The orc, too scared to speak—not to mention that Wolstan's arm had prevented the guy from taking a good breath for the last minute or so—seemed to be trying to indicate the first alternative.

At last Wolstan eased up the pressure.

The orc coughed. "Thank you, thank you," he wheezed. In attempting to sound ingratiating, his voice was an already-irritating whine. "Thank you for sparing my miserable life, great noble sirs, great noble ladies. Great *brave* noble sirs, great *brave*—"

"I'm beginning to regret this already, you unctuous little worm," Cornelius said.

"Yes, sir," the orc said. "Thank you, sir."

Cornelius stuck his face into the orc's. "Let us even suspect you're trying to trick us," he warned, "and I'll let Wolstan here eat you alive."

"That's the only way I don't hate orcs," Wolstan said, sounding sincere.

The orc's head bobbed up and down in total agreement. "Yes, sir. Thank you very much, sir."

We made him remove his armor—he had a metal breastplate, but nobody wanted it because it smelled as bad as he did—then we took off his shirt and used it to tie his hands behind his back. He assured us that it would be another four hours' walk to the exit on the Sannatia side of the caves.

"I can't," Mom said. She began to cry. "I want to go home."

"Aw," the orc said, but he wasn't quick enough to hide his triumphant smile. "Poor lady. Poor, poor lady. Rest for the poor, tired lady. I'll take you to a place you can rest."

I didn't like the sound of that, but none of us was going to make it much farther. We'd been on our feet for at least twenty-four hours.

"We'll go on a little bit," Cornelius said. "I don't like this tunnel. There may be more orcs." He turned to the orc. "You understand, you little rodent? You find us a safe, out-of-the-way place where we can take turns sleeping. And remember, if anything happens, you'll be the first to die."

The orc bobbed his head up and down. "Yes, sir," he said, the picture of happy subservience. "Thank you very much, sir."

CHAPTER 19

Night Watch

"THIS IS A GOOD PLACE, great, brave, noble, gentle sirs," the orc said after a trek of no more than five minutes. Except that he was bound, he would have looked like a smarmy bellhop expecting a tip. "This is a nice, dry place for the poor lady to rest. Nobody comes here. You won't be disturbed here, honorable sirs."

"Yeah, and we won't have any way to get out if somebody does come," Cornelius said. "There's only one entrance, you revolting piece of slime."

"Nobody ever comes this way, great wizard. And the entry's so narrow, anybody passing by couldn't see you if they did come by, which they won't. And the poor lady needs—"

"Just keep away from her," I shouted at the orc. "Don't go near her, don't talk to her, don't talk about her."

"Yes, sir. I'm sorry, sir. Thank you, sir." The orc

bowed and backed away. But behind the gentle words and the wheedling tone was a hardness in the eyes, an expression of loathing that I could see even in the dim light. Orcs abandon sick or wounded members of their own kind. Or eat them if times are tough. I could see his mental wheels turning, wondering why everyone was so solicitous to the helpless member of our group, estimating that she must be *very* important.

If he got half a chance, he'd go after her.

This was stupid, I thought. If we didn't trust the creature to find us a resting place, why did we trust him to lead us outside?

The part of the torch around Thea's hand had faded away, so that it appeared as if the torch were floating about two inches above her clenched fist. Afraid we'd be caught in the dark, we selected a passageway that was near three separate side tunnels and settled down.

"Three tunnels, fine sirs," the orc said as we tried to make ourselves comfortable on the cold, hard ground. "Somebody's sure to come down one of them. Now the place I showed you—"

Everybody yelled, "Be quiet!" or "Shut up!" or something along those lines. Everybody except Mom, who was already asleep, which just goes to show how tired she was.

Robin volunteered for the first watch, then I was to take over, then Cornelius, then Thea, then Wolstan. Each one would guard for what felt like an hour. We figured that even though *we* couldn't tell what time it was, it was probably dawn, or close to. Hopefully that meant that the orcs, and any of the caves' other nocturnal inhabitants, would be getting ready to bed down themselves. *Hopefully* we weren't making sitting—or sleeping—ducks of ourselves. *Our* orc didn't look sleepy at all. He sat against a wall, glowering, his arms still bound. I was sure he was comforting himself with thoughts of eating our brains.

Relax, I told myself. Worrying would keep me awake, robbing me of necessary rest, and wouldn't help anything. The others were asleep already. Every once in a while Mom would make small whimpering noises, but these were interspersed with slow regular breathing. Cornelius was snoring: a gentle rattling wheeze. Thea ground her teeth for a while, but then mercifully rolled over and must have fallen into deeper sleep. Wolstan was twitching a lot, the way dogs will when they're dreaming about chasing squirrels.

I wondered if I should trade watches with Robin, if I couldn't go to sleep.

But Robin was already all settled in, sitting under the last of the torchlight, his sword drawn and resting across his knees. From a pouch at his belt, he took out the cards he had stolen from the bandits' dungeon. "Pick a card," he told the orc. "Any card."

I'd give myself five minutes, I told myself. If I didn't feel sleepy by then, I'd offer to switch with Robin. But I wasn't even awake long enough to find out the orc's answer. Without even being aware of closing my eyes, the next thing I knew, Robin was shaking my shoulder and telling me it was my turn.

"Yeah," I mumbled. "OK. I'm up."

The torch had gone out and we were in total darkness. I wanted to stamp my feet and walk around to make sure I didn't fall asleep again, but I didn't dare. I'd be sure to step on someone. The only light came from the glowing eyes of the captive orc. Still awake. Staring at me.

I couldn't see them, but all around me I could hear my companions, and that was reassuring. I listened as Robin's breathing got slower and slower . . . and slower . . . and . . . slower . . .

My head had been nodding to the rhythm, and I

sat up with a start. I didn't think I'd actually been asleep, but it was impossible to tell. The orc still watched me, his amber eyes never blinking.

I tried to stretch my hearing outward, beyond the rest of the company. Nothing. I'd been awake late at night before, but I'd never heard it this quiet. No cars. No wind. No hum of electricity.

I shook myself, realizing I was lingering longer and longer when I blinked my eyes.

Did I watch one hour? I don't know. Did I fall asleep during my watch? I can't be sure of that either. Certainly our prisoner never seemed to rest.

When I couldn't take it any longer, I got on my hands and knees and followed the sound of the snoring. I just barely avoided putting my hand down on Wolstan's face, my fingers brushing his thick hair and catching on his ear.

He grumbled without waking and rolled over.

I crawled around him. "Cornelius?" I prodded the sleeping form.

"Yeah." I heard our wizard yawn.

"Good night," I said. I lay down right there and yawned myself. I closed my eyes, then forced them open once again, just to check.

The orc was still awake. Still watching.

Day Three

THE DREAM started out nice enough.

I was at a lake, lying on an air mattress with my eyes closed, drifting wherever the wind and the waves took me.

Oh, yeah, I thought, knowing that I was really asleep and dreaming, *I'll stay here a bit.* The gentle up-and-down motion was pleasant, lulling. I thought how odd it was to be asleep and dreaming that I was about to fall asleep and start dreaming.

But where were the other people? I should have heard talking and laughing and splashing.

Instead there was a noise like a squeaky wheel. Like a lot of squeaky wheels.

The dream began slipping away even as I tried to hold on. Instead of fresh air and water, I could smell mustiness, like in our attic, where mice build nests in the corners every spring no matter what Mom does to try to keep them away. Mom . . . Mom . . .

The dream was gone, ruined. I remembered I was really in the Shadow Caves with some gaming companions, a sick mother, and a guide-orc I didn't trust. If I opened my eyes, I wouldn't be able to see anything because we were lost far underground without a light.

At least, I thought, at least I was refreshed. Who'd have imagined four hours' sleep could counteract the exhaustion of last night?

No . . .

No, I was *too* refreshed. Someone had fallen asleep on watch, and we'd all slept a lot longer than four hours.

I opened my eyes. I couldn't see anything, but the rocking motion hadn't stopped. Neither had the sharp squeaks.

I looked down toward the floor. It looked like a sea of red tapioca. Hundreds of little red eyes. I took a deep breath. I gulped. I took another deep breath.

"Rats!" I screamed.

I tried to roll off the rats that were carrying me, but they were everywhere. Blindly I kicked and flailed my arms, all the while remembering that—like orcs—

rats can see in the dark. The squeaking noises they made changed in pitch and intensity. Either they were frightened, or angry.

From around me I could hear noises of alarm and struggle. Then there was a flash. Momentarily the cave lit up, like a night scene frozen by lightning. I glimpsed my companions, borne on the backs of countless dark, furry bodies. Then Cornelius's bolt of Wizards' Lightning faded out.

The rats caught on the periphery of Cornelius's magic—those that were still alive—screeched in pain and fear, an awful noise like nails on a blackboard, like a subway train braking, like the feeling in your mouth when you've got braces and you drink from an aluminum can. Sulfur and singed fur tickled my nose.

There was another flash of Wizards' Lightning. Cornelius was aiming at the front of the mass of rat bodies, to avoid hitting us. But panic was spreading throughout the pack. Even those back where we were screeched and squirmed. They still held on to us, but they'd stopped moving forward.

The next time I rolled, my shoulder brushed the ground. The rats jostled me back up, but there were fewer of them.

Again Cornelius's Lightning flashed.

The rats that had been carrying him had had it: they were gone. Cornelius was on his knees, and the empty space around him began widening.

I twisted as hard as I could, finally got my legs under me, and stood, not that it did much good. My sword was gone, so I did the best I could with blind kicking.

Yet again a light lit the walls of the cave, but this time it was Cornelius's Continual Light spell. A new day, a refreshed set of spells. It was heaven to be able to see again. Apparently reasoning that a bigger light must be a bigger danger, most of the remaining rats took off.

Mom was there, that was the first thing I made sure of. Then I saw that our weapons were scattered on the floor. The rats must have been carrying them separately in case we awoke. Even the box with our treasure was there.

I grabbed up my sword and began slashing at the stragglers. The other members of our company did likewise, and in less than a minute, the only remaining rats were the dead ones.

"Who's the idiot who fell asleep?" Cornelius demanded.

Which was a surprise, because I'd figured it was probably him.

But Thea sheepishly hung her head. "Sorry. I was so tired. I didn't know—"

Mom patted her arm. "No harm done," she said in a hardly audible whisper.

"Except we've lost our prisoner," Robin pointed out.

I saw that our orc was indeed gone. Now that I thought about it, I couldn't remember seeing him during the times Cornelius's Lightning had lit the tunnel. No way to tell if he'd escaped, or if the rats had killed him or just abandoned him.

"Most rats," Wolstan said in his usual slow understatement, "don't act like that."

"Uh-huh," I said.

"They were definitely bringing us someplace," Cornelius said.

"This tunnel's a mess," Mom whisper-said.

That sounded more like her usual self. But then I saw what she was getting at. There were rat droppings all over the place, and marks their sharp claws had worn on the stone ground. They'd been up and down this particular tunnel an awful lot.

"Their lair must be near here," I said.

"And that's where they were bringing us," Thea finished. "But why?"

"No way to tell without going there," Cornelius said.

"Go where they were bringing us?" Mom asked. "Then why did we bother to fight them?"

"Trust me," Cornelius said. He turned to Wolstan. "Better carry her," he suggested.

Mom looked ticked-off to be talked about as though she were too infirm to have an opinion, but she didn't protest as Wolstan picked her up and carried her fireman-style.

We followed the tunnel maybe another hundred yards. The way got narrower and shorter. Up ahead was a low, roughhewn doorway. Carved into the stone above were these numbers: 3:17:8.

"I don't like the looks of this," I said. Whatever we were facing, it was me, Thea, and Robin who'd have to be depended on. Wolstan was carrying Mom, and Cornelius couldn't do any other spells unless he dropped his Continual Light, and none of us wanted that. "I don't like the looks of this at all."

Nobody seemed to care what I liked.

Cornelius walked behind Thea, who'd taken the lead, perhaps still feeling guilty for having fallen asleep. Robin was behind Cornelius, then me, then Wolstan and Mom.

We approached gingerly. If there was anybody there, they'd have seen our light and would have had plenty of time to prepare. So, once we got to the doorway, we leapt through, crouching, our weapons ready.

We were in a small cavern: maybe about as big as a classroom, but the floor was squishy with rat droppings. There were little piles of straw or rags all over the place, perhaps breeding nests.

"Well, now we know where they were taking us." I started to back out so I could breathe properly.

But Robin put his hand on my arm. "Look over there."

At the far end of the room were three steps and a raised platform. More than anything else, the arrangement reminded me of an altar. On the platform was a pile of bones.

"If they were going to eat us," I said, "they could have eaten us back where they found us."

"Yeah," Robin agreed. Without putting his sword away, he strode purposefully across the room. Halfway across he called back to us, "I think you'll want to see this."

Cautiously we followed. Probably for once Mom was grateful for Wolstan's carrying her. If she wasn't, she should have been.

After two steps, I could tell there was more than just bones on the platform. I could pick out shiny, glittery things. Suddenly the smell didn't seem so bad.

We all climbed the steps then leaned in for a closer look. There were coins and gems and pieces of brightly colored cloth. "They must bring everything they find here," I said in awe. The area was clean—no droppings, though the rest of the room was thick with them. Again, the impression of an altar, of offerings, came to mind.

Robin held a pale blue crystal as big as a golf ball to Cornelius's light. "Look at this shine."

"Look at *all* of it," Thea said.

Cornelius finally set down the box of treasure that he'd found in the puddle, and ran his free hand over the new stuff.

"We should get out of here," Wolstan warned.

"Yeah, yeah," I told him, letting a handful of gold coins run through my fingers.

"Where does all this come from?" Mom asked.

"People who've died in the tunnels," Wolstan told her.

That put a damper on things. "Let's just take this and go," I suggested. I tugged on a large piece of satin on which some of the stuff was laid.

I yanked, realizing as I did it that the whole pile would probably end up on me. Luckily the bones stayed where they were, but the cloth came free. Loosened, a piece of parchment fluttered to the floor.

Cornelius snatched it up while Thea pointed to a skull and asked, "What do you think that was?"

"Not human," said Robin.

The thing was big. About the size of a laundry basket. I didn't speculate because I was busy tying knots in the cloth, trying to make a sack of it.

Cornelius glanced up from the parchment he'd rescued. "They're getting their nerve back," he warned.

Four rats were running across the room, headed straight toward us. "Stubborn, aren't they?" I kicked one off the steps and it rolled several feet before lying perfectly still.

Robin stuck his blade into two more, and Thea bisected the last one.

"I don't think they like us messing with their things," Mom said.

"Hmmm." I tied one more knot to finish making the sack.

We swept all the coins and gems off the platform. There was enough here that we could have bought the

Rasmussem Inn and most of the town, even at their inflated prices.

"Put the other stuff in, too," Robin suggested, a little too smoothly, I thought.

"The box won't fit," Cornelius muttered, never looking up from studying the parchment, "and it's safer not to put everything together."

"What have you got there anyway?" I demanded.

"A map of the caves."

We all crowded around.

"I think we must be in this area over here." Cornelius pointed.

A little strangled sound escaped from me when I deciphered the ornate script. "You mean *here*, where it says, 'There be giant rats'?"

"Sure," Cornelius said. "Remember those numbers above the entryway? Those were location coordinates. See, we're not too far from where we want to be. Do you see this long hall? If we—"

"Psst!" Robin pointed to the floor, to the rat I had kicked. The thing was on its feet again. Its front feet anyway; its rear end dragged as though injured. With single-minded insistence it laboriously pulled itself up one step, then another. For a few moments I thought that was as far as it could go. It rested on the step, its sides heaving.

Wolstan elbowed me in the ribs and pointed to the doorway. About a dozen rats crowded there, watching their companion's progress. Waiting.

The rat pulled itself up, heaved itself up the last stair.

Now what? I wondered. I had to admire its persistence. "You going to take us on all together, or one at a time?"

The rat crawled past me, past the sack of goodies on the platform. It dragged itself onto the pile of bones and once again began climbing, inching its way upward. It reached the top of the skull, whatever it was, and balanced on the edge of the eye socket. Then it leaned forward, forward, until it tipped and fell into the skull, impaling itself on a sharp tooth inside.

"Boy, that was smart," I said.

"Suicide leap," Robin said.

We turned back to Cornelius's map.

"What I think we need to do—" Cornelius started.

A bone rattled, perhaps loosened by the rat's fall.

"—is go to the end of the hall where—"

The one jarred bone seemed to have started a chain reaction. I glanced over at the noise and saw that the whole front end of the pile of bones was settling.

"—the rats first attacked, then turn right and—"

I did a double take. The bones were moving all right, but they weren't settling: they were rising.

"Move!" Robin shouted. "Move, move, move!"

We jumped off the platform as the bones picked themselves up and revealed themselves as a single huge skeleton rather than the odd collection we had assumed. "There be giant rats," the map had warned. Sure were.

"I'm going to set you down," Wolstan told Mom as the rest of us spread out, forming a semicircle around the giant rat. "Stay back until we kill it."

"It's a skeleton." Mom's voice shook. "How can you kill it any more than that?"

The rat swung its huge head back and forth as though looking us over, evaluating us. It seemed to settle on Mom, though it was hard to tell, since its eye sockets were empty. It opened its jaws and snapped them.

Wolstan said, to no one in particular, "Well, if you had a cleric with you, clerics can turn the undead."

"You stay back, too," I told Cornelius, who was standing nearest to me. I didn't want to lose his Light again.

As soon as Cornelius started to retreat, the giant rat lunged at me. I jumped away and heard its teeth click shut inches from my ear. I kicked at a leg, too off-balance to use my sword.

Its leg momentarily buckled, then it recovered, coming after me again.

I slashed with my sword across its skull. No reaction. I had to back up yet again.

Thea and Robin jumped in, and from the other side, Wolstan. They hit the giant rat with their swords, knocking loose individual rib bones.

It swung its head to snap at Thea, who skipped lightly out of its way.

I moved in closer, trying to sever its leg, but the creature swung back too quickly.

"Look out, Harek!" Thea called.

I assumed she meant look out for the rat's teeth and thought, *What does she think I'm trying to do?* So I ignored her. And backed into one of the rats' nests and tripped, landing flat on my rear.

The giant rat jaws reached for me and I rolled.

Not quite fast enough.

The skeletal jaws clamped down on my long elvin hair, yanking out a good-sized chunk. Yelping in pain and surprise, I scrambled to my feet.

Wolstan chopped off the rat's tail, and that momentarily got its attention.

What we needed was something big to throw at it, to knock loose more of the bones. But what? There were no loose rocks in this cavern, only the platform with the treasure.

Treasure, I thought. That was it. The treasure we'd gathered here was in the soft sack, but . . . "Cornelius. Throw your box at it."

My shout drew the rat's attention again.

I glanced at Cornelius, who hadn't moved. "Cornelius!" I dodged a swipe by the rat's giant claws. "Cornelius, stop thinking about it and do it."

The rat swung its paw again, and one talon scraped across my leather breastplate. "Cornelius!"

"Oh, all right," he cried in exasperation. He flung the metal box, our first treasure from this expedition. It struck the undead rat's skull and knocked it right off the backbone.

The rest of the body collapsed into a motionless heap of unconnected bones. The treasure box cracked open and flung gems across the room.

I sat down heavily on the cold, filthy floor and rubbed the tingly spot on my scalp where previously a lock of hair had been. "Gee, this is so much fun," I said.

CHAPTER 21

Sand Hands

WITH CORNELIUS'S MAP we found our way back to the main tunnel. Cornelius was moaning and complaining about the lost treasure; we'd refused to give him time to look for more than three or four of the scattered pieces.

To shut him up, I'd handed over the sack from the rats' altar, but he still kept on griping until we reached the place where we had been attacked by the orcs. There we found the remains of cookfires and stacks of bones. The orcs had eaten our horses right there in the tunnel. Our saddles were pushed off to one side, slashed and useless. Apparently our provisions hadn't looked as appetizing as the horses, for those were still there. But the orcs had thrown them to the ground and stomped on them and—to put it as politely as possible—used them as a toilet. The weapons were gone.

Cornelius must have realized that we had gotten off easy, and he gave the complaining a rest.

About two hours later—it's hard to judge time when you're nervous something might be ready to jump out at you from every shadow, and you're worried about your mom, and you're exhausted and haven't had a decent meal in days—we rounded a corner and saw a grayish light streaming in through the back entrance to the Shadow Caves.

"Stop!" Thea jumped ahead of me and threw her arm to block my way.

"What?" Suddenly I realized I had been so excited to see this part of our journey end that I had gotten several very long steps ahead of the others. It *would* be Thea who caught me at it.

She pointed to a slender thread, which stretched from a crack on one side of the tunnel to another crack on the other side.

The others crowded behind us.

"Trigger wire." Robin, examining the spot where one end of the thread disappeared into the stone, motioned for Cornelius. "Can you bring your light over here?"

"Do we *need* to know what kind of trap it is?"

Mom asked from Wolstan's shoulder. "Can't we just step over the string?" She sounded dangerously close to tears.

Robin looked bitterly disappointed. "I suppose," he said. That he was willing to forgo one of his character specialties—trap detection—was a real tribute to Mom. I wondered if she knew it.

In the lead, I high-stepped over the thread. My foot came down on a slab of rock floor that wobbled almost imperceptibly.

Fake out, I realized. The thread wasn't the trap: it was the means to make sure we'd step right where I'd stepped. I threw myself backward, catching my heel on the thread. I felt it yank out of the wall, and I tipped dangerously past my center of balance.

Suddenly everything went dark, and I wondered if I'd knocked myself out. A moment later there was a click, then a hiss and thud that my elvin ears recognized as being about two dozen crossbow bolts releasing and slamming into the tunnel wall.

"Arvin!" Mom's voice was frantic.

"I'm all right," I assured her. *Harek*, I thought. *Is Harek so hard to remember?*

"Harek, you clumsy idiot," Cornelius said, right in

my ear. "Can't you even step over a string?" He'd caught me, I realized, dropping his Continual Light to do so. But we were close enough to the entryway that we weren't in total dark, and already my eyes were adjusting.

I pulled myself back up onto my feet. "It wasn't the string," I said. "The trap was in the floor just beyond the string."

"Yeah, yeah, sure," they all said, chuckling and jovial now that the danger was over. Shaking their heads, they made for the patch of light.

"It was," I insisted.

Robin patted my back as he passed.

"Morons," I muttered.

Outside, it was cold and drizzly. The sun was a patch of milkiness behind the gray sky, a pearl in a mother-of-pearl setting. Midafternoon, I calculated, with a skill I didn't have back home in the city. We hadn't had anything to eat for more than twenty-four hours.

Gone were the woods. Behind us were huge cliffs through which we had traveled. In front of us, there was a river, wide enough that maybe—maybe—a major league pitcher could just throw a baseball across it.

On the other side of the water, and for as far as the eye could see, the land stretched flat and featureless except for little clumps of quack grass.

The first thing we all did was kneel at the river's edge and take long drinks of water. Our waterskins, of course, were gone with the rest of our equipment. I hadn't known how thirsty I'd been until I saw the water and realized my tongue was stuck to the roof of my mouth.

"Which way to Sannatia?" I asked Wolstan as soon as I was able to talk.

He nodded ahead but off to the left. "I've never come through the Shadow Caves before," he said between gulps. "I've always gone around the Sand Cliffs."

I looked in the direction he was looking. The cliffs stretched on forever. Already the drizzle had penetrated my clothes; already I was shivering from the cold.

"At the end of the cliffs," Wolstan said, "is Miller's Grove. You can just see Sannatia from there."

Thea said, "So all we have to do is follow the cliffs."

Wolstan shook his head. "You could. But that's making extra work for yourselves." With his finger, he drew a diagram in the grit. "We're here. Miller's Grove is here. Sannatia is here." He was showing us a triangle. The straight line between where we were and where we wanted to be cut off the angle where Miller's Grove lay.

"If we don't get lost," Robin said.

"Can't," Wolstan assured us. "All we have to do from here is walk straight into the sun."

Or where the sun would be, if it weren't for the rain.

We all looked at each other. "We certainly don't have any time to spare," Cornelius said. Which we all knew already.

"Well, *I* think," Robin said, "we should take the short way, but first"—he stared meaningfully at the sack tied to Cornelius's belt—"we should divide the treasure." He threw Cornelius's words back at him: "It's not safe to keep all the treasure in one place."

"Look," I protested, "can't we—"

"I agree," Thea cut in.

"Fine," I said, throwing my hands up in disgust.

We sat on the ground and divided our treasure. First we drew blades of grass to establish the order in which we'd choose. Then we went round and round, each person picking one piece till all the pieces were gone. Wolstan got to pick, too, because nonplayer characters have to be included or they mutiny. We each had belt pouches, and nobody ended up with more than those could hold.

I was just pulling tight the drawstring on mine, when Cornelius squealed, "My boots!"

I saw that he was standing looking down at his feet in dismay. On his feet were his old regular boots, the ones that he'd been wearing under the ones he had gotten from the troll statue.

"Those stinking rats stole my boots!"

"Hmmm," I said. The thing was, Robin was sitting between us, his legs outstretched before him as though he had nothing in the world to hide. On his feet were Cornelius's boots.

Robin saw me looking and winked.

"Well," said Thea—and as far as I could tell, she hadn't noticed the boots on Robin's feet—"easy come, easy go."

Cornelius kicked at a rock but missed. "Foul stupid thieves," he fumed.

At least his use of the plural indicated he meant the rats, not Robin. I assumed Robin had stolen the boots last night, when he'd offered to take the first watch and the illusionary torch had still been giving some light. If Cornelius was too unobservant to have missed them till now, I figured that was his problem.

"Come on," I said. "Let's get going. Maybe we'll find a nice lizard or snake on the way, and we can fry it up with some crab grass and divide it six ways and have a wonderful feast."

"Oh, shut up," Cornelius grumbled. He kicked at a clump of grass that was no farther than spitting distance from Robin's feet, then walked to the river's edge. He raised his hands and said something in whatever language it is that wizards speak.

"Going to part the Red Sea?" Robin asked.

"No," Cornelius answered. "Fishing."

For a moment I thought he was being sarcastic. Then I scrambled to my feet and joined him, as did Wolstan. One very large fish was swimming around a group of smaller fish. Herding them, I realized. Bullying them toward the shallow edge.

"The trout's an illusion," he said, which I'd already guessed. "Grab the smaller ones."

"Fine," I said. "How?"

Stooping down, Wolstan snatched one of the smaller fish and tossed it, still wriggling and flapping, onto the ground behind him. Then he leaned forward, ready for another.

"Oh," I said. "Like that."

Wolstan turned out to be a natural. Which was a good thing. Thea was too squeamish about holding onto the slippery, squirming fish once she lifted them out of the water; and Robin and I had terrible timing. Wolstan landed more than the three of us combined.

Once we had a pile of them, Cornelius told us to gather some of the grass so he could make a cookfire.

"You'll never be able to get a flame going in this damp," Wolstan said, picking up one of the fish.

My empty stomach heaved as he bit into it, raw and uncleaned.

Cornelius saved us from that fate.

"Sushi only for those who want it," he said. "I can magically light a fire for anybody willing to wait for a cooked meal."

Fish is not one of my favorite things, but this fish smelled wonderful as we waited there in the cold drizzle, each trying to sit as close to the fire as possible.

Robin pulled his cards from his pocket. "Pick a card," he told me. "Any card."

For want of anything to take my mind off my stomach, I picked a card.

Five hands later, I'd lost five coins and one snake bracelet.

"Count me out," I said, and he turned to Wolstan. "Pick a card," he said.

"Careful, he cheats," I warned.

But by then the fish were half cooked, and that was as long as anyone was willing to wait.

As soon as we finished eating, we crossed the river. Luckily it never got much deeper than chest-level, because Wolstan carried Mom piggy-back. On the other side, he switched and put her across one shoulder, the easiest position for him, but the one she hated the most: with her head down and her rear end up in the air. For myself, I was just thankful that between the rain and the river, most of the orc blood and grime washed off.

Eventually we left the drizzle behind, and the ground became hard-packed dirt with great cracks. Our wet clothes gave off steam in the dry heat, and we all smelled like wet dogs. Finally, after what seemed like three or four weeks, but was only hours, we could see something ahead, something besides endless clumps of grass in endless sun-baked earth.

"The desert," Wolstan said. "The Un-named Desert."

"Wonderful," I said.

"We have to cross the desert to get to Sannatia."

I knew that. But I didn't have to be enthusiastic about it.

As we got closer, much closer, we saw something else, but at first we couldn't tell what it was.

"It looks like signs," Thea said eventually. "A series of signs just beyond where the desert starts."

"Sure," Robin said. "They say KEEP OFF THE GRASS."

We were all too exhausted to laugh. Not that it was that funny.

We couldn't make out the wording until we reached the actual edge of the desert, which was a distinct boundary, a strip no more than ten yards wide, where the ground got sandier and the grass got sparser. Beyond that, the sand was as thick and white as in a brand-new sandbox.

What each of the signs said was BEWARE OF SAND HANDS.

"*Sand hands?*" Robin said. "*Sand hands? What in the world are sand hands?*"

Wolstan shrugged.

We all looked at each other. We all shrugged.

"I never heard of anything so ridiculous in my

life," Robin said. He took a step into the sandy area before the desert. And another. Glancing back, he grinned at us. He crossed the not-quite-desert strip. Still nothing happened. Again he glanced back to grin. He took another step, which brought him abreast of one of the signs, and he drummed his fingers against it to show his contempt. He took another step and his foot sank deeper in the sand than he had anticipated, causing him to stumble. He pulled himself upright, then pitched forward again. "Hey!" he yelled, surprised. Then, "Hey!" he cried again. And that was fear in his voice.

From where we stood, we saw . . . Well, it sure looked like a hand to me. A human hand. It had hold of Robin's right ankle, and it tugged. Robin's entire foot disappeared under the sand.

Robin pulled out his sword and jabbed into the sand by his foot. No reaction that we could see. He suddenly jerked forward. The sand came up to his right knee.

Suddenly another hand popped out of the sand and grabbed his left ankle.

"Help!" Robin screamed. "Harek! Cornelius!"

It was like his calling us by name stung us into action. I started running across the strip that divided us.

Robin was tilted over, his right side sinking faster than his left. He continued to plunge his sword into the sand all around him, but still without effect.

The sand was up to his hips by the time I reached the sign. I reached forward with my left hand.

He dropped the sword, which was no use anyway, and a hand surfaced to grab it.

I slashed at the hand with my sword, but it was too quick. *Forget that*, I told myself. The important thing was Robin. Grabbing his hand with my left hand, I tugged. He was waist deep, and I wasn't helping at all.

Cornelius had come up behind me and seized hold of my belt. "Use both hands," he commanded me.

I dropped my sword on our side of the sign and reached for Robin. He was buried up to his chest.

"Do something!" he screamed.

More hands broke the surface of the sand, reaching for Robin's shoulders, pulling him down. Thea had run up beside us and struck at the hands where they came out of the sand, but there were too many of them. Any one of the hands could dodge down out of her way, and there were all those others, pulling Robin down, down, till his chin was resting on the sand, till his chin was disappearing under the sand, till more hands pressed down on the top of his head. And then I remembered the boots. "Say the magic word, Robin! Say *'That!'* "

The hands gave a final tug and Robin's head popped under the surface.

CHAPTER 22

Change in Plans

I SAT DOWN HEAVILY on the hard, sandy ground. After all the fighting and snarling and sarcasm and one-upmanship and cheating at cards, there was a hollow spot in the pit of my stomach that had nothing to do with lack of food.

Wolstan came up behind me, having put Mom down at the boundary where the sand began. Stubborn as always, Mom wasn't going to be left behind and was walking toward us, slowly, seeing that it was too late for rushing to be any use.

"Gone, eh?" Wolstan said. "Terrible waste." He sighed. "Too bad you didn't bring a cleric. Clerics can raise the dead."

I rested my head in my hands. I was beginning to get a headache myself.

"*That?*" Cornelius said in a dangerous tone of voice. He stooped down to put his face on a level with mine. "'Say the magic word, *that*'? Did Robin have my boots?"

"I—"

Cornelius grabbed the front of my shirt and dragged me to my feet. I was too surprised to resist. "Did you help Robin steal my boots?" he screamed at me.

I shoved him away. "Don't you touch me, you incompetent sleazeball. Why didn't you use your Levitation spell?"

"Oh yeah?" he said. Obviously things had happened too swiftly for him to think of it. *I* hadn't thought of it till a moment ago. "Oh yeah?" he repeated. He started to raise his hands for a spell, and I went for my sword an instant before I remembered I had thrown it down to help Robin.

Thea kicked the back of Cornelius's knee, and he staggered. He had to use his hands to keep himself from falling, and that ruined his spell.

"Stop it," Thea commanded. "Both of you." She gave me a hard shove. "You're acting like boys."

Cornelius rubbed the back of his leg and said with a pained expression, "We *are* boys."

"Well, you're acting like *stupid* boys. Robin was a thief. We knew that all along. So knock it off."

I rubbed my chest where she had stiff-armed me. "Yes, ma'am," I said.

"Now," she said, "if Robin used the magic word in time, he's back at the troll statue. But we certainly can't go back for him. Maybe—if our timing has gotten lucky—when the others come back from the town, they'll pass by there and pick him up."

"Since when has anything about this—" I remembered Wolstan in time and bit off the word *game*. "Since when have we been lucky about anything?"

Thea ignored me. "In any case, there's nothing we can do. We have to press on. Agreed?"

"Agreed," Wolstan and I said.

Cornelius grunted.

"Agreed," my mom started to say. But then she swayed, and before anybody could move, she dropped to the ground.

"I'm all right," I could hear her weak voice protest as we crouched around her. "I'm sorry. I just felt so tired . . . And . . . dizzy . . ." She closed her eyes, and I could see her chest heaving as though she'd been running around the block. "I'm sorry," she mumbled, "I'm sorry I'm . . . such a burden."

"Take it easy," Cornelius said, patting her hand.

"We need to find someplace for her to rest,"

Thea said. "We need to find someplace for all of us to rest."

I shaded my eyes from the sun, which was low enough to be turning the edge of the sky pink and orange. The row of warning signs extended as far as I could see. I turned to Wolstan. "This Miller's Grove, will we reach there before nightfall?"

"I thought Miller's Grove was out of the way," Cornelius interrupted.

"Yeah, but obviously we can't cross the desert here. Does the land get any more hospitable between here and there?"

"Miller's Grove is long and stretched out." Wolstan gestured, indicating parallel to the desert. "We'll be in the surrounding woods long before we get to the mill, beyond the cliffs. There's always something to eat in the woods. And we won't be in the open."

The longer we waited to eat, the less fussy any of us was going to be. "Well, if you could carry . . . Felice again."

I wasn't sure how much Mom was aware of. Wolstan picked her up, the head-down, rear-end-up technique she loathed, and she looked awfully limp.

As we started walking, an idea occurred to me. "Mom," I said. "Mom."

Mom opened her eyes and raised her head.

"Do you still have that necklace, the one from the troll statue? If Robin said the magic word in time, the crystal will be gone."

"Of course," Thea interrupted, "if Robin said the magic word in time, the sword would be gone too. *Of course*"—she raised her voice for Cornelius's benefit— "there's no telling where the sword is, since a certain member of our party made me throw *that* away."

Never turning back, Cornelius grunted like a pig.

Mom groped around her neck and the opening of her dress. "It *is* gone," she said.

Wolstan, ever the optimist, said, "A hundred opportunities for you to have lost it in the Shadow Caves."

Mom let her head drop back down without a word.

I hoped for all I was worth that Robin had made it—even though the chances were that, even if he had survived, he'd never catch up and we'd never see him again.

CHAPTER 29

By the Light of the Moon

OUR SHADOWS got longer and longer until they disappeared entirely. To our right the BEWARE OF SAND HANDS signs, posted one every several hundred feet till the land met the distant horizon, melted into the evening darkness. To our left we were vaguely aware of the looming Sand Cliffs, despite the fact that they were miles away.

Eventually we reached the forest, where we were too exhausted to care anymore.

We debated whether to light a fire, weighing the attention it would draw against the warmth and security it would provide. But even Thea, who was the only one raising any objections, seemed to be hoping for a fire. She just wanted us to be aware that she had lodged a complaint; that way, in case anything went wrong, she could remind us that she had told us so.

Of course Cornelius had already lit a fire magically that day, so we had to use flints.

"I'm going to see if I can find any game," Wolstan announced as Thea and I struggled to set spark to dried birch bark.

He disappeared into the blackness of the night. Not that I could see he'd have much luck: the orcs had made off with our bows, and I couldn't imagine anybody—even Wolstan—sneaking up close enough to a forest creature to be able to stab it with a sword.

There was a full moon, though it was playing peekaboo with the clouds. When it was out, I could see Mom sleeping on her makeshift mattress of leaves. Waiting for the fire, Cornelius had fallen asleep still sitting up.

I helped Thea arrange the fish. We still had six of them: one for each of us, plus one that would have been for Robin. Too bad, I thought for the tenth or twelfth time that day, there had been no way to carry some of the river water with us.

We sat warming our hands at the fire, saying nothing to each other. I wondered how long we should wait for Wolstan before we ate without him, and tried to decide who would have first watch. And I didn't want to ask Thea what she thought, because she was obviously more patient than I was, and she'd probably take it as weakness on my part if I did.

From alarmingly close a wolf howled.

Close enough that Cornelius sat upright, instantly awake.

Close enough that the hairs on my arms sat upright, too.

I slipped my sword out of its sheath. Next to me, Thea mirrored my action. Cornelius stood, his back to the tree, his fingers flexing. Mom groaned in her sleep, as though the wolf's call had pierced through to her dreams, and she rolled onto her side.

Then the cry—of loneliness or challenge or declaration of territory—faded till it seemed to sink beyond my threshold of hearing rather than to cease. My heart thudded in my chest. The wolf repeated its howl. And again a third time. Never changing, never coming closer. Telling other wolves about us? Telling them dinner was near?

I waited for yet another cry. And waited. Locusts grated noisily. Branches settled in the cooling night air. The campfire crackled, no longer as cheery as before. But whatever the message had been, it was over.

And suddenly I had an awful thought. What if the wolf had already found its dinner?

"Wolstan?" I called.

Behind me, from the opposite direction Wolstan had taken, the opposite direction from which the wolf had howled, there was a whisper of leaves and underbrush that was more than just branches settling. I motioned for Thea to stay where she was, in case it was wolves, in case they were circling us in.

Cornelius moved to my left. *Should I wake Mom?* She wouldn't be able to help. She might in fact get in the way. Still, if we had to make a sudden escape, being awake would give her a head start.

Before I had a chance to decide, a figure stepped out from behind a tree at the rim of our firelight. It was a lot closer than I had estimated from the noise, and the fact that the shape was human didn't make me any less anxious. But then it said, "Cornelius, Harek," and stepped closer.

Anxiety evaporated into relief. "Nocona!" I sheathed my sword.

Nocona motioned for the others behind him to hurry up—Marian and Feordin. That was why I had been confused by their distance: it was the two of them

I had heard; Nocona, Indian-stealthy, could have come up behind me and tapped me on the shoulder before I'd have been aware of him.

We all hugged and said how happy we were to see each other and asked, "Did you hear that wolf?" and everybody said, "Sure did," and we speculated how close it might be and wondered how safe these woods were at night. Then they asked, "How's Felice?" and we said, "No better," and they were shocked and dismayed and said they had been unable to find the town—that they'd kept riding and riding, and no matter which direction they went, they always found themselves back where they'd started—and they had been sure *we* had been on the right track and that she must be cured by now. We told them about Wolstan, and that orcs had eaten our horses, and they said they still had theirs, but they had tied them back in the woods when they had come to investigate our fire. Then Marian asked, "Where's Robin?"

"Ahmmm," Thea said, "I better tend the fire."

"Ahmmm," Cornelius said, "I better keep an eye out for Wolstan."

"Ahmmm," I said, but my mind went blank.

Marian put her hands on her hips and tapped her foot. "Where's Robin?" she repeated ominously.

I could have said I had to check on Mom, but it was too late for that now. One step and Marian would grab me by the shirt, I just knew it. "We . . . ah . . . sort of . . . lost him . . . Sort of."

"You *lost* him?"

"Sort of."

Marian grabbed me by the shirt after all. "*WHAT DO YOU MEAN, YOU LOST HIM?*" she screamed at me.

Nocona and Feordin stepped closer. I got the impression they might pull her off me if she started beating me up too bad—after all, we were short on players and getting shorter all the time—but they too seemed to take Robin's loss as a personal and intentional provocation.

I explained about the sand hands, stressing how Robin had chosen to ignore the signs and walk ahead of us. Thea and Cornelius nodded vigorously. Then I told the other things that had happened. About halfway through, Marian let go of my shirt. She sat down on the ground, resting her head in her hands.

"So you see," I finished, "it may just be that Robin is fine. We may be worrying needlessly."

Marian sighed. "Idiot," she muttered.

I didn't ask who.

"What about you?" Thea asked. "What happened to you after you realized you couldn't get back to the town?"

Marian just sat there, sulking. Nocona was poking at our fire with a stick, listening to all we said, but quiet himself. It was Feordin who spoke. "Well, we wasted about half the day at it. We kept thinking maybe if we circled around, or if we tried walking backward, or I can't remember what-all we tried. But finally we gave it up as another bug in the computer and took off after you four. Late afternoon we came to this old guy's cottage."

"Yeah?" I said. "Tell me about it." I had only explained that we'd gotten the boots, sword, and crystal from a sun-petrified troll. I hadn't brought up about how the old coot had stiffed us for six silver pieces, nor about how he'd conned us into fixing his stupid door.

Feordin shrugged. "Nothing much to say. Sweet old guy."

"*Sweet old guy?*" I croaked.

Feordin glanced at Marian for confirmation. "How would you describe Fred?"

Fred?

"Sweet old guy," Marian said.

Feordin glanced at Nocona.

"Sweet old guy," Nocona said.

Feordin continued. "Sure. He was full of useful information. Real friendly. Shared his dinner with us and everything. We fixed his front door. Some hoodlums had done a real job on it. He gave us six silver pieces for our help, even though we said he didn't have to. So I guess you could say that was the first treasure we earned."

Thea and Cornelius had the sense not to say anything.

"He had this statue in the back that he said was good luck if you rubbed it, which we did, and I guess we've had pretty good luck since. Wouldn't you say?"

Nocona nodded.

Marian said, "Until now."

"Say. Feordin turned back to me. "Fred's troll statue wouldn't be the same troll where you got your magic objects, would it?"

Thea, Cornelius, and I all nodded.

Before he could say any more, the skin-prickling howl of a wolf brought us all to our feet. It sounded as though it came from the same spot as before. Once again it howled three times.

"I don't like this," Thea said in the thick silence that followed. "Where's Wolstan?"

My thoughts exactly. "I think I should go look for him," I said. "Just in case something's happened."

"We're fresher than you are," Nocona pointed out.

"But he doesn't know you."

Nocona wasn't interested enough to argue.

"I'll come with you," Feordin offered to me. "Which way was your friend headed?"

I led him out of the little clearing, aware that while I might not step as lightly as Nocona, Feordin crashed through the underbrush like a dazed buffalo.

"Anyway," he picked up the story where he'd left it, despite my instinct to proceed silently, "come nightfall we camped just outside of the Shadow Caves, which was what Fred recommended. Only a fool would go there at night, he said. We got a good night's sleep, passed through the caverns at first dawn. No problems. Saw what was left of your horses. Nocona said there weren't any human or elf bones in the lot, so we figured you'd made it through. When we got outside, Nocona couldn't pick up your trail. Said he didn't think you'd passed by yet. But we knew you had half a day's lead on us, so Marian and I figured you *had* to be ahead of us."

"Yeah," I muttered. "That was probably about the time we were rolling around in rat dung."

"Uh-huh," Feordin said. He stopped talking while we climbed a small but steep hill.

I looked back and could just barely see the light from our campfire, despite the fact that we were only a minute's walk away; that's how thick the trees were.

"Fred had warned us about the sand hands, so we pressed on, figuring that's what you must have done. When we got to the mill, come about midday, the miller said he'd never seen you, and that's when we had to face the fact that we must have bypassed you in the caves."

"It didn't take you since noon to get here?" I asked. I'd been hoping we didn't have that much farther to go.

"Naw, the pixies threw a feast for us."

"Pixies?"

"Yeah, we had a real nice little adventure. That's where we picked up our treasure."

"Treasure?" I was getting pretty tired of his dropping this on me piece by piece while we dodged low branches and pushed through clinging bushes. The shirt under my leather breastplate stuck damply to my back.

"Oh, yeah," Feordin said, "I forgot you didn't see

our horses. They're pretty well laden down, what with the reward the pixies gave us and the sprites. And the dragon."

"*What?*"

"You see, the pixies were having this May Day celebration, even though it's June—you know how pixies are—anyway, a bunch of sprites came along and captured the May Queen and her attendants. We rescued them."

"Sounds like a hard two minutes' work," I mumbled. Sprites are never, ever, even remotely dangerous. They have a weird sense of humor, but they wouldn't harm anyone.

"Hey, don't take it out on me just because we got pixies and sprites, and you got orcs and rats." Feordin snorted and stuck his big wedgy nose in the air.

"Sorry," I conceded. "What about the dragon?" *Don't tell me*, I mentally begged, *they met a dragon. Not a real dragon. Not without me.*

"Well, the dragon gave us—"

Not more than a dozen yards away, a wolf howled.

Feordin and I put our backs to the nearest tree, knowing there wasn't time to actually climb it.

The wolf must have heard us and cut itself off midcry.

The trees were too thick for us to see anything, but we heard the crackle of branches and twigs, as though the creature might have jumped down from a tiny hill, or an outcrop of stone, or a tree stump, onto the forest floor. Then nothing. Just the hammering of my heart, the smell of the rich soil, the taste of sweat when I licked my lips.

"Wolstan!" I shouted, since it was for his sake that I was out here, and the wolf knew where we were in any case.

"Here." Wolstan stepped out of the shadows so close that I jumped. We both jumped.

"Half-wit," Feordin snarled. "There's a wolf loose."

Wolstan cast him a disdainful look. "It's gone."

"What were you doing?" I asked. "Tracking him?"

"Yes," Wolstan said, his usual slow, measured speech. It seemed to infuriate Feordin, who repeated, "Half-wit."

Wolstan looked at him levelly, then asked me, "Who is this?"

Oh no.

"I," said Feordin, "I am Feordin Macewielder. Son of Feordan Sturdyaxe, grandson of Feordane Boldheart, brother to Feordone the Fearless, great-grandson of Feordine Stoutarm who served under Graggaman Maximus."

Never glancing at Feordin, Wolstan asked me, "How come he's Feordin Macewielder if he doesn't have a mace?"

Feordin turned purple—I could see it, even in the moonlight—but he never made a sound. He turned on his heel and headed back toward camp.

"Good question," I told Wolstan as we followed after. "Better not ask it again."

CHAPTER 24

In the Dark of the Night

BACK AT THE CLEARING, I saw Feordin hadn't been exaggerating about the treasure he and his group had won. There were huge bulging sacks: gems, loose or set in jewelry; coins from most of the realms of man, elf, and dwarf; intricately worked golden combs, buttons, statuettes. The pixies, evidently, had been *very* grateful, the sprites *very* repentant, and the dragon . . . The group, Feordin explained, had gotten into a riddling contest with a dragon. A real dragon. Riddles have always been my specialty, something I took pride in doing well.

But apparently they hadn't needed me.

The dragon had been forced to give each of them one demand. Marian had asked for a cure for Mom's headache. The dragon said it didn't know anything about it, so Marian settled for gauntlets of power, which would increase the wearer's strength threefold.

She had already made Mom try them on while Feordin and I were out looking for Wolstan, but they'd had no effect on her condition.

Feordin had asked for and received a magic rope—fifty feet of uncutable twine that could climb up any surface on its own and tie itself into knots.

Nocona had been less specific. "Whatever we'll need to complete our quest," he'd said. The dragon had smiled and then handed over a tiny gold key. It had come with its own tiny golden box, exquisite work despite the fact that it was the size of a contact lens case. The key itself was no thicker than tinfoil.

"I think he got taken," Feordin informed us. "Seems totally useless to me."

"Fancy box," Nocona observed, "for a totally useless key." He tucked it back into his belt, not trusting any of us to touch it.

"What about you?" Marian asked us. "Did you bury your treasure or hide it or what?"

Thea, Cornelius, and I looked at each other. "What?"

"You said you had treasure, too. What did you do with it?"

"Oh." Thea, Cornelius, and I indicated the pathetic little bundles hanging from our belts.

"I see," Marian said, positively dripping with politeness. If she had *really* been polite, she would have offered to share some of their treasure with us. Of course, for us to be equally polite, we'd have had to refuse, since we'd had nothing to do with the earning of it, but apparently she wasn't willing to risk that much on our manners.

Our group ate our dinner of fish, grateful for the extra portion that had been meant for Robin. Since Marian, Feordin, and Nocona had already had three feasts that day—one with the pixies, one with the sprites, and one with the dragon—they couldn't possibly eat another bite. Thank goodness. They hadn't thought to save any for us, but at least they had waterskins, which they were willing to share. The way things had been going, I'd half expected them to charge us.

Feordin and Nocona offered to take the first watch since, as Feordin pointed out—three times he pointed it out—we'd walked all day while they'd ridden. Wolstan and I pulled second watch, Thea and Cornelius third. Marian, who was still sulking about Robin, refused to be assigned.

Gratefully I fell asleep right away.

What felt like two minutes later, Feordin nudged me with his foot and told me it was my turn.

"All quiet?" I asked.

"Wolves," Feordin said, snuggling into his blanket—he still had a blanket, of course—and was half asleep already. "To the west. Not very near."

I poked at the fire, just something to do to keep awake. Sparks flared hotly, fragrant smoke billowed. Sitting with his arms wrapped around himself, Wolstan scowled into the flames. Lack of sleep, I thought. Or maybe disenchantment with our company, now that he'd met all the members of it.

I moved off to one side because from where I was sitting the fire seemed to reflect redly in his eyes, an unsettling effect.

The moon had set, but at least the clouds were gone. Maybe tomorrow would be dry. I tried counting stars, but there were too many, too close together.

Farther away than before, but still closer than what I would have called "not very near," a wolf howled.

I saw Wolstan turn in my direction, as though to see if I had heard, to gauge my reaction.

Another wolf, somewhere to the north of the first, answered and was in turn answered by yet another, definitely to the east. And a fourth, from the south.

Wolstan stood, looming big and dark. He was kind of stooped over, as though maybe he'd gotten stiff from sitting. The fire was little more than glowing embers and I couldn't make out his features, even when he took a step closer to me. I figured he was probably going to ask whether we should wake the others, and as he took another step I decided I would tell him I felt maybe we should. It was a risk: the others would probably scoff and say we were jumping at shadows. Wolstan looked like a shadow himself, now that he had moved closer still and the fire was behind him.

And since when had I been afraid of the dark and of shadows?

I scrambled to my feet, intending, I told myself, to meet him halfway. I took a step back.

Wolstan growled at me, a loud, deep-throated growl like nothing that had ever come from a human throat. I saw a glint of teeth, then he lunged for me and his fingers brushed my arm. There was a hot, thick smell about him, which he certainly hadn't had before and which put me in mind of the cages at the zoo back home.

That was my first sensation.

Half a heartbeat later, a sound sank in—or rather,

the meaning of the sound I'd heard as Wolstan's fingers had grazed me. It was the fabric of my shirt sleeve tearing.

Then, only then, did I feel the pain.

Jagged flames seared my arm, from the inside of my elbow, through my wrist, into my palm. *The left arm*, reminded a detached part of my brain, which would be the computer's version of a warrior elf's subconscious. *Luckily not the sword arm*. And Wolstan didn't have hold of me: it'd been only a glancing slash. I threw myself back and tugged on my sword, all the while screaming, "Cornelius! Feordin!"

How come I was always bawling for help?

"Thea! Nocona!"

Behind me I was aware of the others, scrambling for their own weapons even before they were fully awake. Marian too, and Mom, who I hadn't had a chance to name.

Wolstan threw his head back and howled, a long drawn-out howl, like any one of several we had heard already that night. Then, from all around us, came answering cries. And after that the sound of dozens of bodies crashing through the woods, coming toward us.

Though I generally used my sword one-handed,

I felt awkward now that I knew I *couldn't* use my left. I tried to bury that feeling by charging at Wolstan.

He sprang away, raising his hands menacingly but never going for his own sword. Even without light to see more than the outline of his form, I could make out that the shape of his head was all wrong.

And then we did have light. I heard the *crackle-zap* which was Cornelius's Wizards' Lightning, and our campfire surged with temporary extra energy. Wolstan stood there in light as bright as day, looking like a creature from darkest nightmare. Instead of a separate mouth and nose, he had a muzzle, from which the lips were drawn back in a vicious snarl that revealed pointed teeth. He had hardly any forehead, and massive brows over yellow eyes that showed no white. His hands were a combination of human and wolf, with patches of fur on the backs and long, curving claws extending beyond flexible, individual fingers. His body and part of his face were covered with a thick gray pelt, like his wolfskin vest.

Metal scraped on metal as swords were drawn, and suddenly the wolf pack was on us, fifty or sixty of them with snapping jaws and slashing claws and bodies that hurtled at you when your back was turned and you were busy fending off the five or six you could see.

Wolstan seemed fixed on me.

He still stood on two feet, and that made him less agile, less maneuverable than his four-legged friends. But he had two things going for him: he was more intelligent than the full-fledged wolves, and he seemed willing to let any number of them get skewered in order to reach us—me. For some reason he wouldn't back off from me.

In no time I was covered with sweat and blood from battling the wolves, and my injured arm throbbed. Each time I lunged, each time I was jostled, arrows of pain shot up toward my shoulder.

Wolstan was always at the fringe of my sight, directing the attack. He had some sort of mind-link with the wolves. We had seen it, though we hadn't recognized it, in the clearing by the lake. Two wolf-mangled corpses in the road, a third man running, twenty or more wolves at his heels: we had interpreted everything from the wrong perspective. He hadn't been running *from* them. He had been running *with* them.

Exultant. Full of their own life. Celebrating a kill.

That was why Wolstan hadn't run to us right away. Not panic or confusion because of the wolves, but fear of us, because we were the enemy. We had beckoned to him, shouted encouragement while picking off his companions, until finally he had realized our mistake. Realized, if he bided his time, he could have us where he wanted.

We had put words into his mouth for him: that the wolves were pursuing him, that the dead men had been his companions, that the blood on him was from wounds, wounds we never actually saw, wounds he insisted on treating himself. He had spat out blood, and we had never guessed. We had said we were going to Sannatia, and so he had said that was where he was going, too. He had tried to persuade us to spend the night in the forest rather than entering the Shadow Caves. Not bad advice in itself, but now I knew the wolves would have set on us then and there. Instead they had circled around, gathering in number until he had called them during the evening when he was supposedly hunting. He had rescued us from the orcs, from the rats; he had carried my mother—all for us to end here.

I'd been backing away, trying to avoid him, hoping somebody else would get him with long-range weapons: Cornelius with his magical bolts or Nocona with arrows. But he was just going to wait until I was distracted. He had enough wolves to spare. Then he was going to reach in with those incredibly long claws and disembowel me or rip my head off as a souvenir.

I reminded myself that with my sword I had a longer reach than he did with his claws. I swept the head off a wolf who ran between us, and moved in.

Wolstan's lips curled back in imitation of a smile.

I jabbed my sword at him and he danced out of the way, moving to my left, where I hugged my injured arm close to my side. Wolstan's claws raked across the back of it. I heard the tear of fabric and skin. In the fraction of a second that his momentum was slowed by his claws catching in my flesh, I swung my sword.

It was pure instinct; I never expected to make contact. The sword shuddered to a stop with a disgusting noise. No, take that back—"noise" is too strong a word. It was more like a *sensation*, sort of between a thud and a squish, so that even then, thinking I was about to die, it set my teeth on edge.

Wolstan's eyes widened in shock, but he had enough strength to throw me down to the ground and land on top of me. I thought, OK, *here's the part where he eats my throat out while I'm still mostly alive,* because he had his face buried in my neck, and I closed my eyes real tight.

Nothing happened.

I managed to drag in a shaky breath, when suddenly Wolstan rolled off me. I scrunched my eyes even tighter.

Still nothing.

I gave a quick peek, ready to close my eyes again if I saw something I shouldn't. I saw buckskinned legs, and moccasins.

"Nocona," I whispered, my windpipe too battered to do any better.

Beyond him, Wolstan was flat on his back, his arms spread out, totally still. Nocona had rolled him off me, I realized, then stepped in to make sure I was all right. Around us, the sounds of battle were not nearly as fierce as before. I could hear sounds that I was willing to guess were the wolves hightailing it away.

"Whew!" someone—Cornelius? Feordin?—breathed.

Nocona stooped down beside me. Out of the corner of my eye I caught a flutter of motion, Wolstan's hand. "Look out!" I wheezed.

Nocona pitched forward onto me, knocking back out the air I'd just managed to drag in. I heard him cry out, or maybe it was me. There was a sharp *crack!* then the smell of sulfur and charred flesh that indicated Cornelius had scored a hit.

I started, "I can't . . ." but couldn't get any more out.

Luckily—considering the word I was trying for was *breathe*—Nocona rolled off me.

I started to sit up, but somebody tackled me: a flurry of arms and hair and sweaty body. Everything was kind of swimming around, but I didn't need to see. "I'm OK, Mom," I said. "I'm OK."

CHAPTER 25

Aftermath

SOMEBODY PULLED MOM OFF ME—Marian, I think. Everybody was shouting and crowding and demanding to know if I was all right, and I couldn't breathe and my vision wouldn't focus and there was an awful pain in the calf of my leg where I couldn't even remember being injured.

"Harek, Harek." My mother's voice cut through the buzzing in my ears. I couldn't make out her face for the black motes that were dancing in front of my eyes.

Feordin bellowed, "Everyone shut up."

Everyone did.

Gently, Mom said to me, "You're hyperventilating. Breathe slower."

Breathe slower? I couldn't get a breath at all.

"Harek!" She shook me. I thought of all those war movies, where the wimp goes hysterical and someone gets to slug him.

"My leg," I wheezed, so that they could see how bad I really was. I wondered if it was still attached.

"It's just a cramp," Mom assured me. "Breathe like this . . ."

"Mom."

"Come on, exhale like you're trying to blow out three candles, one at a time."

"What is this, the Natural Childbirth Method of Fantasy Role-Playing?" But just talking to her forced me to breathe more slowly, and the cramp in my leg was already dissolving. I breathed the way she wanted me to. In a few seconds, her face sharpened into clearer focus. She was pale and grimy and blood-splattered. "Are *you* all right?" I asked her.

She smiled, a soft, gentle smile, though her eyes filled with tears. She put her hand to my cheek and nodded, perhaps not trusting her voice.

I hugged her to me.

"I hate this," she whispered damply into the space between my shoulder and my neck. "I hate it, I hate it."

My own eyes were filling. "I'm sorry I got you into this," I said.

She bridled at that. "You did not," she said, pulling away, "*get* me into anything. In fact, I practically begged to play." She wiped her sleeve across her face, smudging it even worse.

Helplessly I looked at the mess in the clearing.

Dead, Wolstan had reverted to the appearance of a regular wolf—a large, charbroiled, regular wolf. There were twenty or thirty other wolf bodies scattered about the clearing. As for the people in our company, they all looked terrible: dirty, sweaty, bloody. Thea had twigs and leaves in her hair like she'd been rolling around on the ground. Her pale blond hair was singed short and ragged on one side, as though she'd rolled too near the campfire. Cornelius's fancy robe was all tattered at the edges and hanging loose over one shoulder. Marian, pulling off her gauntlets of power, had a gash on her cheek. Nocona was still sitting next to me, holding his ankle as though he didn't dare try his weight on it. Feordin was wrapping a length of cloth around raw and bloody knuckles, watching me suspiciously.

"You get bit?" he asked.

I shook my head, afraid that this close he could tell I'd been getting weepy.

He didn't look convinced. "Are you sure?"

"Yeah." I held my arm for him to see, sure he'd be grossed out and back off. "Just clawed."

He didn't back off. He took a real close look, like he didn't trust me.

"What difference does it make?" Mom asked.

"Werewolf," Feordin said.

That was a cold chill up my back.

Marian explained, "Player who's werewolf-bit has a one-in-three chance of turning into a werewolf himself in the next two to twelve rounds."

Mom gulped. "What's a round?"

"Hard to tell without dice," Cornelius sighed.

"I was bitten," Mom said, real soft. She showed a cut on her arm. "One of the wolves—"

"Only the werewolf," Cornelius told her. "Wolstan. Not one of the ordinary wolves."

Mom shook her head.

Feordin let go of my arm. "Yeah, just looks like a nasty clawing to me." To Mom he said, "Good thing, or we'd have had to keep him tied up for the rest of the game. Werewolves can't help what they are. But what they are is treacherous."

"Knock it off, Feordin," Marian said, seeing that he was scaring Mom. "Luckily, everybody is OK. Is everybody OK?"

We all nodded that we were OK.

"What we've got to do is rest as much as we can

to regain our strength for tomorrow. Harek, I'll finish off your watch with you." She helped me to my feet. "Need help with that ankle, Nocona?"

"Just twisted," Nocona told her.

Marian was into her bossy mode again. "OK, everybody try to settle down as fast as possible," she said. "Tomorrow's going to be a big day."

"Yeah," I sighed. "That's what I'm afraid of."

CHAPTER 26

Day Four

CONSIDERING THAT I WAS ON WATCH with Marian for a good hour and a half and she didn't say more than two words to me, it came as a shock the following morning when she announced to the group that she had decided to turn back.

I choked on the warm water that was all we had for breakfast, and couldn't get a word out.

Cornelius set Nocona's waterskin down with a slosh and said "What?" in a tone that should have frozen Marian's blood.

She sighed. "If Robin got carried off back to the clearing behind Fred's house, there's no way he can ever make up the time on his own. If I go and get him, with horses, we can join up with you in twenty-four hours."

"Marian," Thea said, "we're already"—she glanced at Mom, who was still curled up, asleep after having been sick to her stomach during the earliest hours of the morning—"we're already four people short."

"That's why we need Robin."

Thea made a sound of mingled disgust and exasperation. She got up and went to help Nocona ready the horses. He was favoring one leg, limping when he thought no one was watching. As for my injury, my arm had improved significantly during my few hours' sleep. It was still sore, and weak, but it looked as though it'd been healing for five or six days. So did the gash on Marian's cheek. Even Thea's scorched hair was growing back. Only Mom never recovered at the accelerated rate. Only Mom got steadily worse.

I glared at Marian. *Being with Robin is more important to her than taking care of my mom,* I thought angrily.

"And you'll take the horses?" Feordin said. "Two horses? There's already only four horses for seven of us, and you want to cut that down to two for six?"

"Look," Marian said, "either way, some of you are going to have to walk. Either that or you'll double up, which'll kill the horses once you get to the desert. Felice won't be able to stand a lot of jostling either."

"I suppose," Cornelius agreed, as though it were up to him. "There's two more days to this adventure, and we certainly haven't been breaking any records. The big encounter won't be till tomorrow."

"If we live that long," I said. I looked to Feordin, hoping he'd back me in saying that dividing was foolhardy, but he just shrugged.

"Felice is awfully weak," Cornelius said. "We'd probably better strap her to the horse."

Feordin got up to help him, leaving me alone with Marian. *Jerk*, I thought. *You think like a girl.*

"Harek," she said, "you know I'm right."

"Hey, listen," I told her. "You're going to do what you want anyway; you don't need to convince me you're right." Robin wouldn't be so silly, I thought. He'd put the good of the group before his need to be with his little sweetie.

Marian sighed again. "I'm real worried about your mother, Arvin."

"*Harek*," I screamed at her. "My name is Harek. And you sure have a funny way of showing your concern."

"Has it occurred to you," Marian said softly, unaffected by my temper, "*Harek*, that there's something seriously wrong here?"

"It's a stupid game," I grumbled. "I wish I'd never joined."

"It is not a game. It has nothing to do with a game. *That's* why I've got to find Robin. So we can work to-gether to get out of here as soon as possible. Harek, if you can think of any way to speed this up, to get out of here entirely, say it now."

She wasn't just trying to justify herself. She was talking about my mom and she was scared, and that scared me. "What are you getting at?" I asked.

She glanced away, reluctant to look me in the face, and that scared me even more. "I don't know." She shook her head, then stole a quick peek at me. "I don't know anything more than you do, Harek."

I sat there watching her.

"It's just . . . I'm worried that there's something wrong with her—really wrong with *her*, nothing to do with her character as Felice or the quest or Ras-mussem."

This was something that had been poking at the borders of my mind, too, though I didn't say that. I said, "You're crazy, Marian."

"The program has direct contact with our brains," she said. "Which is why we feel we're here when we know we're not. But it's all condensed, concentrated. That's why we experience five days when it's only an hour. Harek . . . Harek, what if there's something going on in your mother's body so that her brain is trying to send signals that something is wrong?"

"That's stupid," I said.

"I hope so."

I chewed on my lip. "Something wrong like what?"

Still Marian wouldn't meet my eyes.

"Something wrong with her brain?"

Marian tugged at her sleeve.

"Marian," I begged.

"I don't *know*, Arvin. It's just that that's what my mother died of, a stroke. It happened just like that." She snapped her fingers. "There was no warning because it happened so fast. I'm just wondering if your mother's getting a warning because time here feels so stretched out." She made a vague gesture like pulling a giant rubber band.

I shook my head. "My mother isn't having a stroke," I said. "Her headache is just . . . another glitch in Shelton's program."

Marian couldn't bring herself to say the thing she was obviously trying to get out.

Good, I thought. *Marian at a loss for words*, I thought.

And then something struck me.

My jaw dropped. "Your mother *died*?" We'd just

been over there a couple weeks earlier. For a moment my mind flitted to the idea that she was talking about her *character's* mother.

Marian looked at me as though I were a slug. "Of course she died, you stupid little measle pustule of an eighth-grader. You were at the funeral home."

"No, I wasn't," I insisted. "The only times I've ever been to a funeral home were when my Uncle Lennie died and when Noah's mo-mo-mo . . ." I must have looked as spastic as I sounded. Things suddenly fell into place. Marian put her hands on her hips and looked exasperated.

Just like a girl.

"Noah?" I squeaked. "You're *Noah?*"

"Measle pustule," Marian answered, sweeping to her feet.

CHAPTER 27

Miller's Grove

So, RIDING ONE HORSE and trailing another, Marian—who was Noah—headed back to find Robin—who was not. And we walked to Miller's Grove, leading the remaining two horses, the one with Mom tied on, and the one carrying the treasure.

I watched Mom's limp frame sway with the rhythm of the horse's steps and thought back to when I'd been a little kid; how, if I had the flu or an earache or something, my mother would get this worried look on her face. Sitting on the edge of the bed while she put cold washcloths on my forehead, she'd say, "Don't be sick," and I'd promise to try hard not to. "Don't die," I wanted to tell her. But I didn't want to scare her.

I didn't want to scare myself.

Marian's crazy, I told myself instead. It was a nice thought, but it didn't help.

It took us almost three hours. The only thing that kept me going was the thought that we could buy something to eat from the miller. First we heard the rushing of the River Gan, then the creak of the mill wheel, then the thumping of the machinery inside.

The miller must have seen us from a window, for he came out, wiping his hands on a cloth he wore tucked into his belt like an apron. At first he looked worried. No wonder: we were dirt- and blood-splattered, a desperate, rough lot. But then he recognized Feordin and Nocona.

"Greetings. I see you did finally meet up with your friends. Nocona, wasn't it?" He took Nocona's hand and shook it, although Nocona was simply trying to hold his hand up in Indian-style greeting. "And, ah, let's see . . ."

Feordin didn't give the amiable miller time to grope for the name. "Feordin," he said. "Macewielder. Son of—"

"Yes," the miller said, pumping his arm, still smiling, "Feordin." He started to turn to Thea.

Feordin didn't let go of his hand. "*Feordin Macewielder,*" he repeated more loudly, slowly, and distinctly. The miller froze, realizing what he had done. "Son of Feordan Sturdyaxe. Grandson of Feordane Boldheart.

Brother to Feordone the Fearless." Feordin was getting louder with each generation. "Great-grandson of Feordine Stoutarm who served under Graggaman Maximus." His eyes were beginning to bulge, and you could see this one vein on the side of his forehead throbbing.

The miller gulped.

"I don't," Feordin said, "have a mace with me."

The miller gulped again. "No, you don't," he agreed shakily. He waited several long seconds to be sure Feordin had finished. Finally he cast a furtive glance at Thea, at the rest of us. "Well"—he took a step backward—"welcome to all of you. It was good to meet you. I've got to get back to my work."

"Wait," I said. "We have an injured member in our party."

The miller's gaze drifted over all of us.

"Here." Impatiently, I indicated Mom, asleep, tied to the horse.

He watched me with a wary expression. "The horse is injured?" he asked.

I gritted my teeth. "The lady on the horse." Technically speaking, Mom was a female thief, not a lady, but I was getting ticked off at the way he kept looking right through her like she wasn't even there.

"The lady," the miller repeated, only glancing at Mom, his eyes roving over me. He stole a quick look at the others then took a step away.

It was almost like icy spiders scurried up and down my arms.

Thea grabbed him by the scruff of the neck and shoved his face practically into Mom's. "The lady," Thea said. "Can't you see her?"

"Yes," the miller assured us. "Of course. The lady. Ahhh, no cleric with you?"

"NO!" we all screamed at him.

He was obviously getting pretty rattled from being shouted at all the time. I consciously tried to speak calmly. "We're in desperate need of food. All of us. We're willing to pay."

Thea let go of him, and the miller shook his head. I mean, he shook his head no. The rest of him was shaking already. Even his voice quivered. "I'm sorry. We have nothing."

"We're not picky," I said. The last couple of miles, the bark on the trees had begun to look good.

"I don't mean we don't have much. We don't have anything. My wife just left for Packett's Corners"—he indicated southeast, exactly the opposite direction we were interested in—"to go to the market."

"This is a mill," Cornelius pointed out. "Surely you have bread."

The miller shook his head. "You don't understand. My wife, she took all the bread to market to sell. I have raw grain. And stone-ground flour. No bread."

I thought he looked genuinely distressed, but apparently Nocona wasn't buying it. "Is it immoral," he asked philosophically, looking at no one in particular, "to knock down someone who doesn't really exist outside of one's own mind and ransack his house?"

Mom groaned in her sleep. All of us turned. About five seconds later, out of the corner of my eye, I saw the miller turn also.

He hadn't heard.

He hadn't heard.

He only turned to see what we were looking at. His eyes went straight past Mom, to the horizon beyond her. "Look," he told us, "the wife will be back by midday with meat and fresh vegetables. And she'll start baking too. You're welcome to wait."

We all looked at each other. Cornelius said, "Surely we shouldn't waste a whole day."

"No," I said, real quick.

"No," the others agreed.

The miller shifted his gaze from one to the other

of us. Suddenly he snapped his fingers. "There is . . ." Then he shook his head. "No, well . . ." Again he became more animated. "But on the other hand if you're really desperate . . ." He debated himself out of it. "Still . . ."

"What?" Feordin looked ready to shake him.

"There is *some* bread in the house that I'd forgotten about. But I'm not sure . . ."

Feordin grabbed him by the shirt. "This better not be a matter of money."

Considering that the man was half again as tall as the dwarf, and twice as wide, it was a tribute to the ferocity in Feordin's face that the miller turned white and stammered, "N-n-n-no. I-it's a matter of overbaking."

Feordin had pulled down on the guy's shirt so that their noses were touching despite their difference in height. "Beg your pardon?" Feordin asked

"Last week my wife left a batch of bread in the oven too long. We've been using the loaves as doorstops."

Doorstops?

The miller said, "I didn't think to mention them because, really, they're not fit for human consumption." He suddenly remembered to whom he was talking. "Er, uhm, ah . . ."

And so we sat down on the grassy lawn and had bread to eat. Bread that we had to soak in river water before we could even break off pieces. And the miller only charged us one silver piece each for it. The water he let us have free.

"*Six* loaves," I told the miller as I poured the coins into his open palm. I tapped the top coin. "One for each of us."

"Ah yes," the miller said. "One for the lady, too. I understand." He glanced at the horse, smiled, and nodded. "Lady," he said by way of greeting.

Of course, by then we'd already helped Mom down and she was sitting on the grass with the rest of the group.

"Brain-damaged old coot," I muttered as he went to fetch a sixth loaf.

He tried to feed it to the horse, too. Cornelius, who'd given his loaf to Mom, took it from him. "Now," said Cornelius, wiping his sleeve across his mouth where water squirted out as he bit into his bread, "about our sick companion . . ."

"The lady," the miller said, giving his friendly grin to the horse.

"We'd like her to stay here."

This was *not* something we had decided, or even

talked about. I stopped in midchew and glanced at the others to see if they were any less surprised. They didn't seem to be. Except, of course, for Mom, who had taken maybe three bites of bread, then laid her head down on the grass. "Cornelius," I said.

"No," the miller said.

"Harek," Cornelius told me, "it'd be the best thing for her. She could rest. She'll be safe here." He turned his attention back to the miller. "We'll pay you to watch over her."

"This is no boardinghouse." Obviously the miller had had enough. He turned his back on us and headed inside the mill.

"But . . . ," Cornelius called after him.

I said, "He can't even see her."

"Probably," Nocona said, "the program wouldn't allow for it anyway. There's no telling what would happen if you tried."

Again I said, "He can't even see her."

"Somebody would have had to stay with her," Feordin added, "and the group's divided enough already."

"And we're getting pretty tired of you making decisions for us," Thea said.

"Look," Cornelius started, "I just thought—"

Mom opened her eyes and whispered, "Put a lid on it, Corny. I wouldn't have stayed anyway."

"In that case," Cornelius said, "at the risk of getting accused of making decisions for everybody, I'd say we'd better get going."

CHAPTER 28

Desert

THE DESERT CROSSING was worse than I'd imagined, and I can say that despite the fact that we met no one and nothing out of the ordinary.

No sand hands.

No giant snakes.

No killer sandstorms or flash floods or sun-crazed nomads.

On the other hand, it was hot. The sand was hot. The air was hot. We were hot. The sand dragged at our steps, leaving us exhausted even as we were just setting out. I could feel the heat through the leather of my boots and once, when I didn't step high enough and pitched forward onto my hands, I singed my palms in the two seconds before I picked myself up.

We wrapped cloth around our faces, hoping that would filter out some of the sand our struggles churned into the air and maybe give the air we breathed a chance to cool off before it hit our lungs. Before we were farther than shouting distance from Miller's Grove, we'd already lit into our water supply.

Despite the shredded blankets we'd wrapped around their legs, the horses balked just about every step of the way. They nipped and kicked and just generally made themselves unpleasant. Mom had dismounted so we could handle them more easily, and there was no telling how long she'd be able to walk on her own. About ten steps, I estimated.

"This is not going to work," Thea said.

"We need to leave the horses," I suggested. "They're holding us back."

"Oh sure, that's easy for you to say," Feordin told me. "What about our treasure? We can't leave that behind."

I said, "It won't do us any good if we die in the desert."

"Oh yeah?" he said.

"Yeah," I said.

"You think you can make me?"

"I think—"

Cornelius said, "I have an idea."

We all turned on him, even Nocona.

"Now wait a minute," Cornelius said over all the

shouting and hooting. "Will you just listen to me? I can use my Levitation spell."

I said, "I don't see how that would help. Levitation can get us up off the sand, but it won't get us closer to Sannatia."

"I could levitate the horses," Cornelius explained, "and . . . say, two riders each. Felice, obviously. Myself, of course. The rest of you could alternate, take turns: two ride, and two pull the levitating horses along. It'll be a lot easier than trying to drag the horses through the sand."

"Uh-huh," Nocona said, mulling it over. "Why do you get to ride?"

"Because I need to concentrate on the spell."

"Figures," I said.

We used Feordin's magic rope, tying each end to one of the horses. Thea and I lost the draw and got to be the guinea pigs. Or draft horses, however you choose to look at it.

Cornelius shared a horse with Mom. She was looking a little better. The miller's bread must have done her good, for her face had lost that pinched hollowness. But her hair, not combed in the four days we'd been here, no longer hung halfway down her back. It was so tangled, it barely reached her shoulders. And it was coated with a fine layer of sand so that it looked less like the dark and glossy gypsy hair with which Felice had started out and more and more like Mom's own brown-and-gray hairstyle.

Cornelius closed his eyes and concentrated. The horses didn't look too happy about being three feet off the ground, but they soon caught on that this way their hooves were out of the burning sand.

Thea and I started pulling on the rope and Cornelius was right: It wasn't like pulling the full weight of the horses. It wasn't too much harder than just slogging through the sand on our own.

CHAPTER 29

Sannatia

W E ARRIVED AT SANNATIA shortly after midday.

Sand from the desert had blown into the streets. Scrubby grass and weeds had sprouted in unlikely spots, like between the steps in front of buildings and in somebody's window box, where they'd crowded out the flowers.

"Looks like nobody's been here in years," I said.

Nocona, who with Feordin had been guiding the horses, stooped down. "Goblin tracks," he pointed out irritably. "Obviously *goblins* have been here."

"Nobody besides goblins," I corrected. I waited for Cornelius to lower the horses. Mounting and dismounting had been like being four years old again and picking a carousel horse stuck at the top of its leap.

Thea helped Mom down. "You all right?" I asked.

"I just need to sit on something soft that doesn't move," Mom whispered.

"We really should begin," Cornelius said. "There's a lot of territory to cover."

I gave a hand to Nocona, who hadn't stood up from examining the tracks. I half expected him to consider it an insult to his Indianhood or something, but his ankle must have been sore enough so that he didn't care. He'd probably done more than sprain it; he'd probably chipped or cracked the bone, or it'd have healed by now. Even my arm was half healed. He lugged himself up heavily and turned his face away so I wouldn't see him wince.

"Let's try the barracks first," Feordin suggested, "since that's right here."

It was spooky walking down the streets that the inhabitants had deserted—or from which they'd been snatched—twenty years earlier. Goblins had vandalized the place. Doors were kicked in so that they hung on their hinges and rattled in the breeze. Feather mattresses had been tossed out of windows and gotten sodden from the rains. Wooden furniture had been used for bonfires in the middle of streets. There hadn't been a systematic looting: goblins aren't interested in treasure the way people are. But it explained the lights at night: goblins don't like daylight. Whatever they do, they do at night. It just didn't explain what had happened to the townspeople.

At the barracks we all got out our weapons, to be ready just in case. We assumed the defensive position. I kicked in the door and Feordin and Thea went in ahead of me; Mom dragged herself in after me; Cornelius and Nocona guarded the rear.

No need for SWAT team tactics. The dust was thick enough to taste, and our feet left footprints. Obviously we were the first to pass in years. Storerooms, sleeping rooms, dining hall. Nobody and nothing. All the weapons were gone, though little else seemed disturbed.

"What do you think?" Feordin asked, indicating the stairs to the second floor.

"I think it's a waste of time," Nocona snapped.

The rest of us all looked at each other, anxious that Nocona, the most levelheaded of us, was becoming short-tempered with the pain of his injury.

"Well," Thea said, a study in diplomacy, "where do you think we should look?"

It didn't work. "Don't you get snippy with me,"

Nocona warned. He turned on his heel and stomped out. Well, it was more like stomp, step gingerly, stomp, step gingerly.

Cornelius said, "Maybe we should try the Wizards' Guild HQ."

"How will we know it?" I asked.

He shrugged. "Shouldn't be too hard to find."

He was right. It was the one that was a big, black hole, about twenty feet deep in the ground and wide enough to hold a midsized playground. There was a sign in the front, which said WIZARDS' GUILD, and it was only slightly singed by whatever had taken down the building.

"Ooops," Cornelius said.

Mom leaned against me.

Nocona sat down on the curb and massaged his ankle.

"Do you think we should go to the Street of Temples?" Thea asked.

"Sure," Feordin said. "Why not?"

"Because," I said, "there have got to be hundreds of places we *could* go that are 'sure-why-not?' places. If we go to every one of them, we'll still be looking tomorrow evening when we get zapped back to Shelton's basement."

"So?" Cornelius said.

"So, we've got to slow down and analyze. What have we got so far? Someone—we don't know who—has kidnapped Princess Dorinda and, apparently, brought her to Sannatia. Right?"

They all looked at me with varying degrees of impatience.

"So, what are the possibilities? One: the princess is dead, killed during the abduction or after."

"Oh, no," Mom said.

"What're you getting at, Harek?" Nocona asked.

"Possibility number two: the princess is alive but being held captive. I prefer that possibility, because if she's dead, then this whole thing is pointless."

Cornelius sighed and muttered, "Talk about pointless . . ."

"I'm trying to look at this logically," I said. "If you'd rather just flail about blindly—"

"Just say what you've got to say," Thea told me.

"If Princess Dorinda's being held captive, the question is why."

"*Why?*" Thea repeated.

"Why is anyone held captive?"

"For the ransom?" Cornelius suggested.

"Good. What else?"

"To force the relatives to do something," Nocona said.

"Or to prevent them," Thea countered.

"Maybe," I said.

Feordin said, "Perhaps the princess has some information about something, which somebody wants."

"Could be."

"I can't think," Mom said. "Which is it?"

"*I* don't know," I told them. "I'm just exploring the possibilities."

"Harek, you idiot—" Nocona started.

"What it seems to me," I continued, "is that whatever the reason they want her, they probably want her safe."

"So?" Cornelius said.

"So we've got to figure where someone would keep a ten-year-old girl safe."

Thoughtfully, Thea murmured, "In a town with goblins . . ."

"Even if you were a goblin," I pointed out, "you wouldn't go through all the trouble of kidnapping a princess just to lock her up in a dungeon and terrorize her. Where would you lock up a ten-year-old kid?"

"In school," Feordin said. "That's what our parents do to us."

"No schools here," Thea said. "Children would be taught at home until they were old enough to learn a trade."

"Royal children would have tutors brought in for them," Cornelius said.

Thea shook her head. "Yeah, but the princess didn't live in Sannatia."

"The royal governor did," I said. "If he had any children, there'd be a nursery at the governor's palace."

"Sure," Feordin said to show he wasn't impressed with my reasoning. "Why not?"

As soon as we walked into the main hall of the governor's palace, we saw it was a lot cleaner than the barracks. Not *clean* in the sense of they-must-have-a-housekeeper, but there were definite paths through the dust and grime.

"Goblins," Nocona told us after a quick glance at the footprints.

"Are you sure?" Thea asked.

Nocona sighed real loud and took a closer look at the floor. "Mmm-hmmm," he said in what sounded like thoughtful surprise.

"What?" Thea asked.

He ignored her, moving on instead to check the

furniture, which had obviously been climbed on, and the walls, which seemed to have been bounced off. "Uh-hunh," Nocona said.

"What?" Thea repeated.

He stepped around her to place a chair under the chandelier, which had pieces broken off and scattered across the room as though someone had been playing Tarzan on it. "I see," Nocona said.

"What?" Thea demanded.

"*Goblins!*" he screamed at her.

Very calmly, very quietly, she said, "All right." She gave him the overly sweet smile girls do when they're feeling especially superior. "Thank you."

Nocona stepped off the chair, wincing at the movement.

"Now that you've got the attention of everyone in town . . . ," Cornelius said.

Nocona shrugged, as if to say, When you surround me with fools, don't blame me for the results.

"Can we please stop bickering long enough to finish this?" Mom asked.

I pulled out my sword and Thea her knife. In a moment, Cornelius stepped closer, then Feordin, finally Nocona. Mom just hung onto my arm, which would be the death of both of us if we ran into trouble.

We followed the path the goblins had made through two decades' worth of dust. Certainly there were sidetracks, where individual goblins or small groups had gone into other rooms—and some of these even looked recent. But obviously a great number of goblins passed through here repeatedly. At one end of the path was the front door. All we had to do was find the other end.

We walked through the banquet hall, where there had been a food fight decades ago: food stains on the walls, broken dishes on the floor, shriveled and dusty pieces of who-knew-what underfoot. We went up a curved marble stairway. There were doors along the hallway, splintered where they had been kicked in. At the far end of the hall a set of double doors were wide open the normal way, and that's where the goblins' trail led.

For a moment we just stood there, listening.

Nothing.

Stealthily we made our way down the hall. Thea pushed ahead of the rest of us to take the lead. Pressing herself against the wall next to the door, she motioned for us to keep back. Once we were all in position, she bobbed forward to peek inside the room, making herself as quick a target as possible.

Nothing.

She repeated the motion, a fraction slower.

Nothing.

She held up three fingers to us, folded one down, folded the second one down, folded the last one down, and leapt into the room. We jumped in behind her.

There was no one there.

It had been a nursery, that was obvious by the faded pictures on the walls. There were animals, more cute than realistic, and rainbows and stars. One entire wall was a tapestry: a fantasy castle with airy spires and turrets coming out of the building at impossible angles, and a very friendly-looking moat monster in the background.

The room had a canopied bed—too dusty to tell what color—and the canopy sagged almost to the quilted covers. A few toys lay in the corners of the room—a painted top, a rag doll, a puppet. More toys overflowed out of a wooden chest at the foot of the bed. The floor was rubbed dust-free by the passage of countless goblin feet, but there was no telling where they'd come from. Only one doorway opened into the room, and we were standing in it. Why would goblins come up here, walk around the room, then go back downstairs and disappear into the town?

"Now what?" Mom sank down onto the floor. "Do we just wait until they come back?"

"No." Cornelius stepped forward. He raised his hands and sputtered in his obscure wizards' dialect.

"What are you doing?" I asked wearily.

"Reveal Magic spell."

"I don't feel anything," I protested.

Cornelius shoved past me and zeroed in on the wall, the one with the tapestry. He began running his hands across the weaving.

I rested my hand against the cheerful moat monster. "I don't feel anything," I repeated.

Cornelius ignored me. He stooped down for a better look at the bottom half of the picture.

I examined the tapestry more closely. I still felt no telltale tingle of magic. But I did suddenly notice that the wall hanging wasn't dusty. "Hey," I started.

"Bingo," Cornelius said. He tapped his finger against the door of the castle.

I got down on my knees and ran my hand over the same area and got just the faintest sensation like I'd been leaning on one arm too long. There was a warding spell here, to prevent the magic from being casually detected.

"Yes," I said. "Now what?"

The others huddled closer. "Try knocking," Feordin suggested.

"Ask the moat creature if anyone's home," Thea said.

Nocona cleared his throat and held up the little golden box, the one he'd won riddling with the dragon. "'Whatever we'll need to complete our quest,'" he reminded us.

We all cleared a space while he got out the tiny key and looked for a place to insert it. A tinfoil key in a woven-cloth door. Sure, I thought.

Cornelius's head was in my way, but I heard the click.

The castle door, about as tall as my hand, swung open. Light poured out, but we couldn't see anything.

Take that back.

Looking inside was like looking into a candle flame, or into the sun: not really a color, but a presence.

"Oooo," we all breathed.

Nocona reached his hand in, and it disappeared up to his wrist. He pulled back and wriggled his fingers. Apparently that was proof enough for him that it was safe. He reached in again. His hand disappeared up to the wrist, the elbow, the shoulder. He stuck his head through the door, which should have been too narrow, but somehow he was gone up to the shoulders, then he crawled forward and disappeared up to the waist.

"Ahm, Nocona," I said, grabbing hold of his ankle. It was his injured one, all wrapped up in a makeshift bandage. I must have hurt him, for he jerked his leg away. If he cried out or said anything from the other side of the doorway, we couldn't hear. I caught just a glimpse of blood on the bandage—which shouldn't have been there, not on a sprain—then Nocona crawled the rest of the way in through the door and disappeared as completely as Robin going down in the sand.

We waited what felt like half an hour. It was probably closer to a minute.

"He would have come back," Thea said. "If everything was OK on the other side, he would have come back to tell us so. Something must be wrong."

Mom, looking like an overwashed dishrag, said, "Does that mean we go after him, or does that mean we stay here?"

"Maybe he's safe," I pointed out, "but he *can't* come back."

Feordin said, "We need a line." He eased his magic rope off his shoulder. "Go," he commanded it. At first slowly, then more and more quickly, it uncoiled itself and snaked into the bright doorway. Anxiously we watched as it hurtled itself away, looking for something on the other side to tie itself to. Coil after coil disappeared, until finally there was hardly any rope left, and Feordin had to say, "Stop."

But apparently the rope could only keep track of one command at a time. The last two coils whipped straight and the end of the rope whizzed across the nursery floor toward the tapestry.

Feordin stamped down hard onto the rebellious rope. It twanged taut, caught between where it was coming from and where it was going. Then it slipped out from beneath Feordin's boot.

Thea dove for the loose end, grabbed hold of it inches short of the wall, and was dragged through the castle doorway. Cornelius grabbed her foot at the last second, didn't have the sense to let go, and disappeared half a moment later.

We stood there listening to the dust settle.

"My, that was certainly a fine idea," I told Feordin.

He gave me a look that indicated if he had still had a mace, he would have made mashed potatoes out of me. "Untie," he ordered the rope. "Return."

Nothing.

We all—take that back—*we three* looked at each other. Mom sighed. "Well, I think we're meant to go through."

"Yeah?" I said. "What if there are goblins waiting on the other side?"

"Then they've captured Nocona, Thea, and Cornelius and know we're here. I don't see how it can hurt to go, and we're certainly not doing anybody any good here."

"Yeah, but . . . ," I started.

She gave me the same look she would have given if I were trying to weasel out of doing my homework.

Feordin pushed ahead of both of us. "I'll go," he announced. "I am Feordin Macewielder . . ." His head poked through the tapestry and already his voice came back faint and faraway, though his rear end still stuck out on this side of the castle. ". . . son of Feordan Sturdyaxe . . ." We could only see the bottoms of his feet, and I was straining to listen, holding my breath so that the noise wouldn't interfere. "Grandson of . . ." I might have just heard "Feordane," or it may have been only that I knew what came next. In any case, my ears heard no hint of Feordin's voice saying "Boldheart."

I gulped.

Mom said, "Me next."

"Maybe you should just stick your head in, then come back out and tell me what you see," I said. I would have gone first, but she was in my way.

"All right." Mom crawled partway in, then backed out. "Nothing," she said. "Just light."

"Maybe—" I started.

She crawled through the doorway and disappeared.

I sighed. "Maybe," I said, "I should go through, too." I answered myself, "Gee, Harek, that sounds like a good idea. Why didn't I think of that?"

But I got the final word in. I said, "Stupid game," before I crawled through.

CHAPTER 30

The Other Side

CRAWLING THROUGH the castle doorway, I was aware of light ahead of me and darkness behind and a thickness to the air, like in a dream when you're trying to run and you can only move *verrrrry* slowly.

I was just wondering what would happen if I veered right or left, when the ground gave out under me. I braced myself for a plummet of two or three hundred feet and the ghastly *splat!* that would follow, but I hit the ground in less than a second, before the picture was complete in my head.

"Harek—you all right?" Feordin's voice asked.

It took a few seconds before my surroundings registered. I was in the cobblestoned courtyard of a castle, which looked for all the world like the castle in the tapestry. Which was ridiculous, because the castle in the tapestry looked like a cartoon drawing. But both castles were pink and purple, and the building blocks looked more like stitches than real construction, with horizontal and vertical blocks alternating like the weave of fabric. For another thing, there were windows all over the place, which as an inhabitant of this time period I knew would be impossible to defend. And there were all these pointy towers which came out of the main building at angles that would give an architect nightmares. And the cobblestones on which I'd landed *looked* like cobblestones, but they weren't hard. They were, in fact, almost bouncy.

"Harek?" Feordin repeated.

"Yeah, yeah, I'm fine." Beyond the outside wall, through the gate door that Nocona had unlocked and through which we, presumably, had passed, I could see the moat, sparkling as though with silver threads. No sign of the moat monster, which, in the tapestry anyway, had been way off to the right. Beyond was a uniformly green lawn dotted with vaguely shaped but colorful flowers. Over all was a rainbow in the sky, not pale and elusive the way rainbows are, but bright and solid.

Feordin? I suddenly thought. *Feordin's asking how I am?*

I turned my attention from my surroundings and looked for my mother.

She was sitting on the ground, Thea, Nocona, and Cornelius bending all-solicitous over her. Feordin was right next to them, as though he'd only now taken one step away toward me.

I scrambled to my feet. "Is she all right?" I asked.

"Just shaken from the fall, I think," Cornelius said.

I looked back and up, and could see no evidence of where I had dropped from, but there was a big red X on the cobblestones where I'd landed. The X looked embroidered.

"We were going to stand there," Thea said, "to break her fall. But we counted on you coming through before her."

"Really," Mom assured us all, assured me, "I'm OK."

"It's only about six feet," Nocona said. "I watched all of you. If she wasn't sick to begin with . . ."

Yeah, I thought. A lot of things would be different if she wasn't sick to begin with.

Mom used Cornelius's and Nocona's arms to pull herself up, swaying for a moment, like she was on her way back down. She closed her eyes and depended on the others to hold her straight.

"Let's get inside," I suggested.

It was a fine idea. Until we stepped through the front door.

Around the corner came a goblin serving-girl carrying a silver dinner tray. At least, I think it was a girl—with goblins it's hard to be sure. They all have mushroom-pale skin and tufts of shoulder-length hair the color of dragonflies' wings. Their faces are lumpish, having none of the expression of people's faces, like a Play-Doh project given up halfway through. But what looked like a goblin serving-girl came around the corner and saw us. And what sounded like a goblin serving-girl threw the dinner tray into the air and screeched.

By the time the white linen napkins floated down to the flagstone floor, she had disappeared down one of the four halls branching from the entryway.

"Whatever we're going to do," Thea said, "we better do it quick."

Each of the hallways looked as good as the others, and there was also a set of stairs leading down, probably to the dungeon. All the passageways were well lit and painted in what could only be described as designer colors—colors like aquamarine and fuchsia. There were life-size family portraits lining the walls too: families of humans and elves and dwarfs and halflings. The whole thing looked like a little kid's idea of a castle, a picturebook version.

Just then a squad of ten or twelve goblin guards leapt in from outside, their swords already drawn and their pikes already leveled. Mom gasped and backed away.

And not a single one of them even looked at her.

Cornelius crackled a bolt of Wizards' Lightning at two of the guards who were close together, but the others spread out immediately.

One of them came straight at me as I was still pulling my sword from its sheath. He practically stepped on Mom on the way.

"Move," I commanded her. My sword was about three quarters of the way out, and the guard would reach me before I was ready

But he hesitated. He glanced warily to either side, and that gave me time to draw my sword. All I could see of his face were his eyes, for his helmet had cheek-guards, a nose protector, and chin strap. The eyes were orange.

"Get back," I snapped at Mom. "Stop crowding me." I gave her a shove toward a doorway. "Stay there."

Yet again the guard looked distracted, missing the opportunity to move in.

I moved in and swept off his head, spattering thick yellow goblin blood.

I checked my companions. Mom seemed OK, huddling in the doorway. Cornelius had just let loose another volley of Wizards' Lightning. Feordin was by his side, protecting him, since he'd be helpless to protect himself if any of the goblins should get in close. Considering that the mace was Feordin's weapon of choice, he was doing quite well with a sword: two goblin guards lay dead at his feet. Thea had used my knife to kill a goblin with a bronze sword, which she'd taken and was now using on another goblin.

However, Nocona was in trouble. This was too close-quarters for him to use his bow, so he was forced to use his dagger. Backed up against a wall and dangerously close to the steep dungeon stairs, he was hard pressed by three goblin guards with swords. I stabbed one of them in the back, but one of the others whipped around, nearly taking my nose off with his sword.

I dodged. The guard came after me, coming in close, his sword striking sparks off mine. He was real fast, real strong—and I had all I could do to keep him off me.

He growled, showing his teeth, and strong-armed

me yet again. *Where were those stairs?* I'd lost track of them and only knew they were behind me and close. The air was hot and thick with the smell of Cornelius's Wizards' Lightning, sweat was pouring off me, and I was having trouble catching my breath. Killing people is a lot harder work than it looks in the movies. Even if they are goblins.

The goblin swung at my face, and I got my sword up just in time. Our blades locked. While I was concentrating on getting loose, he reached in with his left hand and grabbed a fistful of my hair. Twisting my head back, he exposed my neck. Then, with his right arm, he pushed both our still-locked swords toward me.

I fought back using both hands, but my left was still weak from where Wolstan had gouged me, and I couldn't get my sword free from the goblin's.

And then I felt a tremor start in my elbow.

I saw the goblin's face when he realized it, when he knew for a fact that my arm was about to give and he had won. My entire arm was beginning to shake with the strain. Who was going to take care of Mom? Who was going to see to it that the game ended as quickly as possible so that she could be rushed to the hospital? At least my death would be fast. My arm wasn't going to bend slowly back to the point where the edge of my own sword pressed agonizingly into my throat; it was going to give all at once, sweeping through me in another second, two at the most.

Except that suddenly the goblin had this weird look on his face, like someone had scraped fingernails across a blackboard, and he hadn't exactly stopped leaning against our two swords, but he wasn't pushing quite as hard as before.

Over his shoulder I saw Nocona. *Don't just stand there*, I thought. Because that's exactly what he was doing. He was maybe six or seven yards away, standing with his arm outstretched, not even holding a weapon. What'd he think he was—a wizard?

The goblin coughed, spitting up yellow blood onto my shirt. *Oh*, I thought, finally catching on. Nocona had thrown his dagger into the guy's back. The goblin's eyes rolled upward. I stepped back.

Mom screamed. Just as I realized there was nothing under my foot.

The goblin's weight tipped me backward, and the next thing I knew, we were bouncing down the stairs, me and the corpse together.

We slid to a stop maybe a dozen steps later, still on the stairs. I was on my back, pointed down headfirst with my blood rushing to my brain, the guard on top of me. I didn't dare move, for fear I would cause us to tumble even farther.

My companions clattered down the stairs. "Are you all right?" several voices asked before someone thought to roll the goblin off me.

I swayed dizzily for a moment before they came entirely into focus. "I'm . . ." I couldn't manage *fine*. ". . . OK." The only thing that had saved me from cracking my head wide open was that the stairs had the same bouncy texture as the cobblestoned courtyard. I made sure Mom could see me, though a couple days ago I would have avoided her attention. "Really, I'm OK." I clasped her hand.

"We better get out of here," Cornelius warned. "Down is probably best. We've made enough noise to raise the dead."

In her strained whisper-voice Mom said, "Can't raise the dead: we don't have a cleric."

I gave her hand an extra squeeze. But then the seriousness of the situation set in. "They can't see you," I said. "None of the nonplayer characters can see or hear you anymore."

"Wolstan could," she said. "The old man with the troll. Those other two . . ." She gestured vaguely, too headachey to grope for the names Brynhild and Abbot Simon.

Yeah. But not since yesterday. I glared at Cornelius.

He gave a guilty, noncommittal shrug.

"This is all your fault," I said.

He looked ready to protest, but Thea whacked him on the arm and gave a warning scowl.

The thing was, she didn't look so much angry with him as anxious that he not say anything stupid in front of Mom.

CHAPTER 31

Dungeon

Nocona, stepping around me because I wasn't moving fast enough, gave me a long, hard look. "Listen," he said to the others in an urgent whisper, "anybody down there heard us coming a mile away." He nodded to where the stairs disappeared around a curve. No shadows as far as we could see, indicating more torches in the walls, same as up here. Indicating, maybe, occupancy.

"Yeah?" Thea said.

"First one down may well get his head chopped off."

"Yeah?" Thea repeated. "So?"

Nocona shrugged. "So the first one down should be someone who wouldn't notice if his head got chopped off."

We all looked at the dead goblin. I must have

made a face, because Nocona gave me another of his looks. "It's just a goblin," he said.

Yeah, and the wolves were just wolves, and the orcs were just orcs, and the bandits were just bandits, and I was the next gentlest thing to Mother Teresa.

"Nothing to it," Feordin said. He and Nocona picked up the dead goblin and heaved him down the stairs. He thudded and clanked and sounded like a whole squad racing down.

There was a moment of silence.

Then another.

And another.

"Nothing to it," Feordin repeated.

Still, we were careful on the way down, leaping out into the guard area at the ready, assuming the defensive position.

The torches in their wall sockets sputtered and hissed. That, and the thudding of my heart, was all I could hear.

Nobody home.

At least . . . nobody we could see.

We were facing four doors arranged in a semi-circle around the deserted mint-green guard area. Like the rest of the castle, the dungeon seemed the brain-child of an interior decorator gone over the edge. The doors to the cells were colored rose, turquoise, violet, and acid-yellow.

Cautiously, we approached the rose door. Like the doors to the cells in the bandits' fortress, these had little barred windows through which the guards could check on the prisoners. Cornelius opened the peek-hole door.

"Well?" I snapped.

Cornelius put his finger to his lips, then moved on to the turquoise door.

Self-important jerk, I thought. I had to stand on tiptoe to look through the rose door's window.

Empty.

Behind me, I was aware of Nocona, Thea, and Feordin lining up for a look also. Mom sat on the bottom step, pale and listless, with her head leaning against the wall, her eyes closed.

I caught up to Cornelius at the window of the turquoise door. Nothing: I could tell by his lack of expression. I lingered to check anyway, since I didn't put it beyond Cornelius to miss something.

I was right the first time: nothing.

And nothing at the violet cell either. Just a perfectly normal, perfectly empty dungeon room.

When I looked up, the others were crowded

around the yellow door, Nocona, Thea, and Feordin elbowing each other for a chance to look through the bars. Cornelius, who'd spent an average of three seconds per window, was hogging the middle.

"What did you find?" I asked. I figured if it was Princess Dorinda, somebody would have said something to her by now: "Don't worry." "We're here to rescue you." That sort of thing.

I stood on tiptoe to see over their heads.

The fourth cell was a treasure room: golden coffers overflowing with coins, gems, golden crowns and tiaras; a golden table standing in the middle of the room, with a golden chair behind it, a half dozen golden carrying buckets stacked beside it, and golden measuring scales on it. A crystal chandelier hung over all, glittering in its own right, reflecting back the dazzle of gold.

In a voice made husky by awe, Cornelius intoned, "The Mother Lode."

"Yeah," I said. "*If* we were looking for treasure."

"But of course we are," Cornelius told me. "There may well be something in here we need for the next step of our quest. Like Nocona's key."

"How would we know it if we found it?" I asked. "I think we should go check the rooms upstairs."

"Stop worrying," Cornelius said. "Everyone step back."

I looked at Thea for support, but she shrugged. "He might be right." Then to the others, she said, "We'll take a quick look for magic items. We can always come back for the gold."

Talk about not taking a definite stand on issues. "Fine." I stood back, furious.

Cornelius leveled a concentrated blast of Wizards' Lightning at the door. The thick metal disintegrated, revealing even more gold. A huge golden platter hung on the wall—big as the table in our kitchen back home. I could see our life-size reflections in it. *Look at us*, I thought. *We're too grungy to be recognized.*

"Felice," Thea called. "Come take a look at this."

Mom didn't appear interested, but was too polite to say so. As soon as she got there, she sat on the floor.

The others were running their fingers through the coins and jewelry.

"Magic items," I said. "Remember?"

"Ta-dah!" Cornelius sang out. He held up a box labeled MAGIC ITEMS.

"Oh, that's very generous of someone," I said.

The thing was as big as a stereo speaker lying on

its side, and apparently not very heavy. Cornelius sat down on the floor with it and pulled back the hinged cover. It opened about two inches, then stuck. "Hmmm." He put his eye up to the opening.

"What do you see?" Feordin asked.

"Nothing." Cornelius tipped the box and shook.

Something—some*things*—rattled and thumped, but nothing came out.

"Must be caught." Cornelius reached his right hand into the box. Then, "Wonderful," he grumbled. "Now my hand's stuck." He wiggled the fingers of his left hand into the space between the box and the cover. "Hmmm. Can't feel anything."

"Wonderful treasure," Nocona sighed.

"Harek," the wizard said, inexplicably turning to me. "Both my hands are stuck."

How could they be stuck? I wanted to ask him. The right hand, conceivably, since he had shoved it in all the way up to the wrist; but his left hand only had the fingers in there. But he had this panicked glaze to his eyes, and I didn't think he was kidding. "Take it easy," I told him. I leaned over and looked, but I couldn't see anything. The left hand wasn't caught on anything. It had enough room that it should have slipped out easily.

"Can you close the lid?" Thea asked.

"Hey! My hands are in there."

"I mean just a little bit," she explained. "Sometimes that works to get a zipper restarted."

The lid didn't budge in either direction. Cornelius was beginning to sweat. You'd have thought that would make his hands slick and able to slip out, but no, nothing.

"Here." I picked up a long, thin candlestick holder from one of the piles of golden treasure. "Let's pry it open."

"Yeah," Cornelius said, "what if you put that in here and can't get that back out either?"

"Better this than one of our hands." I wedged the holder in between Cornelius's right hand and the hinge. I pushed. I twisted. I shoved it as close to the hinges as it would go.

Nothing.

And it came away from the box as easily as it should have.

"What am I going to do?" Cornelius said.

Mom, who I hadn't thought was with us, so to speak, said, "Can't you use one of your magic spells?"

Cornelius shook his head. "I need to use my hands for my spells," he explained. "Each spell has its own words and gestures. I can't do any magic with my hands . . . locked up like this."

"Felice," Thea said, "you're a thief. You're supposed to be able to open things."

"I can try," Mom said. She leaned forward. And her hand passed *through* the box.

"Whoa!" Feordin exclaimed. "Neat trick!"

But he was wrong. I knew it right away. It wasn't the box: *I* had touched it when I'd shoved in the candlestick holder.

"Mom." My voice quivered like I was talking through an electric fan. "Can you touch this?" I picked up a piece of treasure, it didn't matter what. I think it was a golden bowl.

Her hand passed right through it.

She was fading away.

I dropped the bowl, turned to look for something else—as though that would make a difference. I saw the huge mirrorlike platter on the wall. I saw my reflection, smack in the middle. And Thea's. I saw Feordin, Nocona, Cornelius with his hands caught in the box. I didn't see Mom.

"I hate this stupid game!" I yelled.

And then I saw something else in the platter, a

blur almost off the edge of the shiny surface. A movement by the stairs.

"Look out!" I shouted.

But that was useless. In the doorway, five steps away, impossibly distant, a heavy metal grate emerged from a crack in the ceiling and slammed down to the floor.

CHAPTER 32

Prisoners (Part I)

WE LEAPT TO OUR FEET, but of course we were already too late. The gate was down, and the single goblin soldier who had released the lever on the back wall of the guard area dropped behind the heavy oak table to hide from any possible retaliation. A squad of goblin guards charged down the last several steps and stood there aiming . . . nine, ten, eleven, twelve loaded crossbows, two pikes, five swords, and what looked like a miniature catapult at us.

"Drop your weapons," one of the goblins told us.

Each of us waited to see what the others were going to do.

"Drop your weapons, or we start picking you off one by one."

Our weapons weren't going to be any good to us in this situation anyway, so I let my sword drop. The others did likewise, including Nocona with his bow, which was probably the only weapon the goblins, out there, were really worried about.

"Don't," I told Mom as she reached for the knife she wore at her side.

She hesitated.

"They can't see you," I said.

I could see the goblins giving each other sidelong glances, like they were thinking they'd caught themselves a load of psychiatric refugees. "Everybody drop everything," the one in charge commanded, which I guess he figured covered every contingency.

Mom folded her arms defiantly. She would have looked more convincing except that she was wincing, like her head hurt so much she was afraid it was going to burst open.

Not that it made any difference. The goblins looked right through her. "Now the one with his hands caught," the goblin said. "Somebody toss his knife down. Now kick everything over here." He indicated the grate, whose bars were spaced widely enough that the stuff could fit through. "Now back off." Apparently we didn't move fast enough. *"Back off."*

Two of the lackeys rushed forward to gather up our weapons.

"What about this?" Cornelius said, indicating his hands trapped in the box.

"Tough," the goblin commander said. He pointed out three of his men. "You, you, and you. Watch them. Any funny business—kill them all." He led the rest of the squad upstairs with never a glance back for us, like we were lower than grubs.

Our three guards brought our weapons into the guard area. They took off their helmets, revealing bland, almost identical, Silly-Putty faces. They cleared a space on the wooden table, pushing aside apparatus for inflicting pain—thumbscrews, branding irons. I began to sweat, but all they had in mind was a game of mumblety-peg. They tossed a knife repeatedly into the wooden table, using Nocona's knife so as not to dull their own.

I motioned for the others to gather around Cornelius, where we sat, our backs to the guards. I reached and touched Mom. She felt solid to me. "This is weird," I whispered, so the guards couldn't overhear what we said.

"Felice," Nocona said. "Can you . . . Does your hand go through your knife?"

She picked it up, handed it to him.

He turned it over in his hand to show us that it was solid.

"Better give it back to her," Thea said. "The guards can't see it if she's got it."

"But it's no use to us if she's got it," Nocona argued.

"Give it back to her." Feordin's voice was a soft but dangerous rumble. "It's her knife."

Nocona was going to fight us for it, I was sure. But then he flipped it into Mom's lap.

"Idiot," I whispered. "You could have cut her."

"But I didn't," Nocona snapped.

"Knock it off," Cornelius said. "We're in deep enough trouble as it is."

We all glared at each other, as though we were the enemy. From the guard area, we could hear the murmur of the goblins making calls, the thud thud of Nocona's dagger hitting the table.

"What are we going to do?" Mom asked.

"Can the knife," Thea asked, "with you holding it, inflict damage?"

Mom tried to pierce a link in a gold and ruby necklace, but the point passed right through.

"Can you . . ." Thea glanced at the rest of us, as

though concerned about our reaction. "Can you leave the cell?"

Slowly, for fast motion made her dizzy, Mom stood. She walked to the barred door.

And walked through.

I motioned her to come back. "What good is it," I asked, "if she can't touch anything?"

One of the guards cheered at a point gained.

Mom sighed as she sank down to the floor. "No good," she said. "It's no good at all."

CHAPTER 33

Prisoners (Part II)

T HE HOURS CRAWLED BY, minute by minute.

The guards changed.

Dinner was shoved under the door, a meat stew we didn't dare touch because there was no telling what meat goblins would serve.

Dinner was taken away.

The guards changed again.

The hours crawled by, second by second.

Nocona selected an emerald, tossed it and caught it one-handed several times to get the weight and balance of it. Then he lobbed it through the bars of the door at one of the goblin guards.

The guard picked that moment to score in the game of dice he was playing and raised both hands above his head in a winner's cheer. The flung gem struck his armored shoulder rather than his head. With orcs, they wouldn't have noticed. Or even if they had, with the emerald ricocheted away into a dark corner, they wouldn't have known what had hit and wouldn't have made the connection with us, ten yards away.

But these were goblins, not orcs.

All three leapt to their feet and went for their crossbows. They aimed. Cornelius, with his hands caught in the MAGIC ITEMS box, obviously had an alibi. Thea and Feordin had both fallen asleep: Thea sprawled in the golden chair, resting her head on the table, Feordin leaning against the back wall. Mom, also asleep, they couldn't see anyway. Nocona had whipped around so that his back was to them.

Leaving me looking right at them.

They aimed at me.

It was no good protesting my innocence; they wouldn't believe me anyway. In the absence of innocence, I went for repentance. "That was a mistake," I said. "Sorry. It won't happen again. Sorry."

They glowered, evaluating my sincerity.

My heart pounded in my throat and I couldn't swallow. Behind me, I was aware of Cornelius sitting up sharply, suddenly aware that something had been going on while he wasn't paying attention. One of the others was snoring softly. Nocona didn't twitch.

"Anything," one of the guards said, "*anything* happens, and you die first."

"Yes," I said. "All right. I understand." Then, because it couldn't hurt, I again added, "Sorry."

Slowly, very slowly, they backed off. They put the crossbows back down on the table, first one, then the other, then the other. They sat down. They resumed their game of dice.

Periodically they would glance at me, glaring.

"What happened?" Cornelius whispered.

"Nothing." Nocona whispered also. "Go back to your magic box, old man."

"Jerk," Cornelius said.

One of the goblins glanced up then, and we sat there looking saintly. At the first chance I punched Nocona in the arm. "Thanks a lot," I whispered between clenched teeth.

Nocona had the sense not to make a noise. "You handled it," he said.

"What were you trying to do anyway?"

"Knock out his eye."

"How would that have helped?"

"It wouldn't have," Nocona admitted. "Just something to pass the time."

"That's sick," I told him.

Cornelius seemed no longer interested, now that the excitement was over. He resumed trying to extract his hands from the box.

"Give me a break. Give us all a break." Nocona's voice had gotten louder and the goblins glared again. He waited till they returned to their game. "You're acting like an old woman, Arvin."

"Harek," I corrected automatically. "And what—"

"You liked the game well enough before. Now all of a sudden your mother's here and you're going"—he switched to a sissy singsong, "'Oooo, bloodshed, I can't stand it.' And—"

"This has nothing—"

"And, 'Oooo, let's try to get through this without hurting anybody, can't we, guys? *I'm* too nice a person to get involved in all this barbarian stuff.'"

"This has nothing—"

"I've had it up to here—" He indicated beneath his chin, and I grabbed his hand to shut him up. Practically shouting, I told him, "This has nothing to do with my mother."

"Shh," Cornelius warned.

I didn't even check to see if the goblins were watching.

Nocona said, "Well, what *does* it have to do with,

Arvin, besides you thinking you're so good and pure and superior to the rest of us bloodthirsty savages?"

"I never said that." I glanced around the cell and saw that Thea and Feordin were wide awake and listening. Mom was still zonked out, looking so pale and fragile, I was beginning to think *I* could almost see through her. And she was Mom more and more, Felice melting away almost as I watched. "I never said that," I repeated. I groped for the words to describe how I felt: that the danger was too real to be exciting any longer, that it had become too personal.

But that wasn't it exactly.

Was it my mother? Embarrassment that she could see what I really was? That didn't seem quite right either. Embarrassment that *I* could see what I really was? Melodramatic. I realized I didn't know how I felt.

Well, maybe I felt like when you're at the amusement park on the Over the Falls ride and you've just gone over the edge and you know it only takes three, four seconds to hit the water at the bottom, but it seems like your heart's stopped and your eyes don't register what you're seeing and you know you're going to be falling forever, and then you do hit the water and your friends say, "Wow, neat ride!" and you say, "Want to do it again?"

All I could get out was, "I-I-I—"

Nocona said, "You're just taking things out on us because you're worried about your mother."

Without stopping to think, I said, "And *you're* just taking things out on *me* because you're worried that you're turning into a werewolf."

Nocona stiffened and went white.

"What's all this?" Feordin asked.

Instantly I regretted my hasty words. "Nothing. Just . . . Never mind." Dominic was my friend. I felt like one of those scuzz-balls in the movies who turns his neighbor in to the Nazis or the KGB or the Ku Klux Klan.

But Feordin was already on his feet. "What are you talking about? That sprained ankle? That *has* taken an uncommonly long time to heal. And he *has* been uncharacteristically surly. I think it's time one of us took a look at that, Nocona."

Nocona drew his leg under him. "Leave me alone."

I glanced at the goblins. They were watching us. Apparently their dice were less interesting than the possibility that we might knock each other's heads against the walls. "We've got to stick together," I started.

Thea said, "Nocona, just let us see your ankle. You're not helping your case by acting this way."

"Don't you touch me," he warned.

She took a step toward him and he leapt to his feet.

Still sitting, Cornelius swung his leg around and smacked the back of Nocona's knee. Nocona staggered and Feordin tackled him. Together they slid into a pile of treasure, which rained down on them.

The goblins whipped together a quick wager on the outcome.

Nocona wriggled away from Feordin, but trying to get up, he set his foot on some loose coins. He went down on one knee, and Feordin grabbed that foot. Nocona pitched forward.

Feordin threw himself on Nocona's back. Both went down in another flurry of treasure.

Thea stepped on Nocona's right leg, the injured one. Once she had him pinned, she leaned over and pulled up the pants leg. We could all plainly see his ankle was bloody. She unwrapped it anyway, just to be sure.

Puncture marks, obviously a bite.

"I'm not a werewolf," Nocona protested.

Thea took off her belt, and between her and Feordin, they tied Nocona's hands behind his back.

"Come on, guys," Nocona said. "It's me. Don't do this to me. Please. You can't leave me tied up for the rest of the campaign."

I asked, "Can't we just watch him?"

"Yes," Nocona said. "Please. I promise to tell you if I start to turn. Really."

Nobody bothered to answer.

"If you had a cleric with you," one of the goblins said, "you wouldn't have to worry about it."

That was it. I'd had it, I'd had it, I'd had it. "We don't have a cleric!" I screamed at him. I hurled a golden goblet at them, but wasn't as good a shot as Nocona had been. The goblet hit the bars of the door and bounced off, striking my own leg.

The goblins sniggered. "Wooo, that'll teach us," one of them said.

I grabbed a handful of coins and flung that. Mostly they fell far short of the guards. I don't think any of them actually hit, and I certainly didn't inflict any damage. The goblins didn't even go for their weapons.

The goblins didn't even go for their weapons.

That thought suddenly sank in. And what could have happened—what *would* have happened—if I'd gotten them mad instead of amused. If they killed me, what would Mom's chances be?

I turned to check on her, to see if our racket had woken her.

And I couldn't find her.

"Mom?" My voice shook. This cell wasn't big enough to misplace anybody. "Mom?"

"Harek," Thea warned between clenched teeth.

"Thea," I answered in the same tone. "She's gone, and that's more important than anything that happens in this stupid . . ." I didn't dare say *game:* if the program looped at this stage, there was no telling what might happen.

I took a step forward, to grab Thea and shake her.

And stopped when I saw Mom, sound asleep on the floor, right where she'd been all along.

I stepped back and she flickered out of view again. I sank to my knees. From that angle I could see her again.

"Does everybody see her?" I asked. "Nocona?"

Obviously he was worried that this was some sort of trap, that we'd use what he said against him. I discounted his answer even as he said it. "Yeah. Sure. How not?"

"Cornelius?"

"Yes," he said very softly. "But she's kind of shimmery."

Feordin said, "I can see her from here. But if I tip my head, I . . . sort of . . . can't."

She was beginning to fade out for us, too.

For me.

"I hate this," I screamed.

One of the goblins tapped his head. "I think they *all* should be checked for werewolf bites," he said.

CHAPTER 34

Prisoners (Part III)

Hours . . . MINUTES . . . SECONDS . . .

Trying not to call attention to ourselves, we examined our cell. There were no loose blocks of stone, no hint of tunnels under the floor. The bars didn't feel like metal, which I suppose was good, because if they had been metal, they probably would have been iron, and who knows what effect being surrounded by iron would have had on Thea and me?

At first we thought, Oh, boy. The bars are just needlepoint: we could rip our way out of here. But when we tested our strength against it, the fabric might as well have been metal for all the damage we caused.

And I couldn't see that we'd ever be able to overcome the guards anyway.

Hours . . . minutes . . . seconds . . .

I was no longer able to convince myself that it was all part of Shelton's programming glitch.

My mind began skittering around the idea that my mother could die. *Really* die.

I mean, looking at it logically, normally parents do die before their children. It'd even happened to a few of my classmates, besides Noah Avila. But I'd never really considered it happening to me, never imagined day-to-day life without Mom.

For the first time, it occurred to me that some day I was going to have to face both my parents' dying. Unless I died first. For the first time, it occurred to me that someday *I* was going to die. Oh, sure, I'd *thought* of dying before. As in: And then they'll be sorry they didn't treat me better . . . didn't let me go to the rock concert . . . didn't increase my allowance. I'd *thought* of it. But I'd never *Thought* of it. And suddenly there was nothing grand or noble or romantic about it.

Hours . . . minutes . . . seconds . . .

The torches burned low and were replaced.

The guards changed.

Breakfast arrived.

The goblins who delivered the food were noisy, or at least one of them was. It was morning in Sannatia, he announced in a voice even more gravelly than the average goblin's. Were they going to get a chance to execute the prisoners?

The others didn't know. Didn't care. Didn't look up from carving their initials into the wooden table.

The kitchen goblin whistled a monotonous tune as he ladled what may well have been yesterday's stew into what may well have been yesterday's tin bowls. Perhaps his helmet's cheek protectors interfered, or maybe he was just a lousy whistler. It got on my nerves after about ten seconds.

His companion kicked stray coins back into the cell from the batch I'd thrown last night. After the fourth one hit my kneecap, I realized he was aiming at me.

I scooted back on my rear end. I avoided their eyes, trying not to look annoyed, which they might take as provocation. Or scared, which they might also take as provocation. The others were all sitting farther back and were pretending not to notice. Mom hadn't awakened since the previous evening.

The talkative one shoved the bowls under the door. "One for you," he said, sliding a bowl toward me. "One for you." He shoved one in the general direction of Nocona. "One for you." The stuff was slopping over the sides and onto the floor. He should have just left them by the door like last night's guard. "And one for you, and you. And—oops, one left over. Anybody else in there?"

I sucked in a cold breath, but he wasn't looking at where Mom was. Just an idiot goblin who didn't know how to count. Quickly I averted my eyes again.

"So," he said to the other three goblins. "What do you guys do for entertainment?"

Our guards had been on duty for four hours. They were one-third tired and two-thirds bored out of their minds. They'd taken off their helmets and loosened their armor straps, and the highlight of their watch had been when they'd had a contest to see who could spit the farthest. They didn't like these bright and spiffy new guys any better than I did.

"I've got an idea," the talkative goblin said, and that made me nervous, because I sure hoped *we* didn't have anything to do with his idea of entertainment. I pretended to be engrossed with the tip of my boot, but out of the corner of my eyes I watched him reach into his pocket.

"Pick a card," he said. "Any card."

Pick a card?

Slowly, very slowly, I looked up.

The talkative goblin had his back to the cell. He wasn't wearing the troll boots, but that could just have meant Robin had smartened up. His companion was watching me. Were the eyes orange? It was hard to tell in this light. I mouthed the name "Marian?" figuring, if not, what could it hurt? She gave me a look like "Well, finally," then winked. Then, in a very gruff voice, she growled, "Hey!" like I'd tried something, and drew her sword.

The guards jumped to their feet, grabbing their crossbows up from the table.

But Robin had been waiting. His sword was out a fraction of a second before they even started to move, and there was nothing to warn them that it wasn't just a case of his reflexes being faster than theirs.

Until he swept off the head of the nearest guard.

The others let their crossbows drop with a clatter; there was no time for setting up. Instead they whipped out their swords and closed in.

Marian was real good; Robin, now his advantage of surprise was gone, was already backing up, giving ground.

He was marking time, I realized, waiting for Marian to finish off the one guard then come and help him.

And there wasn't enough time.

Already the guard had Robin backed up to the bars of our cell.

I grabbed a handful of the coins on the floor and threw them at the guard's face.

He barely flinched, but it was enough to give Robin an opening. He lunged forward, skewering the hapless guard with his sword.

A moment later, Marian finished off her man, too.

It happened fast, about ten seconds from the time Marian had yelled, "Hey!" The group inside the cell cheered, though I'm not sure they really knew what was going on till Marian removed her helmet. Then they cheered even louder.

"Thank you, thank you," Marian said, trying to fluff up her helmet-flattened hair. It took me a moment to remember that she was Noah, that Robin, kneeling in front of the lock mechanism, was Dawn Marie. Marian looked us all over; then, real quiet, she asked, "Where's Felice?"

"Here." I pointed, though it was obvious she wouldn't have asked if she could see from where she was standing. Despite all the excitement, Mom was still asleep. "She's beginning to fade. You have to stand just right to see her."

Marian glanced at the others, to make sure that I wasn't the only one who thought she was there. She shifted, first one way, then the other to align herself with the position from which I could see Mom. She sucked in her breath sharply. It might have been because she still hadn't believed me, or it might have been because Mom had lost almost all the characteristics of Felice. Instead of a gypsy bar wench, she looked like somebody's mother, except for the fact that if you looked at her straight-on you couldn't see her at all.

Marian closed her eyes and whispered something. I didn't catch it, but then again, I didn't figure I was supposed to. To Robin she said, real snappy, "What *are* you doing?"

"I'm trying to unlock the gate."

Marian reached under her goblin tunic and pulled out her gauntlets of power. "Step aside," she warned. Holding her sword two-handed, she struck the bars. They separated like strands of yarn.

"Now," she said to Cornelius, "what in the world happened to you?"

"I'm stuck," our wizard said.

"No kidding. Here, do you trust me?"

"No," Cornelius said, watching her approach with her sword.

She stuck the point into the box and worked to jimmy the cover open.

"If you cut my hand off, that's not going to help."

"Be quiet. I'll have you out in a second."

There was a loud *crack!* But what had happened was that the sword had snapped.

"Hmmm." Marian grabbed the box with one hand and the cover with the other. She strained to pry them apart but finally had to give it up.

"Maybe I can help," Robin said.

"It's magic," Marian pointed out.

Robin, kneeling next to one of the dead guards, held up a ring of keys.

"Which one though?" I asked impatiently.

"Probably this one, marked 'Magic box key.'"

"If the key's as good as the box . . ." I started, but Robin inserted the key into the lock before I could finish. There was a *click*, and the cover swung loose.

There were none of the promised magic goodies; in fact, the box was empty despite the fact that it rattled, but at least Cornelius's hands were free. He rubbed his wrists gingerly.

"How about you?" Marian said to Nocona. "Those bonds magic, too?"

"*We* put them on," Feordin explained. "He's been werewolf-bit."

Nocona said, "And I haven't turned into a werewolf yet. Can't you see I'm not going to? Please. Let me loose. If I start to feel funny or anything, I swear I'll let you know."

Marian shook her head.

"Please," Nocona said, sounding more angry than pleading.

"Sorry," Marian said.

Nocona scrambled to his feet. I don't know what he thought he could accomplish, with his hands tied behind his back and her wearing her gauntlets of power. She shoved him back, and he went skittering across the width of the cell.

"Come on, Nocona," I said, "my mom's really sick. The most important thing is that we get out of this game as fast as possible."

"I want to help," he said.

"Then stop taking up our time." Sure, I felt sorry for him, but I'd be a lot more sympathetic if he'd just shut up and come along quietly.

"I wouldn't do this to *you*," he said.

And he probably wouldn't have.

I probably wouldn't have, if I wasn't convinced this had stopped being a game when Mom's headache had started.

"Felice," Thea said. "Felice, you have to get up now."

Nothing.

"Mrs. Rizalli?" Thea went to shake her shoulder, and her hand passed right through her.

I could see Mom was breathing, which was the only thing that kept me from going into total panic. "Mom. *Mom.* Mom, get up. We've got to go now."

There was absolutely no reaction. It wasn't like she was too sleepy to respond. It was like she didn't hear us at all.

"Harek," Marian said. "We're going to have to leave her."

"No way."

Cornelius said, "The goblins can't see her: she'll be perfectly safe here. I can put an Invisibility spell on her to be sure."

Abandon my own mother?

"The other choice," Robin pointed out, "is for us to just sit here until the next shift of guards comes on. But that's not going to do her any good."

"I guess," I said. I wished that she was awake so

that I could ask what she thought. Not that I was in the habit of asking my parents for advice, but adults have a way of always sounding so sure of themselves. I wondered how old I'd have to be before I'd know all the answers. "What if she wakes up, and we're all gone, and she's scared?" Did parents ever get scared?

Nobody said anything.

"All right," I said. "The Invisibility spell."

Because *I* was scared.

Because I thought that if we didn't end this game sooner than its natural run, she wouldn't ever wake up to *be* scared.

CHAPTER 35

Day Five

WE DEBATED LEAVING Nocona locked in the dungeon, in a separate cell from Mom, but in the end decided we'd feel more secure if we had him where we could see him. We even tied a gag around his mouth because werewolves are chaotic, which means they don't care whose side they're on. He might decide at an inopportune moment to yell a warning to the goblins.

"I wouldn't—" he started, but the rest was a muffled mumble of complaint. Werewolf or not, by then he looked mad enough to kill all of us.

The troll boots, Robin explained, were back on the troll. Marian had brought the crystal though, and they gave Thea the sword, Orc Slayer.

The rest of us retrieved the weapons the goblins had taken from us.

"Back where we started," Robin announced chipperly.

"Except my mother's sick," I said.

"Except I don't have my mace," Feordin said.

"Except we're weak from wounds and from not eating in I-can't-remember-how-many days," Thea said.

"Except we don't have Brynhild and Abbot Simon," Marian said.

"Except we don't have Nocona," Cornelius said, for which Nocona scowled.

"Yeah," Robin said, "except for that."

Even Marian gave him a dirty look.

Cautiously we went up the dungeon stairs. Nobody there, in any of the brightly colored hallways, nor in what we could see of the courtyard outside.

"It's midday," I groaned, noting the shadows.

"It's always midday here," Robin said. "That's why the goblins go through the tapestry when it's night in Sannatia. It's the only chance for darkness they get. When we came through, it looked like about six, seven A.M. outside."

"How *did* you get in, by the way?" I asked. "I never thought Marian would get you back here in time."

"Ah, well. I bought a horse from the old man, Fred,

with the money I won playing cards with you." He flashed a smile and wiggled his eyebrows at me. "I was halfway through the caves when Marian and I ran into each other."

"We got to Sannatia just about dusk," she interrupted, "and hid in the old granary. We watched the goblins until finally a couple came close to where we were, and we jumped them and took their stuff. We mingled until the captain ordered everyone back in."

Cornelius said, "You mean that all the goblins are doing in Sannatia is just exercising and getting R-and-R and that sort of thing? They aren't really doing anything?"

"You got it," Robin said.

"What a bust." Cornelius wasn't the only one disappointed.

"Yeah, but," Thea said, "that can't be the only reason they did away with all the inhabitants. Besides, if it had been only goblins, they would have just slaughtered the people. And there weren't any bodies. And what about the treasure in the dungeon? Goblins don't collect treasure like that."

Marian shrugged. "We didn't find out anything about that. We heard the captain order one of his men to get food for the prisoners, and we figured that had to be either you or the princess and her Grand Guardsmen. So we followed the goblin to the kitchen, then ambushed him on the way here. The rest," she gestured expansively, "is history."

Feordin said, "This is all *very* fascinating, but what next?"

"Ah-ha!" Robin said. "We have the answer to that, too. When we were peeking into the kitchen, we saw another goblin in there besides the guard we'd followed. This other guy had a silver tray—with crystal dishes, no less—a flower on the tray, linen napkins with gold embroidery, and *much* fancier food than what you guys got."

"So?" Feordin asked. "The chief goblin?"

"At the least, I'd say," Thea said.

"Maybe the mastermind behind what happened at Sannatia?" I suggested.

"We won't find out here," Robin said. "The kitchen's this way." He started down the aquamarine hall and we followed.

All along the hallway, twin rows of portraits watched our progress. Elves, dwarfs, members of the various races of humans: the pictures were very realistically done in needlework, much more realistic than the castle tapestry that had led us here from the nursery in the governor's palace. I thought of those spooky old haunted-house movies where the eyes in pictures follow the people around.

Luckily the eyes in these pictures stayed where they belonged.

The first two doors we passed were closed. The third was open. Robin peeked in, then looked back at us with his finger to his lips. Quickly but quietly he tiptoed past. One by one we followed. Last in line, hustling Nocona, I peeked in. A library. With a goblin dusting the books. Fortunately he—or she—had his back to us. Nocona gave no indication that he wanted to get the goblin's attention.

Several closed doors later, Robin motioned for us to halt at a point where the hallway went around another corner. He gathered us in real close, then whispered, "There's about six more yards—"

"Three," Marian interrupted.

"Whatever. Not very far. Then there's the open door to the kitchen. We've got to pass through there, because the goblin with the silver tray went out into a hall that way."

"Any kitchen staff?" Cornelius asked.

"Yeah," Robin said. "Maybe six or seven."

"Closer to ten," Marian said.

Robin sighed.

"What we've got to do," Feordin told us, "is take them totally by surprise. Wipe them out fast before they have a chance to make an outcry."

From the kitchen came the clatter of pots and pans, the sizzle of fat dripping into a cookfire, the voices of goblins carrying on the day-to-day chores of a scullery. The smell of fresh-baked bread and savory meat pies was almost enough to make me cry.

Robin got out his slingshot and a stone about the size of a cherry. The rest of us held our swords ready. Stealthily we approached the corner, rounded it together, and spread out across the width of the hall so that each of us could see what the others saw. What we saw was a busy morning's kitchen. Eight of them to six of us. Not counting Nocona.

We were halfway to them when one of the goblins looked up from scrubbing a pot and saw us.

Before he could utter a sound, Robin's slingshot twanged. The goblin pitched forward onto the counter. For another two seconds nobody noticed, and by then we were in the room.

"Escaped prisoners!" the cook yelled. He picked

up a carving knife as long as my arm, but Cornelius blasted him long-distance with Wizards' Lightning.

It took less than a minute to kill them. They'd all been real old or real young, and for the most part they'd been so disconcerted, they tried to fend off our swords with spatulas and colanders. I felt sick about it, and it didn't help when Feordin referred to the cook as being deep-fried. I fought a wave of nausea and looked up to see Nocona watching me with pure loathing. If he could have talked, he probably would have asked how come I had sympathy for goblins—who weren't even people—and yet could heartlessly tie *him* up and keep him out of the game.

Angrily, I gave him a shove down the hallway where Robin and Marian said the goblin with the silver tray had gone. This hallway was lavender.

Not knowing where he'd delivered that tray, we had to check each room. We passed a pantry, a linen closet, and a study. There was a goblin sitting at a desk in the study, and Cornelius shot him with a blast of Wizards' Lightning from the doorway. The next door opened on a set of stairs leading up in a tight circular twist, obviously one of the turrets we had seen from outside.

On the second floor, the walls were the color of lilacs. As on the first floor, there were life-size pictures lining both sides. We crept up to the nearest door and Thea, first in line now, peeked in.

Frantically she gestured us back to the stairwell.

"What?" we whispered at her.

She made shushing motions and gathered us in even closer. Barely audible, she whispered, "It's her— the princess. But there's half a dozen goblins in there guarding her. We can't just burst in, or they might hurt her."

"Burst in is exactly what we've *got* to do," Feordin said. "Just like in the kitchen: neat and clean."

"Yes," Marian said. "We've got to be super quiet."

Behind me there was a crash. I whipped around and saw that Nocona had knocked one of the pictures off the wall. Perhaps he had simply leaned against it accidentally.

Perhaps not.

Feordin put his knife under Nocona's chin.

The rest of us stood poised, waiting to see if anybody would come to investigate.

My heart beat so hard I had a coppery taste in my throat. I wanted so much for this to be over.

We waited.

And waited.

I glanced back at Nocona, whose eyes dared me to accuse him. Another picture hung crookedly on the wall as though he'd brushed against it too. I noticed because the wall behind was a darker shade of purple, as though the picture had been hanging a long time. I picked up the one that had fallen to rehang it—no reason to let anyone see we'd come this way.

The first thing I noticed was that this was the last picture on the wall, though there was room for maybe three more before the stairs.

The second thing I noticed was that the picture had been hung recently enough that for this one there wasn't an outline on the wall.

The third thing I noticed was that the picture was of a group of men dressed in what I suddenly recognized as the uniform of King Ulric's Grand Guard—Princess Dorinda's bodyguards.

Nocona, also looking at the picture, raised his eyebrows.

Before I could mention any of this, Marian nodded impatiently toward the room and took off without us.

Feordin finally removed his knife from Nocona's

throat, with a look warning that next time he wouldn't take any more chances.

We crept after Marian to the door. I got the briefest of glances, but it was enough. There were six big goblins wearing all sorts of glittery medals and epaulets. Veterans. War heroes. Tough guys. They were all holding their swords up in the air, standing around the princess, who was sitting on the edge of a large canopied bed. She was small for her age, looking no more than six, though I knew she was ten. Her light blond hair was a tangled mess around her heart-shaped face, which was incredibly pale. No wonder, considering the goblins looked like they were about to chop her to pieces. She was facing us; the goblins had their backs to the door.

For the briefest moment I thought we were in luck. If only the princess didn't react to our presence. I saw her eyes focus on us. I put my finger to my lips.

She screamed.

Probably I would have too, if I'd seen somebody who looked like me, who looked like any of us.

She jumped off the bed, even with those armed goblins standing there, and tried to crawl underneath the overhanging comforter.

The goblins, naturally, whirled around to face us.

Two fell right away, one vaporized under Wizards' Lightning, the other with a stone right between the eyes. As the rest of us moved in—me, Thea, Feordin, and Marian—I heard Robin call out, "Don't be frightened, Princess Dorinda. We're here to rescue you."

The goblin I was matched up against swung his sword distressingly close to my midriff.

I parried, and our swords came together with a clang like someone whacking a flagpole with a metal two-by-four.

He was a lot fresher than I was, and a lot stronger. I found myself hard pressed just to defend myself, parrying instead of thrusting, and backing up. We rounded the corner of the bed, me trying to escape, him trying to pursue, and I stepped on Princess Dorinda's fingers as she tried to crawl out from under the bed to make *her* escape.

She scurried back under the bed, which was where I would have put her if I had the choice, but meanwhile I felt the wall at my back and still that goblin came.

My right arm began to ache from wielding the sword, and I knew I didn't have the strength in my left arm to switch, not since Wolstan. I slid along the wall and backed into a piece of furniture, a low table with the silver serving tray we had been following and some sort of tiny cage.

If he'd only let up for a second, I thought, I could reach behind me with my left hand, fling something from off the table at him, then—while he was distracted—finish him off.

He didn't let up for a second.

I kept backing up, and the wooden table scraped across the flagstone floor with a skitter-screech I could feel in my jaw.

And still from the goblin there was this flurry of sword thrusts and swings and jabs, and I was breathing through my mouth and still not getting enough air, and the table leg snagged on a slightly raised flagstone and tipped, and I went down with it.

There was a flash of light and a smell of sulfur. I listened—once I could hear above the pounding of my heart—and realized the fighting was over. Wonderful. The climax of our adventure, and here I was flat on my back, once again rescued by the superior ability of the others.

From under the bed, Princess Dorinda looked out at me like I was a princess-eating ogre.

"It's all right," I said. I switched my sword to my other hand and reached out to her.

She flinched.

"We're going to take you home," I said, trying to sound as gentle and reassuring as I could, lying there on my back among the ruins of the splintered table, covered with sweat and grime and orc, wolf, and goblin blood.

"Home?" Her voice was a scared little kid's voice.

Thea came round to the near side and stooped down closer. "We've come to take you to your father. We've come to rescue you."

Slowly, still not completely trusting us, Dorinda crawled out from under the bed. "You're not going to hurt me?" she asked, looking pathetically at each of us with her pale blue eyes.

"Of course not," we all assured her.

Except for Nocona, who was gagged.

Suddenly Marian gasped. "Oh, no!" I thought she was extending her hand to help me up. But she was pointing at something on the floor: the cage I had glimpsed on the table. It was made of gold, and it held a little chipmunk. "Look what you did, Harek. The poor thing."

"Everything's all right," I said. "Don't worry, I'm

fine." But I picked the cage up anyway. The brown-striped creature looked at me with its tiny black eyes. "And you're all right too, aren't you, little fellow?" I smiled encouragingly, and the miserable beast sank its teeth into my finger. "Yow!" I let the cage drop.

"Harek!" Marian picked the cage up by its wire handle. From talking to me in a growl, she shifted to a friendly salesman purr. "Is this your pet?"

The princess nodded.

"What's his name?"

"Chipmunk," the princess said.

"Clever name," I said.

Robin, helping me to my feet, stomped on my toes.

Marian said, "Do you and Chipmunk want to go home?"

Dorinda nodded.

"All right, then." Marian handed her the cage. "We've got to go quickly and quietly."

Dorinda nodded solemnly. Although her size made her look younger than she was, her sad eyes were of someone who was much older, someone who had seen more of the world than any ten-year-old should have.

Take-command Marian put her arm around the princess's shoulders.

The princess said, "Do you know about the back way?"

"The back way?" We all looked at one another.

"It's a secret shortcut."

I shook my head. "We left one of our people in the dungeon," I said. "We have to go back for her."

"The dungeon's where it leads," she said. She nodded toward the back door.

"I'll check it out," Cornelius said. He opened the door. Beyond was a deserted hallway, a mauve-colored one. There was only one door, way down at the far end.

"This way." Dorinda dashed ahead of us.

"Dorinda," Marian said, not quite daring to shout. "Honey."

Dorinda got to the door a full five yards ahead of us. Robin and Feordin were in the rear, dragging Nocona between them.

"Wait!" I called.

She flung the door open anyway.

My heart almost stopped, but she said, "See, nobody here," and disappeared through the door.

We followed her, all of us.

And found ourselves in what had to be a goblin barracks room.

Filled with goblins.

Dorinda stood in the midst of them.

I heard the door slam shut behind us. Dorinda said to the goblins, "Arrest these clowns."

CHAPTER 36

Prisoners (Part IV)

W E COULD HAVE PUT UP a fight. After all, *we* already had our weapons drawn.

On the other hand, *they* outnumbered us about five to one. And they had us surrounded. And they were rested and well fed and uninjured. And it took them about two seconds to get *their* weapons drawn. Other than that . . .

"Here we go again," Cornelius muttered.

We let our swords clatter to the floor.

Several of the goblins hustled forward and searched us for hidden weapons. They took my dagger, which Thea had just gotten around to returning, and relieved Robin of several knives and files and assorted whatnot. They also found Cornelius's knife and Marian's gauntlets of power.

Dorinda sat down on one of the cots. Her feet dangling over the edge, not quite touching the floor, she said, "They have a companion in the dungeon. Somebody go fetch her, too."

I should have known, I told myself. Given the way this game had gone at every other stage, I should have known Rasmussem wouldn't give us an ordinary blond-haired, blue-eyed princess to rescue.

"What about this one?" one of the goblins asked, indicating Nocona, his arms bound behind his back with Thea's belt. "Is he one of ours?"

"No," Dorinda said. "But it's a good idea. Tie them all, then bring them up to the tower. I'll meet you there." The goblins saluted by raising their swords. Just like they'd been doing in her bedroom. She left, carrying her nasty pet chipmunk with her.

The goblins jostled each other for the privilege of tying us up, and naturally those who won were the strongest and meanest. The one who did me almost broke my arms getting them behind my back—despite the fact that I was cooperating—and tied my wrists tight enough to cut off the circulation.

We ended up with three guards; the rest settled back to doing whatever it is that off-duty goblins do. Our guards had knives that were almost as long as our swords, and these they never put away. In the hall, they waved the knives under our noses and shoved us and bounced us off the walls and called us names rather than just telling us where they wanted us to go—which would have been easier on us, but I guess not so much fun for them. Where they wanted us to go turned out to be back to the turret with the stairs. Up we went.

And up.

And up.

And up.

The higher we went, the narrower and steeper the stairs became, especially after the fifth-floor landing, which was where the castle building ended and the tower corkscrewed out and up into one of the absurd towers we had seen from the ground. We went single file, which was all there was room for: first a goblin, then Feordin, then Cornelius, Robin, Marian, the second goblin, Nocona, me, Thea, the third goblin.

Ahead of me Nocona tugged and strained at the belt around his wrists—the belt Thea, and not one of the goblins, had tied. Which probably meant it wasn't as tight as our ropes. I know I couldn't budge my hands. I stayed close, hoping to hide his struggles from the goblin behind Thea.

Finally his right hand came loose. Nocona caught the belt with his thumb to prevent it from dropping and becoming obvious. He was quick enough that I was certain even Thea behind us hadn't noticed.

Now what? I thought.

Nocona stepped on the heel of the goblin ahead of him.

The guard stumbled, half falling into Marian, right ahead of him. He whirled around, holding his long knife to Nocona's throat. "You eager to die?" he asked.

I stood real close to Nocona to hide his loose arms from the rear guard, who was crowding us to see what the excitement was.

Nocona, gagged, said nothing.

"Crazy man is eager to die," the goblin said to his companion, to both companions: the guard who'd been in the lead had stopped to watch, too. The goblin sliced his blade through the gag, just hard enough to draw beads of blood across Nocona's cheek.

Nocona never flinched.

"Crazy man," the goblin repeated. He flipped one of Nocona's braids.

Nocona looked past him. He looked at Marian. He spat out the remnant of gag and said to Marian, "Sorry, *Feordin*."

Marian's eyes widened slightly, that was all. I

didn't see any reaction from Feordin, and I didn't look at any of the others.

"No talking," the guards chorused.

"I was just worried about Feordin's *rope*," Nocona said. Then, to have it seem to make sense to the guards, he added, "Being too tight."

"Never mind and no talking." The middle guard spun Marian around to face forward. "And you"—he jabbed Nocona with the index finger of the hand that still held the knife—"you'll look just the same in the Lady's picture whether you have a tongue or not."

We started back up the stairs. Again I kept close enough to block Nocona's hands from the rear guard. The trouble with that, of course, was that I blocked his hands from Thea, too, so that she couldn't see what was going on. Nocona slipped the belt off his right wrist. He moved both hands to the front. I took that as my signal. I threw my weight backward, falling onto Thea, who fell on the rear guard.

Nocona whipped the belt around the neck of the middle guard and yanked.

I heard a scuffle at the front of the line, but the curve of the stairs prevented me from seeing what was happening. Not only that, but the guard Thea and I had landed on was trying to squirm out from under us.

Somewhere under all that cursing and flailing was a knife long enough to skewer Thea and me both.

"Hurry up!" I yelled. I pressed back, knowing I was squashing Thea, but hoping to hamper the goblin. Together we slid down another two stairs, but the curved walls kept us from ending up all the way down on the fifth-floor landing.

Nocona whirled around with the dead goblin's knife.

My words played back in my memory: *You're just taking things out on me because you're worried that you're turning into a werewolf.* Seeing Nocona standing there over me with that knife in his hand, I suddenly had a mental image of the moment I'd betrayed him. When I pushed the image away, I got Wolstan, watching me from across the campfire, his eyes red and hungry.

As Nocona's were now.

He raised the knife.

I rolled to the right, slamming myself into the wall, digging my elbow into Thea's stomach.

There was nowhere to go.

I kicked Nocona's knee and he pitched forward, breaking his fall by putting out his left hand, which slammed into my face. A wave of nausea swept over me, and for a second I thought I was going to pass out.

Do that and you'll die over a broken nose, I told myself and forced things back into focus.

Nocona's attention had momentarily been diverted from me. He was on his side, but I could see him jam the knife down with both hands and remembered, too late, how I'd instinctively rolled out of the way of that knife. And left Thea exposed.

I kicked him in the small of his back, and he let go of the knife and rolled toward me. I heard Thea groan, which was wonderful—proving she was still alive. But the next moment Nocona brought his knee up sharp into my groin. I curled around the pain, then tried to whack his head with mine, though the entire area around my nose was throbbing. I only hit his shoulder. He put both hands around my neck and started to squeeze. Each breath brought the taste of my own blood, and there wasn't anywhere I could move.

Somebody grabbed hold of my hair, which was weird because Nocona had both his hands around my neck. *The goblin!* I thought. In all our grappling with each other, we'd forgotten the goblin.

But there was a hand in Nocona's hair too, and both hands pulled in opposite directions.

"Marian," I gasped. Evidently they had overpowered the lead goblin and freed themselves. Of course it was too late for poor Thea. "Let go."

"Knock it off, you two," Marian snarled.

And Thea, her voice muffled, said, "And get off me."

Obviously she wasn't as badly dead as I had feared.

In a moment Robin and Cornelius came around the corner. "Everything under control?" Cornelius asked.

"Yeah," Marian said shortly. "Right."

We finally got untangled, and I saw that it was the goblin guard that had Nocona's knife in him.

Oops.

Nocona pulled it out of the goblin's chest to cut Thea's bonds, and then mine.

"I'm sorry," I said, holding my hand to my nose, trying to stop the bleeding. "I thought—"

"I am not," he announced to all of us, "a werewolf."

Cornelius said, "Harek, I think we're going to have to overrule you on this one."

Me?

"But . . . ," I sputtered. "I never . . ."

Silently Nocona slipped the knife into his belt.

Then he took the second knife from the corpse's hand and tossed it to Robin. Not that I could have used it—it was probably iron—but it sure didn't look like the thought ever crossed his mind. Still never saying a word to me, he headed back up the stairs.

"You all right?" Marian asked, tipping my head back to look at my nose. She grimaced. "Looks broken to me."

I touched my nose. Definitely broken.

"Here," Robin started, tucking his new knife away.

"Don't touch me!" I yelled, throwing my arms up to ward him away from my nose.

"All that tipping your head back is going to do is make you swallow the blood. Put your head like this and hold here." "Here" was just below the bridge of my nose.

"I'm not—"

"Just shut up and do it," Marian said.

I shut up and did it and the bleeding stopped.

"It still hurts," I said.

"You're welcome," Robin said.

We went back up the stairs and joined Feordin, who'd commanded his magic rope to tie itself around the first goblin's neck. At this point he was sitting next to the goblin, holding onto the rope and holding onto the knife, which was also pressed against the goblin's neck.

"Now that we're all here," Feordin told the goblin, "how about if you start at the beginning?"

The guard's orange eyes glanced our way, evaluating the situation. I saw his Adam's apple bob as he gulped. "What," he asked, "beginning?"

Feordin gave the rope an extra twist. "You might want to start by telling where the real Princess Dorinda is."

"There isn't one," the goblin gasped.

"What?" Feordin demanded.

"Ease up," Marian said. "You can't get answers from a dead man."

"Or a dead goblin," Robin corrected.

Marian shot him a warning glance.

Feordin loosened the rope a smidgen.

"Who's the little blond sweetie?" I asked.

The goblin licked his lips. "She's Dorinda, but she's not a princess. I mean, she's the only princess there is and she's the person you know as Dorinda, but she's not really a person. I mean—"

Feordin said, "I think we're just going to have to kill him and start again with somebody else."

"No, wait," the goblin begged. "I'm trying to ex-

plain. She's a shape-shifter. She was accidentally created when the Wizards' Guild magically built this
castle as a playground for the governor's children. The
wizards put too much power into it. At first she was
just a shapeless ball of excess magical energy. Then the
High Mage came through the portal to check on everything, and the energy wrapped itself around his
wizard's staff. It hid in the faceted crystal knob at the
top." The goblin held up his fist to indicate the size.
"Each time he cast a spell she got stronger, and finally she
gave herself a form outside of the staff. She destroyed
the Wizards' Guild—if you came in through Sannatia,
you probably saw the hole where it used to be."

Feordin tightened his grip. "Keep talking," he
growled.

"She found that she could use the staff to take the
life force from the people of Sannatia. It left them . . .
flat, looking like portraits, but it gave her the ability to
change her own appearance."

Skeptically, Robin asked, "Then why aren't *you*
hanging over the mantelpiece?"

"We goblins swore allegiance to her," he said,
cringing away from the point of the knife. "We promised to help her."

"To help her what?" Feordin asked.

He gulped, knowing we wouldn't like his answer. "To rule the world. But she knew she had a lot to learn first. That was all right: she was patient. She decided that the best way to learn, and to be in a position of power when she was ready, was to pose as King Ulric's child. First she used her magic to kill his surviving sons and his latest wife. Then she took on the form of a tiny baby and had one of the goblin women bring her to the king, saying that she was the daughter of a farm girl with whom the king had spent a night the previous summer. It's happened often enough before that he couldn't remember one way or the other. He was told the mother had died in childbirth. The king believed the story and raised Dorinda as his own."

So much for Ulric the Fair. I didn't say that, I said, "But why did she return to Sannatia?"

"To change. To grow. Once she takes on a form, she keeps that form forever unless she casts another spell. So, she came to Ulric looking like a month-old baby. A month later she had to cast a spell to look like a two-month-old baby. Human young change rapidly. She used up all the power stored in the staff from the original inhabitants of Sannatia. Us goblins"— he cringed, knowing our reaction—"we gave her new people. Every time someone came to investigate the town, we'd take them prisoner and hold them in the dungeon until Dorinda returned. She'd come and she'd use the staff on them. That way, she was able to give herself the appearance of growing older. But this time some members of the Grand Guard got in the way. They thought she was being kidnapped and raised a fuss."

"But in the end," I said, remembering the latest portrait, "she used them to power her staff."

The goblin nodded.

"So why is she still here?" Robin asked.

"She needs more people to advance to the next age. The dungeons were empty and the guardsmen weren't enough."

"Us?" Cornelius squeaked incredulously. "She's going to use us as raw material for her shape-shifting spell?"

The goblin nodded.

Cornelius pursed his lips, considering. "This doesn't make sense," he muttered. "A magical staff isn't like a battery that needs recharging."

"Cornelius," I warned between clenched teeth. The last thing we needed was a looping goblin.

He turned on the goblin. "Using the staff shouldn't drain it of power. I think you're making all this up."

The goblin cringed. "No—really. The staff was damaged, that's why it doesn't retain power. When Dorinda and the High Mage were fighting, the staff dropped. A piece broke off the crystal. She didn't notice right away, and by the time she did, the piece was lost."

Incredulously Cornelius said, "The staff broke and she didn't notice?"

"It was a very small piece," the goblin explained.

Marian cleared her throat and we all looked at her. And no doubt we all were thinking the same thing—that this explained the tiny crystal we had gotten from the troll statue. But nobody said anything, not in front of the goblin. As unobtrusively as possible, Marion tucked the crystal into the neck of her gown as Cornelius said, "So she's waiting for us to be brought to her at the top of the tower. Who's likely to be with her?"

"Nobody," the goblin assured us. "She doesn't like anyone to see exactly how her spells work."

Robin said, "Except that eventually those guys who went to fetch Felice from the dungeon will be coming up to let Dorinda know they couldn't find her."

I *hoped* they couldn't find her.

"We should go up now," Marian said. "The longer we wait, the worse it'll be. We don't want to be caught on the stairs between Dorinda coming down and guards coming up, and us with only three knives."

Feordin put his face right up to the goblin's. "I think we should slit your throat here and now," he said. "But my softhearted friends probably won't let me. But if I even *think* you're going to make a sound"—Feordin tapped the knife on his shoulder, the blade grazing his neck—"that'll be the end of you. Understood?"

The goblin nodded.

Feordin pulled him to his feet, and we started back up the stairs.

CHAPTER 37

Dorinda

THE DOOR WAS JUST far enough away that we couldn't be sure if Dorinda had heard the fight and was waiting for us, or if we would take her by surprise.

We decided to assume she hadn't heard. Instead of bursting in, we opted for stealth.

Very gently Nocona eased the door open a crack. I was too far back to see what he saw, but Marian, looking through the space between Nocona and Cornelius, turned to give the rest of us a short nod. Silently Nocona opened the door the rest of the way. I tried not to wheeze, though with the state my nose was in, each breath sounded like a snore.

The room was dominated by a huge wooden table cluttered with scrolls and papers and assorted wizardly-looking apparatus: animal skulls and mysterious tin

boxes and vials of colored liquid, some of which bub-
bled and smoked. Eight-foot-tall picture frames were
stacked against the walls, blank white canvas turned
out toward us. Directly across from us was a door,
which led outside to a balcony. We only had a narrow
view of the balcony through the doorway but were
relieved that Dorinda was in plain sight. Standing on a
box so that she could look over the edge of the parapet, she was throwing pieces of toast, presumably to
the moat monster.

I glanced around and couldn't spot anything that
looked like a wizard's staff. Dorinda's chipmunk was
there on the table, still in its cage. Still in its wonderful
mood. As I watched, it walked over to a chunk of bread
that had been placed inside the cage and peed on it.

Carefully we stepped into the room.

Our goblin prisoner didn't make a sound.

We didn't make a sound.

Dorinda whirled around, pointing the staff at us.
There was a crackle of pink light and the faint smell of
ozone like you get during a lightning storm.

My muscles froze halfway between one step and
another. I felt my heart stop beating, my lungs stop
taking in air. I knew the others were similarly affected,
for there wasn't a sound out of any of them.

"Stubborn troublemakers," Dorinda said, jumping down from her makeshift stool.

Two goblins came in from that part of the balcony we hadn't been able to see.

Liar! I thought at our goblin, immobilized with the rest of us.

Dorinda walked beyond me. I strained my eyes to follow her. Nothing. She said, "This one has betrayed us."

The goblin. Good.

One of Dorinda's goblins asked, "Will you put him in a picture?"

"No. The life force of goblins doesn't get absorbed properly." She must have gestured, for the two goblins stepped behind me, then came out, carrying their compatriot, Feordin's rope still trailing from his neck. You'd think that'd be a pretty clear indication that he hadn't betrayed her willingly, but Dorinda nodded to the parapet. Without a word the two guards tossed him over the side.

If my stomach hadn't been freeze-dried like the rest of me, it would have turned over at the thought of our prisoner, fully aware but unable to twitch, plummeting to the ground.

"Now," Dorinda said, "my pictures. Let's see." She

walked among us, occasionally tipping her head or holding her thumb out the way you see artists do. Evaluating. My eyeballs were beginning to dry out from not being able to blink. "I think . . . not all together. That would be too cluttered. This one and this one." She pointed out Robin and Nocona. "With this one in the middle." That was Thea. "And . . . All right, this one too in front." Feordin. "The walnut frame with the metallic trim, I think. With the stairs as background."

The goblins picked people up and rearranged them.

"The two men to the rear," Dorinda instructed.

The goblins set one of the huge frames behind my friends.

"Fine. Only . . . they all have weapons except the woman." She turned to her two goblin guards and looked them over. "Here, give me that." She took the spiked mace one of them had in his harness and approached Thea. Then, as though on second thought, she pried the goblin knife from Feordin's fingers and placed that in Thea's hand and bent Feordin's fingers around the handle of the mace. "Somehow that looks more appropriate."

Dorinda pointed the staff at them. There was, as the goblin had told us, a crystal knob at the end, cut into hundreds of facets so that it sparkled madly. There might have been a chip missing; I couldn't tell. Not that it made any difference now.

Again there was the delicate tracery of pink around the head of the staff. And almost instantly after, a blue flash.

"*Oh*," Dorinda snarled, obviously annoyed. "They moved."

I had thought so too, but feared it was my imagination, wishful thinking. Apparently Dorinda had to thaw us out before immortalizing us on canvas. For on canvas was where Robin, Thea, Nocona, and Feordin were. But they'd only had half a second. What could I do in half a second? I was about to be flattened, and Mom . . . whatever was wrong with Mom would have to wait until the game played out to its natural end without us.

Dorinda stood there caressing the staff's crystal. Finally she roused herself. "All right. These three get an outside scene."

"What about the one in the dungeon?" one of the goblins asked.

"She'll get her own frame," Dorinda said. "I like these three together. They look like a family. Husband and wife and grandfather."

Husband and wife? Me and Marian? Me and *Noah*?

The goblins carried us onto the balcony and put a frame behind us. Dorinda aimed the staff at us. *Half a second*, I thought. *Half a second*. Had Cornelius and Marian seen? The staff sparked pink, and I threw myself onto the floor and rolled.

In my tumbled view of floor and ceiling and floor and ceiling, I saw that Marian had dodged to the left. I heard a *crack!* and smelled Cornelius's trademark sulfur. A moment later there was a roar like a cannon had exploded half an inch from my ear, which was Cornelius's magic and Dorinda's colliding midair.

I scrambled to my feet, launching myself at one of the goblin guards before my brain had time to register how dizzy I was. I more fell on him than tackled him, but in any case he lost his footing and we both went down.

He didn't have any weapons in his hands—after all, he'd been busy carting us and the frames about—and that was the only thing that saved me.

I grabbed his helmet by the nose protector, raised his head, slammed it down on the pavement. The tapestry-like ground gave slightly, but still his eyes crossed, then rolled up. I did it once more, just to be sure. I rolled off him, putting his unconscious bulk between me and the others, and looked up.

Cornelius and Dorinda were still flinging magic at each other. I couldn't tell who was winning, though possibly they had a feel for it. Both had sweat pouring off them, and you could see the tendons sticking out in their necks as they concentrated.

Marian, however, looked in serious trouble. She was grappling with the second goblin guard, but he had managed to get his knife out. Flat on her back, she was holding him away with straightened arms, but when her strength gave out, that knife was going to plunge right into her throat.

I grabbed the knife from the unconscious guard but didn't even have time to stand, before the pain of holding iron numbed my fingers and made me drop it.

OK. So no weapons. I didn't dare hit the goblin on the back of the head, because I was afraid that extra force would be enough to collapse Marian's arms. So I kicked him in the side, which wasn't enough to disable him, not with the chain-mail tunic he was wearing, but I hoped it would distract him enough that Marian could push him off.

It didn't.

Marian's arms were beginning to tremble with the strain, and the knife inched that much closer to her skin.

With all my might I kicked again, just as Marian's left arm collapsed. The knife plunged down. But between my kick and Marian's far arm buckling, the goblin was thrown off center. His knife cut her throat, deeply, but at least it didn't decapitate her.

He was in a position that I could kick him in the face, which I did, as hard as I could. He fell off Marian and put his hands up to protect his face. Straddling Marian, I kicked his knife hand, and finally he dropped it.

Marian grabbed it up and plunged it into his neck.

I dropped to my knees beside her. As soon as it was over, I began to get dizzy from my own viciousness. But it was necessary, I told myself. It was self-preservation, and saving the life of a friend.

It was, in its own way, exciting.

Not fun. Not nice. Not pleasant. But exciting.

"You all right?" I asked Marian.

But I could see she wasn't. She had a gash on her left side, which I hadn't even noticed before, and it was bleeding badly. And she was patting around her neck and chest as though to see if she'd been hit any-place else.

Then I saw what she was really doing. She pulled the sliver of crystal out from where it had fallen when the goblin's thrust had sliced through the gold chain. "Don't let her get it," Marian said in a voice made faint and raspy by the wound in her throat.

A little voice.

A voice I had no problem hearing, for everything around us was quiet.

I looked up and saw the wizards' duel was over. Dorinda watched us with a triumphant gleam in her eyes.

Behind her was Cornelius. He was as flat as the images in the castle halls, as flat as Thea, Robin, Feor-din, and Nocona, except that he hadn't been standing in front of a canvas. He must have been falling at the time Dorinda's magic cut through his defenses, and so he was at an angle, partly on the parapet, partly on the flagstone floor, like a sticker stuck in a corner.

"Give it to me," Dorinda commanded.

I looked at the crystal in my hand. Marian was too weak to stand. I didn't even have a weapon. What could I do?

Dorinda moved in closer, the picture of sincerity. "Give me the crystal, and I will spare your life. I will spare the lives of your friends." She pointed at Marian, who'd closed her eyes, who may in fact have already lost consciousness. "I can heal this one, and I can return the others to their original forms. Give me the crystal."

I thought, Maybe she's telling the truth.

Then I thought, Probably not.

I popped the crystal in my mouth and swallowed.

Dorinda lunged, so she was only the length of the staff away. "You've got to be joking," she said. She no longer attempted to sound trustworthy and reasonable. "You know I can have that cut out of you. Now spit it out."

She thought I was bluffing. She thought it was still in my mouth. And she didn't dare flatten me, because then she wouldn't be able to get to the crystal.

"The guards I sent down to the dungeon for your

last companion will be here any moment," she reminded me. "Will you stand by and watch as we cut her open first?"

I didn't think there was anything *they* could do to Mom. They hadn't been able to see her even before Cornelius had used his Invisibility spell. And there was nothing *I* could do. The only way I could help—*if* I could help—was to end this game as quickly as possible.

I tried to look disheartened, as though her threat had knocked the last of my hope out of me. With my shoulders slumped and my head hanging, I puffed out my cheeks and raised my hand to my mouth as though I were about to spit out the crystal.

Dorinda stepped closer, eager to grab it away from me lest I try something else.

Just close enough.

I grabbed the end of her staff and slammed it down onto the pavement. It bounced off, unharmed.

Dorinda gave a cry of rage and used all her strength to pull back.

Which is one of the major disadvantages of being a kid: the grown-ups, even the tired, hungry, wounded grown-ups, are stronger.

I heaved at the staff and felt it come free of her

little fingers. I turned my back so she'd be less able to grab it away. Then with all my strength I struck it against the ground. Still nothing.

Dorinda's fingernails raked the back of my neck as she continued to howl in rage.

Again I raised the staff and this time brought it down against the metal helmet of the dead goblin. There was a sound and a flash of color like being in the middle of a fireworks blast. The crystal knob had cracked. I hit it again and again, until it shattered and the fireworks dissolved and were no more.

"There," I said, turning to Dorinda, figuring, *Now let her do her worst.*

She wasn't there.

Only another scattering of crystal shards.

With a sigh I let the staff drop. Now what? We had discovered the secret of the goings-on at Sannatia. The princess, though not exactly rescued, had been taken care of. The quest was over. The game should end. But I was still there. I sighed.

Marian was breathing shallowly, and I didn't see how shaking her awake—if I even could—would help. The others were two-dimensional wall decorations. Except for Mom, and there was no way for me to tell how she was. With or without Mom, Dorinda's goblin guards would be trooping up any second, and they'd probably toss me off the castle when they saw what I'd done.

Through the doorway into Dorinda's workroom I could see her pet chipmunk. It'd grabbed hold of the cage bars with its teeth and was shaking the whole cage.

Well, I thought, maybe it was just naturally ferocious, but maybe being Dorinda's prisoner had done that. The worst it could do was bite off my fingers.

I opened the cage.

The chipmunk ran from one side of the table to the other, chattering at me angrily. "Hey," I said, "give me a break." I watched as it teetered on the edge of the table then launched itself at the chair. It landed on the wooden arm, quickly scrambled down to the floor, and headed for the balcony. With its little paws it swept pieces of the broken crystal—both the original knob and what was left of Dorinda—toward the tip of the staff.

"If you're trying to fix that," I said, "pardon me, but I just finished breaking it."

There was a sound like a ten-yard-long zipper getting zipped, and a puff of smoke. Coughing and sputtering and waving his arms, a man stepped out of the smoke, holding the staff, in one piece and bigger than ever. "Well, finally," he said. "Good thing you pointed the far end of the staff at her while you broke the crystal. I was watching you, and frankly, I didn't think you were smart enough to figure it out."

I didn't tell him that the staff was aimed at Dorinda by coincidence because we were playing tug-of-war with it. "Ahm . . . ," I said. "You must be . . . ?"

"The High Mage, yes. Of course you're right. Who else?" He looked around and shook his head. "What a mess, what a mess. Still, it's to be expected. Or at least I expected it. I don't know if you did, because I don't know you, so I don't know what you expect and what you don't. Still, it is a mess."

"Look," I said, "I don't know if you're aware of it, but there's a troop of goblins downstairs, some of whom are due up here—"

"I," said the High Mage, incredulous that he should have to explain, "I am aware of everything. I was turned into a chipmunk, not a half-wit. Goblins are easy to handle. Stand aside, boy. Stand aside." He repositioned me away from the unconscious Marian, then pointed the staff at her.

Immediately her eyelids flew open. She sat up.

She touched her side and her neck, which were still bloody, but the skin underneath was intact.

"*Stand aside, boy,*" the High Mage told me again, and this time he was looking at Cornelius, plastered to the wall and floor. He pointed the staff at him, and Cornelius slid the rest of the way to the floor, a continuation of the action frozen by Dorinda's spell. He sat there as though stunned, then rubbed his bottom.

The High Mage sighed loudly, and I realized I was standing between him and the portrait of the others in the group. "Sorry," I muttered, moving.

One by one, Feordin, Nocona, Robin, and Thea tumbled out of the frame. "Who *are* all these people you brought with you?" the High Mage asked me.

Feordin, holding his new mace aloft, said, "I am Feordin Macewielder, son of Feordan Sturdyaxe, grandson of—"

"Nobody cares," the High Mage interrupted. To me he said, "This is going to take quite a while, restoring people to their original forms, cleaning up after the goblins, twenty years of Guild paperwork to catch up on. Is there anything I can do for you before I get started, or do you just want to wander around the castle, knocking goblin heads together or whatever it is you warrior types do?"

"I want to go home," I said.

"Done," he said.

The castle fell apart with the sound of ripping fabric, and the sky exploded into a color with no name.

CHAPTER 38

Final Scores

A ND SO THE GAME ENDED.

Of course, the Rasmussem program has an automatic system that figures out each player's score, tabulating treasure won, experience points gained, hit points scored against, prestige, etc., etc., to determine an individual's level for the next time he plays. Not a single one of us thought to call the information up onto the computer screen.

As soon as we found ourselves in Shelton's basement, everybody started asking Mom, "Are you all right? How do you feel?"

She seemed a bit groggy, but she said, "I'm fine. What happened? Is the game over?"

"Your headache," I insisted, "how is it?"

"Gone." She pressed her fingers lightly to her temple. "Really. I'm fine."

I knew she was going to refuse to go to the doctor;

I knew she was going to say it had all been a computer glitch.

I knew she was going to wait until it was too late.

Shelton saved the day. "Modem," he commanded the computer, "dial nine-one-one." Because he has cerebral palsy and on bad days finds it hard to control his movements, his computer's functions are all voice-activated. Before Mom could protest yet again that she was fine, Shelton was announcing, "We have a medical emergency."

Mom didn't say anything, figuring, I guess, now that the ball had started rolling, she'd let it go.

Of course, the only way we were able to convince the doctors to even look at her was to explain about how we'd been hooked up to the Rasmussem program. And once the doctors agreed to look at her, it didn't take long for one of them to come hustling out of the examining room all serious and in a hurry, demanding a phone number where he could reach my dad.

They wouldn't talk to me, they wouldn't let Mom talk to me. It wasn't until Dad arrived, about five hours later, that I learned she was already in surgery. They sat us down—they sat *Dad* down; they still wouldn't acknowledge me—and explained that Mom had an aneurysm in one of the arteries in her brain. That means a weak spot where the artery kind of balloons out and eventually breaks. If it's an important enough artery, the person can die, and of course an artery leading to the brain is one of the most important. In Mom's case, the "eventually" was more like "any minute." Finally, after treating me like a smudge on the wall all afternoon, the doctor congratulated me on getting Mom to the hospital when I did.

Dad insisted I was old enough to be allowed to stay, and I wasn't sure which was worse: being forced to wait outside or watching her while she lay unconscious, listening to the awful sounds of the machines that helped her breathe and monitored her life signs. It seemed like we were there forever before her eyelids finally fluttered open.

The doctors had warned that she might be disoriented, unable to remember things, might not, in fact, immediately recognize us. I steeled myself not to be frightened or worried, no matter what.

Dad leaned over and kissed her. She kissed him back, which may or may not have been just an instinctive reaction. But I *knew* she was going to be all right when I went to kiss her cheek and she whispered, softly but clearly, "Who won?"

Actually, we never found out.

We had told the doctors about the Rasmussem program, and apparently one of them told a reporter, and it didn't take any time at all for the Rasmussem people to hear about us.

At first they threatened to take Shelton's whole computer, but here was this poor kid in a wheelchair— and, boy, did Shelton play that up—who couldn't do his homework or dial a phone or communicate with the outside world without his computer. In the end, possibly afraid of bad publicity, they relented and just confiscated the pirated program.

I figure the computer would have given me top billing, since I happened into being the sole survivor of the game. Which just goes to show how dumb computers can be.

The last I heard, Shelton's given up being Cornelius the Magnificent. He's pirated a self-teaching law course, and he's hoping to learn enough to take on the Rasmussem Corporation.

I say "the last I heard" because—between going back and forth to the hospital with my dad while Mom was there, and helping her get around now that she's home—I haven't seen too much of him lately.

The old group has pretty much fallen apart.

Dominic, a.k.a. Nocona, hung around until the

ambulance picked my mother up, but he didn't say much. Two days later he came up to me in school and said, "I'm glad your mother's going to be OK."

"Thank—" I started.

"But I hope a truck runs over your face," he finished.

I've seen him in the halls since, but he won't talk to me.

Cleveland—Feordin—has dropped out of the group, too. His parents heard about what happened, and now he isn't allowed to play with us. They say we're too rough a crowd.

Noah and Dawn Marie are into bigger and better things than Maid Marian and Robin of Sherwood. They're running for Student Council, and they're running, of course, as a team. Instead of calling themselves candidates for president and vice president, they're running as co-chairpersons one and two. Best of luck.

Giannine—Thea—I see every day because we're in all the same classes. Today she walked up to me and said, "Boy, you really made me crazy during that game. Always showing me up. Always being in the forefront of the action. Always knowing the right answers, knowing what to say and do."

Me?

"I kept trying to compete with you, and I kept falling on my face."

Her?

"I was really getting to hate you," she said. "But I've been watching you the last couple weeks, taking care of your mom and all. You're not really a bad guy after all."

Ah . . . thanks. I think.

I was about to try to put into words how I felt I'd been given a second chance, which is kind of hokey and I probably would have regretted it later, so it was a good thing she interrupted, saying, "I'm impressed to see sensitivity and nurturing from a fourteen-year-old male." She said it the same way you might say "from a green-tentacled creature from outer space."

My palms were beginning to get sweaty.

"So," she said, "wanna go to the school dance with me?"

"Noooo," I said slowly, "I don't think so."

"Arm wrestle you for it?"

"I don't think my parents would like me arm wrestling with a girl," I explained.

She hesitated, as though thinking. "Play you a game

of cards. You win and I'll do tonight's math homework for you. I win and you'll take me to the dance."

What can I say?

How was I to know she'd been getting lessons from Dawn Marie?

CHAPTER 1

The Dangers of Higher Education

MY MOTHER isn't normally the kind of parent who comes to school and has me yanked out of class because she needs to see me.

Never mind that the class I was pulled from was trigonometry, which is monumentally mind-numbing and—as far as I can tell—entirely useless to anyone except trigonometry teachers. It is rumored that, on a warm spring day three years ago, our trig teacher, Mr. Petersen, actually fell asleep during one of his own lectures. The speculation is that he has not awakened since, but is still droning on from memory, in a sleepwalking state.

I have never seen anything in Mr. Petersen's demeanor to make me doubt that rumor.

Generally speaking, I'd be eager for *any* excuse to get away from sine and cosine and whatever that third function is whose name I can never remember. But I felt a prickle of anxiety. Despite my mother's inability to come up with even one real-life situation where knowing the difference between opposite and adjacent, much less a hypotenuse would be a benefit to me, she does strongly believe in the theory of education. So I couldn't make sense of the note the messenger from the office interrupted the class to hand to me:

Grace Pizzelli
Go down to Mrs. Overstreet's
office right away.
Your mother is here

My brain instantly zipped to the West Coast, where Dad was attending a sales conference at a hotel I was suddenly convinced was the obvious target for arsonists, kidnappers, earthquakes, flash floods, outbreaks of Lyme disease, and/or killer bees.

My outlook wasn't improved by walking into Mrs. Overstreet's office. Mrs. Overstreet was wearing that I-smell-something-bad-and-I-suspect-it's-coming-from-you expression that must be taught in one of the required courses at principal college—a course that clearly would be more useful than trig.

But my mother had on sweatpants and a Milky Way Galaxy T-shirt she'd gotten when she'd chaperoned my Brownie troop's overnight at the Strasenberg Planetarium seven years ago. This is strictly at-home wear for her. Even for going to the grocery store, Mom's shoes need to match her purse. On this particular occasion, her shoes didn't match each other.

My prickly-all-over worry exploded into panic. "What's wrong? What's happened?" I asked. "Is Dad all right?"

My questions seemed to send my mother into a worse spiral than the one she was already in. "Dad?" she echoed. She glanced around the office, looking simultaneously dazed and frantic, as though not sure whether to level accusations at Mrs. Overstreet or the two strangers in the room—a man and a woman. She settled on the strangers and said in a squeaky voice, "You didn't tell me something happened to my husband!"

The man had a trim little beard, and excuse me, but if you were a casting director looking for someone to play the role of a debonair devil, you'd be giving this guy your card and asking him to come in for an audition. By contrast, the woman might well have been studying for that principal's course on intimidation through facial expression, but she was the one who spoke: "Mrs. Pizzelli, we don't even know where your husband is."

Mom's voice went even higher. "Tyler is *missing?*"

My feelings were bouncing all over the place because I didn't know if Mom was overreacting—which has been known to happen—or if she actually had a reason to suspect the worst.

Mrs. Overstreet went with option number one. "Mrs. Pizzelli, I'm sure your husband is fine." She didn't give my mother a chance to say more than "But—" before she continued, "When I go to conferences, the presenters always ask everyone to turn off their phones. I'm sure once they break for lunch, your husband will check his messages and return your call."

The other woman was nodding as though those were her thoughts exactly. "Please," she said, "now that your younger daughter is here, let's talk about Emily."

Emily?

Before I could ask "What's wrong with Emily?" the woman had stood up and offered me her hand to shake. She was very business-chic and sophisticated. "Hello, Grace. I'm pleased to meet you. Though not under these circumstances, of course."

The man, still sitting, smoothly interjected: "By which we do not mean to imply that Rasmussem Corporation or any of its employees is in any way responsible for those circumstances."

Ah, I thought, putting together that suave but slightly sinister look with his precise wording. *Lawyer.*

I finally noticed that they both had Rasmussem Corporation nametags, as well as school visitor badges.

The woman continued, "My name is Jenna Bennett, and I'm the chief technical engineer at the Lake Avenue Rasmussem facility. This is Alexander Kroll, from our legal department."

Mr. Kroll showed some of his teeth and added, "By which we do not mean to imply that this is a matter requiring adjudication."

Apparently, my principal didn't like lawyers. She leveled an I-am-picturing-doing-you-bodily-harm expression at him and said to my mother, "Yeah, yeah, so it's much too early to talk about suing the pants off them, but that's always a possibility."

Kroll's expression didn't change: proof, if anyone had needed it, about the sincerity of his smile.

Suing didn't sound good. People sue when something goes terribly wrong, and what did all this have to do with Emily—or me?

Ms. Really-I'm-an-Engineer-Despite-the-Fact-That-I-Look-Like-a-Principal-in-Training Bennett put on a pained expression.

But, fashionable and pretty as she was, she didn't know *pained*. My mother's eyes were red-rimmed and scared—*that* was pain. She took my hand and worked it like someone trying to soften up putty.

What a terrible person I am, I realized. *Something awful has happened to Emily, and here I am mentally moaning about a few squished fingers.*

Mom said to me, "Emily's playing a game at the arcade."

"Okay . . ." I said, knowing there had to be more. Emily is a student at RIT—Rochester Institute of Technology. She's studying technical engineering and is in a work co-op program at Rasmussem, which, long story short, means she's slave labor for them this semester, though I'm guessing Mr. Lawyer Kroll would try to qualify that statement. Rasmussem is the company that developed total immersion, the next step beyond virtual reality. When you play their games, sensations are fed directly into your brain: you can feel the warmth of the sun if it's daytime in the world you're playing in, just as you can feel cold and soaked to the bone if it's raining; you can taste the food and smell the flowers; and if you're riding a horse, after a while your butt goes to sleep. The difference between playing a Rasmussem game and a regular old virtual reality game is like the difference between watching an IMAX movie and one of those old black and white silent films.

I thought, *Of course Emily is playing games at the arcade.* No doubt most—if not all—of the people who work at Rasmussem are there because they love games. Well, maybe excepting the lawyers. But if the company wasn't going to pay their interns salaries, they couldn't be surprised at an unauthorized game or two. I assumed Emily was playing while she was supposed to be working, which apparently I didn't take as seriously as the legal department did. Was she getting fired? Was she getting expelled?

But surely that wasn't enough to account for Mom's distress, or for my getting called out of class.

Mom still seemed intent on kneading all my fingers into mush. She said, "They can't get it to stop."

Confused, I said, "The games last a half-hour. While you're playing, you feel like it's hours, but it's only thirty minutes." I figured my mother wasn't sure whether to believe me. She's not a gamer—hard as that is to conceive of these days. She's not into technology and can barely get her cell phone to cooperate. I said, "When the time runs out, the game just stops."

"Yes," Ms. Rasmussem-Engineer-Lady agreed. "Normally."

Okay, well, granted, something was not normal or we wouldn't all be here.

She continued, "Emily hooked herself into the game she was developing, and . . . she did something. She bypassed safety protocols. But the half-hour is up. The half-hour was up more than four hours ago."

"Can't you just . . ."—of course I *have* played Rasmussem's games, but Emily is the tech-type in the family—". . . unhook her?" I finished lamely, thinking of the wires they stick to your head when you lie down on a total immersion couch. Duh. Like the people who could think up total immersion weren't smart enough to think of that?

"We did," Ms. Bennett said, without sounding impatient or condescending at my obviousness. "She didn't revive."

Mom said, "I asked them to just pull the plug on the whole thing, but they won't." Pulling the plug is Mom's cure-it technique for *all* of our computer's ills.

Ms. Bennett said—and I could tell she'd said it before—"It doesn't work like that."

"There should be safeguards," Mom said.

"There are," Mr. Kroll told her. "Your older daughter, intentionally, with forethought, for her own reasons, disabled them. Leaving behind a note clearly showing her culpability."

From his briefcase, he pulled out a piece of paper in a clear plastic bag hand-labeled EVIDENCE.

Evidence? Like from courts and trials and cop shows? What sort of trouble was Emily in?

The note was in my sister's neat rounded penmanship. It said:

Not anybody's fault.
This is MY choice.

While the word *evidence* had set off all sorts of alarm bells in my head, now I think my body temperature dropped ten degrees.

Emily had *chosen* to go into a game and not come out? *Why?*

Mr. Kroll was still talking to my mother. "There may well be loss to company revenues because of her actions, beyond the time of the techs who have been trying to help her, beyond the time taken by Ms. Bennett and myself to explain things to you at your home, and now here again at your younger daughter's school because you wanted to consult with her." His expression clearly showed what he thought of a woman who would seek her fourteen-year-old's opinion.

"Be that as it may . . ." Principal Overstreet said.

We all looked at her, but she didn't really have anything to say; I guess she just didn't like our bickering.

Ms. Bennett stepped into the breach, too elegant to put up with bickering, either. "Be that as it may, we can tell, approximately, where in the Rasmussem-created scenario she is. I myself went in and tried to talk her out. She refused to listen to me."

This was so weird, so . . . *more* than weird. I couldn't even tell what I should be thinking.

I saw Ms. Bennett looking at me, waiting for me to realize she was looking at me. She said, "We're hoping she'll listen to you."

Me? Somehow this was coming down to *me*?

I had caught that part where Ms. Oh-So-Well-Dressed Bennett had said she'd *gone in* to talk to Emily.

"I think it's insane," Mom said. "First one of my daughters gets stuck in their crazy game; then they want my other daughter to just step right in after her."

"Mrs. Pizzelli," Ms. Bennett said, "I've already explained: there's no danger. I told you that I went into the game and was perfectly capable of coming back out again. Emily could come out, too. She's simply choosing not to. We're hoping Grace can get her to see reason."

Liking a game is one thing. Playing into the wee hours of the morning even though it's a school day is one thing. Shouting "Just a minute" when your mother hollers at you to get off the computer *now* because she's called you for dinner twice already—all of that is one thing.

Emily wouldn't come out?

"If," Mom said, "*if* someone from the family needs to do this, it should be me."

Ms. Bennett shook her head. "You're not a gamer. You'd be overwhelmed. Without experience, you wouldn't know where to begin, how to get around, what's important and what's only background. We'd lose valuable time. The programs are meant to last from thirty to sixty minutes. The equipment is rated safe for eight times that exposure. But it's not meant for sustained immersion."

Everything she said made sense, too much sense.

There was no way I could hope Mom would insist on being the one to go—not when I could see so clearly it would be better for Emily to have me there.

In the movies, the good guys always fight each other for the opportunity to do the dangerous stuff. The Rasmussem people were saying this *wasn't* dangerous. And *still* the responsibility was enough to freeze me solid.

Mrs. Overstreet, as a principal in charge of her students' safety, said to me, "Grace, you don't have to do this if you don't want to."

For the first time in my life, I wanted to hug her.

"No," Ms. Bennett agreed. "Of course she doesn't *have to*. But there's no reason she shouldn't. It's not like we're asking her to donate a kidney or something."

Suddenly we were into donating body parts? *Would* I donate a kidney? I wondered. Much as I loved Emily, I wasn't sure I could.

"Oh, I wish your father would pick up the damn phone," Mom said, "and tell me what we should do."

Somehow, that cleared my head. *We SHOULD*, I thought, *be able to make up our minds on our own.*

"No danger of me getting stuck in there?" I asked.

"Absolutely none," Ms. Engineer and Mr. Lawyer said in unison.

"Then," I had to admit, "I guess I don't see any reason why not."

My mother sniffled but didn't try to talk me out of it.

Mr. Kroll smiled his non-smile smile and opened his briefcase again. "Fine. We just have one or two papers for you to sign . . ."

AUTHOR BIO

Vivian Vande Velde has written many acclaimed books for teen and middle grade readers, including two other books about virtual reality games created by the Rasmussem Corporation, *Heir Apparent* and *Deadly Pink*, as well as the Edgar Award–winning *Never Trust a Dead Man*. She lives in Rochester, New York.

www.vivianvandevelde.com